HIDEKI SMITH, DEMON QUELLER

HIDEKI SMITH, DEMON QUELLER

A.J. HARTLEY   HISAKO OSAKO   KUMA HARTLEY

Charlotte, NC

FALSTAFF
BOOKS
WWW.FALSTAFFBOOKS.COM

To my wonderful family, and to anyone else who feels that the world doesn't quite get them.

1

My name is Hideki Smith and I'm a loser's loser.

Except that no one calls me Hideki. They call me Caleb because my parents—I swear to God this is true—actually searched for the most common boy's name the year I was born and went with that. Hideki—my middle name—was added to keep my *obāchan* (my Japanese grandmother) from going ballistic, but my mom was determined to fully adopt my dad's Anglo ancestry, so I got stuck with Caleb. Her goal was to make us the most 'regular American' family in the neighborhood, whatever *that* meant. If you went through our house you'd see nothing, and I mean *nothing*, that gave away the fact that one side of the family was Japanese. I was probably the only kid in my school who didn't read manga or watch anime. I'd never used chopsticks except once at my grandmother's (when I had wallpapered her dining room with food), I'd never eaten sushi (not that raw fish is a highlight of life on the edge of the Great Smoky Mountains), and I'm pretty sure that the only Japanese words I know are all in this paragraph.

I guess they meant well. Portersville, North Carolina isn't what you'd call a cosmopolitan place and I can't blame them for not wanting us to stand out. Apart from my sister and me, the only other Asian kid at either the middle or high school is a Korean girl I've never spoken to called Sue Park. Everyone assumes she's my cousin. The town is little more than a railway crossing and a central square surrounded by half empty strip malls. Population: 6,732. I know that number exactly because someone on the town council is paid to repaint the number on the "Welcome to Portersville" sign by the interstate every six months. Weird, right? Like saying exactly how many people live here will make you stay after you notice that the cotton and tobacco fields have dried up and the furniture industry has been deader than roadkill for twenty years. The only jobs are working for our pals at Southern Shale Gas, who spend their time blowing off the tops of the mountains which is stupid because, if you ask me, the Great Smoky Mountains are the only reason anyone might actually want to live here.

My parents don't work for the fracking company. They run an inconvenience store. It's supposed to be a convenience store, but it's way over on the edge of town behind the Walmart that closed a year ago, so it's not very, you know, *convenient*. That was where I was when this all started, when my status as a loser's loser got . . . complicated.

Actually, I wasn't there so much as I was *leaving* there. Fast as I could run. I worked in the inconvenience store after school, stocking shelves, unpacking boxes of chips and beef jerky, filling the fridge cases with soda, and generally trying not to break stuff while avoiding my classmates. I was supposed to be there till we closed at nine, but I'd had a bad day at school which had gotten worse when I got home.

There had been WORDS. That's what my mom called a screaming match, like that made it into a garden party or something. These particular WORDS had been about my grades, my forgetting to do homework, my utter bombing of the football try-outs my dad had convinced me to take a shot at even though he knew I couldn't catch a ball if the lives of entire peoples depended on it, and my general and effortless skills as a screw up. The usual, in other words. Today, however, I had managed to add an extra special ingredient to the whole nasty mix which I'm not going to tell you about.

Anyway. I took off. Slammed the door and bolted. I might not have wide receiver speed but I can shift when I need to. To tell you the truth, I need to quite a bit.

So, yeah. I ran. Past Desmond's Liquors—one of the few stores around here which did a roaring trade—past the CVS and through the forecourt of the McDonald's where my sister Emily—known exclusively to my grandmother as *Kazuko*—was hoping to get a part-time job next summer, because asking "Do you want fries with that?" was supposed to be solid preparation for her adult future. I went by the boarded-up church on the corner of Main, timed my run between two crawling pickups, and crossed into the parking lot by the old Walmart. When I reached the chain link fence at the back—which was already starting to vanish under a strangling raft of kudzu vine—I checked that no one was coming after me, then clambered awkwardly over. It took me three tries. At least the security lights didn't work anymore, so no one saw me falling into the bushes on the other side like a sloth with its paws tied together.

I didn't mind the dark. It was easier to disappear, which was pretty much my goal in life. The last thing I wanted was for any of the kids from school to spot me, even if I didn't think I had any cool points to lose. So I pushed hurriedly through the undergrowth, avoiding a patch of poison ivy, and onto a deer trail that ran up into the wooded hills that surrounded the town.

This was my spot, the one place I was pretty sure I would be undisturbed. There were hiking trails higher up which drew backpackers and day-trippers from Charlotte, but once the sun went down I had even those to myself. I climbed, listening to the tree frogs and the throb of the insects all around me, wondering how late I would have to stay out to be sure everyone would be asleep when I went home. That was a tough one. Mom and Dad would wait up, and if I stayed out too late, they'd call the cops; then I'd have to deal with Mark Halpern's dad coming over in his squad car and looking at my parents in that way that managed to be both pitying and sort of mocking, like my status as Lord of the Portersville Idiots was somehow their fault.

Which it wasn't.

Dad tended to go stiff and quiet, glancing around like he'd lost something (which he would find by turning on the game or working on—this is real, I swear—his model railway), and Mom would get overly efficient with her cooking or cleaning in a way that was hard to look at, but I couldn't blame them. Mary Montjoy's dad was a drunk who people said lit into her and her mother once or twice a month with a belt, and Jamie Forstegg's whole family were supposed to cook meth in an old barn behind the house, but my parents had never done anything like that. They got mad at me, sure, but mostly they were kind, if baffled, and they had never laid a hand on me or Emily. So yeah, it could have been so very much worse. But in a weird kind of way that only made it harder. I had no one to blame for my screw ups but me.

I said I wasn't going to tell you why I had messed up more than usual,

3

but it's not like saying it can make it any worse, right? And I guess it's only fair that you know the kind of Olympic Moron you are dealing with.

There's an old barn on the edge of the playing fields that the middle and high school share. I say old, because while it's nothing special, it was built a little after the Civil War and is therefore the Oldest Surviving Structure In Portersville. That's how people say it: with capitals, like it's the Empire State Building or the Pyramids of Giza. When people visit from out of town, they are dutifully driven slowly by the barn so they can look and nod and smile while they start planning how to get out of here as soon as possible. At the beginning of sixth grade we were walked over there on a field trip, which was like being taken out to watch grass grow. I mean, you could see the barn from the school, but we were marched over there to gape at it like it was the Taj Mahal or something.

Anyway, that day (that Fateful Day, as I now thought of it) there had been a combination lock on the side door and I watched Mrs Henderson punch numbers to get us in. There was nothing to see inside—an old farm cart and a hay loft with a couple of pitch forks and a rake hanging on the wall—but we walked around like we were in the Louvre and then went back to class to write about 'All We Had Learned'.

What I had learned was the combination for the lock. A few weeks later, while I was busy not being chosen for our recess game of pick-up soccer, I wandered over there and snuck in. There was a little clockwork timer that ran the light in the hay loft, and though it would run out after about five minutes, I found that if I braced the twisty bit with a nail, the lamp in the roof would stay on as long as I wanted. It was a good bolt hole, a place to read, and I got into the habit of sneaking over there with whatever I found in the school library—first Captain Underpants, eventually Sherlock Holmes.

Four years later, I still went there when I needed a bit of alone time. Like today. Tyler—that's Tyler J. Miller the third, if you can believe that—son of the mayor and voted Most Popular In His Own Head, had called me something. He'd said it before loads of times, so I'm not sure why it bothered me today, but it did. I'm not going to tell you what it was, so don't ask.

I had no business trying out for the football team. I hadn't even wanted to. It was another one of my parent's ideas about infiltrating the American dream, or some such thing: "Just join in and have fun, and you'll blend right in," my dad had said. It had, he announced—without a shred of self-consciousness—worked for him. My dad was originally from

England, something he apparently thought no one noticed anymore, though I saw people's faces when they heard him speak for the first time or referred to my "mum." They got that "you're not from round here" look, which could be amused, curious or hostile depending. He either didn't notice or pretended not to, smiling and nodding: blending right in . . .

Anyway, he had talked me into showing up for the stupid football trials even though I had the strength and agility of a drowning mouse. Portersville East wasn't a big school but the powers that be insisted on having Varsity, Junior Varsity and Freshman teams even though there were barely enough students to suit up. I figured that if I made the team I'd sit on the bench, part of the squad but not actually required to play on account of my massive incompetence. Better still, the coach might decide that no shortage of players would ever make them desperate enough to use the likes of me and he'd send me home. That way my duty to my dad would be completed with no harm done and we'd never speak of it again.

Unfortunately, before the coach could give me my marching orders, quietly amazed that anyone could be this bad at anything, I had to actually, you know, *try out*. So I did. I strapped on the ridiculous, gross-smelling helmet, ran races (last!) caught footballs (dropped!), blocked running backs (touchdown!) and generally failed as few people have ever failed at anything. At one point, I realized I had attracted the attention of a cluster of baffled girls up in the bleachers, all watching with a kind of horrified fascination. Madison was with them, which kind of sucked. I mean, I was used to making a fool of myself, but I tried not to do it quite so obviously in front of Madison, who was a junior like my sister, and at least part goddess. She was with Ayisha, DeMarcus Murphy's twin sister. They were sophomores like me, but DeMarcus made no secret of the fact that he wanted to be the quarterback for the JV team, and one day for the varsity squad. Portersville East had never had a black quarterback. And he was up against Tyler J. Miller the third, so you could see how that was going to go.

It was DeMarcus who threw me the pass. We were "scrimmaging," the coach's idea of a reward after our various exercises and drills, and I had managed to look busy without actually getting involved until all of a sudden the pocket around DeMarcus was collapsing and he had nowhere to run; the only person open—wide open because no one ever bothered to cover me—was yours truly. So having waited as long as he dared for a better option, he threw me a pass. He didn't look happy about it, but the ball came out of his hand in a beautiful, perfectly weighted spiral which lanced toward me, bypassing the defense completely and dropping into my outstretched hands like a Christmas present, complete with ribbon.

I'm not sure how I missed it. I am not certain that, even with hours of practice, I could recreate the way it bounced off my helmet as I fell face first into the dirt. I stayed where I was, not wanting to look up and see Madison laughing, DeMarcus raging, or the other team casually running the ball back for an easy, game-winning touchdown, though I know all these things happened. I lay there, wondering if I could burrow to the changing rooms from where I was, waiting for everyone to forget I existed, before getting up and trudging off, trying to make myself small.

That was when Tyler made his remark. He said it casually, smirking, like it was on me if I made a big deal out of it. I looked at DeMarcus, but he was pissed at me for not giving him his touchdown pass, and he glanced away. Tyler's jock buddies smirked too, and one of them—Bobby Davenham who had bullied me since third grade—stretched the corners of his eyes and said "Me Caleb. Me no understandy Amelican Football," in this stupid accent. My face got all hot. I wanted to tell them that I couldn't care less about their idiot game and that I spoke English better than all of them, but what with the hot face and all I couldn't, so I went to the old barn instead.

I shut myself inside and sat really still, sort of pretending to myself that I was hoping to spot the king snake which kept the barn's rat population down, but really I just had to be still. It was hot up there in the hay loft. Hot as my face, probably. I just sat there, motionless, waiting for it to cool down and looking for the snake, which didn't show. Anyway, I lost track of time. One minute it was lunchtime, and the next I was late for Math, a subject where my grade—trust me—could not stand to take a hit.

I slid down the ladder from the hayloft and pulled the nail from the clockwork timer, but instead of it clicking off the seconds toward shutting out the light, it just sat there. I touched it and it span pathetically. I had broken it.

Now, if I'd been smarter and braver, I would have gone right to the principal's office and told Mr. Grealish what I'd done, starting with learning the number for the combination lock four years ago and working my way back to the present. I might have done just that, but I could still see Tyler Miller's sneer, could imagine only too well what he'd say when he heard I'd broken something while hiding from him, which is what he'd think I'd been doing, even though I hadn't. Not really.

So I said nothing. I went to math class and stared at a whiteboard full of equations I didn't understand and imagined what it would be like to be Tyler J. Miller the Third, until I realized that I was jealous of someone I kind of hated, and that made me feel worse.

I didn't know there were security cameras in the school grounds, though it seemed obvious to me later. No one ever looked at the feed, I guess, not unless something happened, so the pictures of me carefully shutting the barn door behind me and trotting back to school didn't get looked at till after the fire trucks had gone. I was in homeroom by then, my face squashed against the window with everyone else watching Portersville's Oldest Surviving Structure burn to the ground. It had survived for almost a hundred and fifty years. Then it met me.

The principal arrived, then the fire chief and Mark Halpern's dad in his sheriff's uniform. Then my parents. And they sat me down and asked me why I'd done it, what I was upset about and what I was rebelling against. Mr. Grealish asked me if I thought causing mayhem and destruction was funny, or if I was lashing out because I hadn't made the football team. My home room teacher inquired what the barn had represented to me. I didn't understand any of that for a while and told them what had happened twice more before realizing they thought I'd done it on purpose. Then I got upset. I mean, I'd been upset before, but this was different. First I felt stupid and guilty, which I'd been feeling for hours. But then I got mad and sad in a wild kind of way, like when old Mrs. Clary died and her dog spent a week on her porch howling at the sky till her husband gave it to a family in Winston Salem. I felt like the dog: sad and confused and angry enough to bite. I didn't say anything about Tyler Miller.

I mean, you don't, do you?

So, you see, when I said I was a loser's loser, I wasn't kidding. I mean, the kids at school all kind of hated the stupid barn and the way we were expected to treat it like it was a Great Landmark, and if it had been anyone else in the class who had demolished it, there would have been some secret congratulating, because anyone who could get rid of something that tedious and annoying in such a spectacular way had to be a little bit cool, you know? But it was me, so it wasn't cool, and even the bullies and incompetents—Barry Johnston who had been suspended twice already this year and Clinton Weeks who had repeated more grades than anyone could remember looked at me like I'd peed on some treasured family heirloom. Then set fire to it. Tyler caught my eye for the briefest of seconds, and the smirk had been replaced by something like hatred, like rage. Even deep in my own anger, I was surprised by it. He had never liked me, and I didn't like him, but this felt different: upsetting, even a little scary.

So when I got home to more parental tears, more baffled anger and demands for explanations, I ran, and that took me into the woods where I felt like staying forever. The woods were where I could think, where I could process what had happened and what was going to happen next. The woods were where the world made sense and where I could be alone.

Boy, was I wrong.

2

Elsewhere

Jed Ashworth, senior engineer, checked the pressure readings on one computer terminal, then the seismograph readings on another.

"Looking good," he said.

Gas production at the Red Scar Mountain site had been slow even after the usual delays brought by local government, health and safety inspections, and industry standards checks. There had also been the inevitable interference by environmentalist do-gooders, though that hadn't been so bad in Portersville, where people needed the work. Southern Shale Gas had been making inroads into this community for years, but the fracking operation had only been up and running for two. Output had been low so far, but they were just getting to the big gas reserves. Jed had heard that these mountains had once been mined for gold, even diamonds, but those kinds of finds had been rare, nothing like what could be made from methane reserves now. And in spite of what the environmentalists said, natural gas was a whole lot better than coal and petroleum.

Jed Ashworth, a big man who grew up less than ten miles from the very spot he was working in now and knew these mountains and forests as well as anyone at Southern Shale, was a believer.

"Increasing pressure," he said, tapping the keyboard, eyes fixed on the screen. "Now at fifty megapascals, seven and a half thousand PSI moving 130 litres of slurry blend per second."

Outside in the Carolina night he could hear the rumble of the truck engines responsible for pumping the water, sand and other additives, via the blender and slurry pump, down the well and three thousand yards under the ground. He sensed the rising tremor of all that power and couldn't suppress a smile of satisfaction.

"All good here," said Vivian Singh, the assistant engineer and seismologist.

It had been a long day, and Jed was looking forward to a late dinner and a beer or two, but this was the part of his job he liked best: the exhilaration right before the pressure hit high enough levels to actually fracture rocks deep under the aquifer. The sense of power was extraordinary and infectious. When they started drawing the resultant gas up through the well head and into the holding tanks, there was a sense of satisfaction, of a job well done, but this part, as you got up near a 100 megapascals and 15,000 pounds of pressure per square inch: that was the real rush.

"Increasing to 70 megapascals," said Jed.

The hum outside increased, seeming to reverberate through the ground and up through his boots.

"Seventy-five," he announced.

"Everything proceeding as expected?"

Jed half turned to find Chris Collington, the company appointed overseer, hovering at his elbow. He was wearing that crisp suit he always wore, like he'd just stepped off one of those TV courtroom dramas. Too slick for Jed's taste.

"All under control," said Jed, a little irritable. He'd done this a dozen times. More. He knew what he was doing. He didn't need some corporate drone standing over him . . .

"What was that?"

Vivian Singh's voice. Jed gave her a quick look. She was staring intently at her monitor, her face tense.

"What?" he asked. "All looks normal here. Increasing to eighty megapascals . . ."

"No," she said. "Hold it. I'm seeing unexpected seismic activity in Sector 12."

"Richter reading?" said Jed. Minor tremors, so long as they were within operating parameters, were considered normal. They were, after all, looking to break up rock deep underground . . .

"1.7," said Singh. "We should shut down."

1.7! That was way higher than anything Jed had seen before. But they'd done all the geological surveys! It made no sense.

"Another. That one was 1.9," said Singh. "Shut it down."

Jed cursed under his breath but did as she said. All around the thrum of engines, the thrilling build-up of energy under tension, slackened to nothing. In the unwelcome silence, Jed scowled at the monitors.

"What the hell happened?"

"There must be an area of instability we hadn't identified," said Singh. "Unless the equipment is malfunctioning."

"Better check it out," said Collington, as if they couldn't have figured that out for themselves.

"I'll take a team there now," said Singh. "Sector 12 is accessible through a cavern on the south side of the drill site. We can be there in ten minutes."

"Do it," said Jed.

He sat down heavily, staring at his computer screen.

"These things happen" said Collington blandly. "The thing to do now is follow protocol to the letter. Hopefully we'll have the site up and running by morning."

Jed said nothing. Tremors were bad news. If anyone in the surrounding area had noticed them, they could be out of action for weeks or more. That was time—and money—down the drain.

"I'm getting a soda," he said.

For the next half hour he sat on the back of his pickup, the Coke can warming in his hand, staring at nothing. Then his phone rang. It was Singh.

"Hey," she said. "I have Peterson and Rodriguez with me. We're splitting up to check the seismographs, but they look like they are working fine."

Damn, thought Jed. More delays.

"I'm gonna set up some new monitors to see what's going on, but we'll have to wait to see if there are any aftershocks."

"How long?" Jed asked.

"A week, to be safe," she said.

Jed blew out a sigh.

"A *week?*" he said, forcing himself to stay professional. "And if it looks like the tremors are decreasing before then?"

"That would depend on . . ." her voice cut off. "Hold on. I think we're getting another." She sounded tense. "Yes. A big one."

And now he felt it, the ground beneath his feet shifting unnervingly, moving like the earth should never move so that he felt weirdly cut adrift.

"We've got falling rock!" shouted Singh through the phone. "Everybody out! Now!"

Still the earth shook, and then, there was another sound from the phone, a strange, distant booming, a thunderous noise which—impossibly —almost sounded like a voice, though the words it roared out were meaningless.

"*Hanashite kure!*"

Then nothing.

"Vivian?" Jed shouted. "You there? What's going on?"

But the phone was dead.

3

Caleb!"

I looked up from the forest floor. Coming toward me was my sixteen-year-old sister, Emily. I turned away, saying nothing.

"Yo, Destructoid!" she said, approaching.

I gave her a hard stare, then relented.

"Hey, Em," I said.

"Having a fun night?" she asked, with a perkiness that was positively frightening. "A real barn burner?"

"Funny," I said, as she sat next to me on a fallen tree. "Don't you have swim practice?"

"They sent me home," she said. "Probably thought I was planning to torch the pool."

"Tough to burn water."

"I have faith in your abilities."

"Sorry."

"No problem. It's not like I'm being punished for something that you did or anything."

"I said I'm sorry."

"And anyways, Portersville has tons of other cherished nineteenth century buildings . . . oh, wait . . ."

"You think you could leave me alone, please?"

"That's a big fat no, there, little brother. I'm here so I can report back to mom and dad that you didn't throw yourself under a train or get eaten by bears."

"Bears keep to higher ground at this time of year."

"Raccoons, then. Possums."

"I don't think I'm in that much danger from . . ."

"You should come home."

I pulled at a couple of leaves sticking out of the mossy trunk which we were using as a bench and listened to the gathering night. For a long moment I didn't say anything, so that Emily turned to me frowning and I could make out the concern in her eyes.

"What happened?" she said.

"I already told everyone like ten times."

"Yeah, I heard," she said. "What happened?"

I gave her a look that was supposed to be defiant and kind of outraged. A *how-dare-you?* look. It didn't work.

"Caleb," she said. Though she was only a year older than me, my sister was pretty good at sounding as if she had been born during the Eisenhower administration, like she knew things, you know?

"What?"

"Why were you in the barn?"

"It's where I go," I said, my face getting hot. "When I want to be . . . away."

"I know," she said.

This was actually a surprise. I hadn't told anyone that I knew how to get into the barn and figured my little lunchtime excursions were a total secret.

"You know?" I asked.

"Spotted you coming back from there months ago. Been keeping an eye on you ever since."

"Spying!" I shot back, but it was like shooting a knight in armour with a Nerf gun.

"Caleb," she said again.

"What?"

"Why were you there? I heard you had a fight with Tyler Miller."

"The Third," I said.

"Did you?"

"No!" I said. My face must have been lighting up the woods like a traffic signal again. Or like an ancient barn burning to the ground.

"I heard otherwise."

"It wasn't a fight," I said

"Then what?"

"He said . . ."

My mouth was dry. I looked away into the gloom of the trees.

"What did he say, Caleb?"

Emily could wait out a statue.

I muttered.

"What?" she said for the thousandth time. "I didn't catch that."

"He called me something," I said. "Happy?"

"What did he call you?"

"Doesn't matter."

"Seems like it does."

"It really doesn't. It wasn't even really an insult."

"Caleb?"

"He called me a *weirdo Jap*, ok?"

Emily sat very still, then nodded thoughtfully to herself.

"It wasn't a big deal," I said. That was a lie, but it felt like it shouldn't be a big deal. I mean, *Jap* just meant Japanese, right? Just shorter. Except that it didn't feel like it was just shorter. "I'm not even really Japanese."

"Half," she said.

I looked at her, trying to read her face, but she looked suddenly miles away. *Half* was true, I guessed. One Japanese parent. One white parent. So, half. But it felt strange, like it meant you weren't a whole person. That was nuts, of course, but I couldn't shake the idea, and I wondered if this was why mom always behaved as if she had never even heard of Japan. But that didn't work either because everyone could see it when they looked at you so . . .

Half. Incomplete. Neither one thing nor the other.

"I didn't burn the barn down on purpose," I added, quietly. "I mean, yeah, I lied about why I went there. I don't know why. But I didn't burn it down. The rest happened exactly like I said."

"Okay," she said. She sounded softer now, and if you knew my sister you'd know how weird that was, and that made the next words I said just come out, like they'd been waiting for weeks or months, queued up in my mouth like people getting off a train.

"You ever wish you were someone else?" I asked.

"Like a Jedi Knight or something?"

"No, I mean like an actual person."

"Like who?"

I shrugged and looked away. "No one particular," I lied.

"Caleb," she said, pushing, a half smile buckling the corner of her mouth.

"I don't know. Jake Sanders."

"Jake Sanders?" repeated Emily, aghast. "That skinny kid from down the street? Why him?"

I shrugged, wishing I hadn't said it.

"I don't know," I said. "He's just… regular."

"You mean he's *white*?" asked Emily.

"No!" I replied. "Well, partly. But it's more than that. He can hit a baseball, just about. Not real bright but gets okay marks in class. Collects bottle caps…"

"He's a nobody!"

"Exactly!" I said. "That's what I want to be. Someone no one notices. Someone ordinary."

"*Jake Sanders?*" she said again in baffled disbelief.

"Let it go."

"You want to be like someone who collects bottle caps?"

"It's a hobby. People have hobbies."

"You really are weird."

"Thanks," I said. "We've established that I'm a weirdo half Jap."

"That's not what I said. And if that's what you are, then it's what I am too."

"I knew you wouldn't understand."

"I understand just fine," she shot back. "I just think you're a dummy."

"No, Em, you don't understand, because you're *you*."

"Only person I know how to be," she quipped.

"You know what I mean. You're a straight A student. Competitive swimmer. You have friends . . ."

"You have friends too," she shot back, before she had chance to really think it through.

"Like who?"

"What about that Goth kid? Joey something. She's your friend."

"Kind of," I conceded. "We barely know each other. And it's *they*."

"What is?"

"Joey's pronoun."

"OK," said Emily. "See? A friend."

"*You know what I mean,*" I said again, not looking at her, staring fiercely into the dim forest, my face hot again, my eyes swimming.

"Caleb, there's nothing wrong with being different."

"Tell that to mom and dad," I said.

"Oh please!" she replied. "Mom and dad aren't upset with you because you're different. They're upset because you burned down a historic building which, frankly, seems fair. But they're also upset because you don't talk to anyone and hide out in abandoned buildings with your head in a book."

"I like books," I muttered.

"Great!" she said. "Me too. Yay books! But if you want to be a regular person, maybe you should put the books away once in a while and say hi to people, kick a ball around, do . . . regular stuff."

"If I wanted a pep talk, I'd go home," I snapped.

"Good idea. Let's do that."

"You go," I said with forced cheerfulness, "and I'll be right behind you." She scowled.

"You think it's odd that the person you like least is the only one you ever spend time with?" she said.

I had been comfortable with the fight so far but this threw me.

"You mean me?" I said, stalling. "That's dumb."

"Is it?"

"Look," I said, giving her a hard look, "right now I really just want to be by myself."

"Too bad," she replied, patting me on my knee and grinning crazily into my snarling face. "I'm here to protect you."

I sighed.

"From the possums," I said.

"And mice," she agreed. "There are probably mice."

I gave up.

"Ok," I said. "Thanks. I guess. Em?"

"What?"

"You think they'll make us pay for it?" I asked.

"The barn? Let's hope not."

"We couldn't."

"No," she said.

The inconvenience store wasn't exactly raking in money.

"I can't believe I actually . . ." I began.

But I didn't finish the sentence. The ground began to shake. Trees rustled and creaked as if a high wind was coursing through the still forest. A low rumbling growl seemed to come from the mountain beneath our feet, like distant thunder coming out of the earth itself. It swelled, ending with a muffled BANG which echoed through the air. The insects and frogs had all fallen eerily silent, and in the sudden hush I heard something else, a faraway cry, somewhere between a roar and a shriek, a terrible, mad animal sound that raised the hairs on the back of my neck.

"What was that?" I said, getting to my feet and looking around wildly.

"Fracking?" said Emily. She didn't sound convinced.

We had grown used to the booming explosions and the constant drone of machinery on the other side of the mountain, but this felt different.

"It came from over there," I said, pointing up the path that weaved its way up to the summit. I took a few steps in that direction.

"You're not going up there," said Emily.

I couldn't tell if she was giving an order or asking a question.

"Just want a quick look," I said. "We won't go far."

"We?"

"There may be possums," I said, grinning at her for the first time.

She gave me a long, searching look, then smiled a little grimly and nodded.

"Not far though," she said, as we set off up the path. "It's almost completely dark and I don't want us getting lost on top of everything else."

"We won't," I said, rounding a bend in the path. "I know these woods like the back of my . . . huh."

"What?" asked Emily.

"Weird," I said.

"What is?" she asked, more urgently this time, but then she saw where I was looking and stopped.

About ten yards ahead the path went through a strange kind of gateway: two red-painted wooden gate posts thick as telephone poles, sitting on stone bases and spanned overhead by a pair of red cross beams whose ends flared up slightly. It was one of the strangest things I had ever seen, strange and a little scary, so the fact that I suddenly wanted nothing more than to go through it was very weird.

"You ever seen that before?" I asked.

Emily shook her head.

"Me neither," I said.

"We should go back," said Emily. "We really don't want . . ."

She fell silent and, feeling her uncertainty, I turned to look at her. She was gazing back along the dim path, the way we had come . . . except that it wasn't. The familiar mix of pines and hickory, sweet gum, maple and rhododendron were gone. In their place was bamboo. Not the little skinny bamboo you saw wilting in pots down at the Home Depot. This was towering stuff, great pale columns thick as tree trunks and twice as high.

"Caleb?" said Emily. "Where are we?"

I stared and swallowed.

"I have absolutely no idea," I said.

4

"Where are you going?" Emily demanded.

"Up," I answered.

It seemed the obvious choice. Or maybe I just wanted it to be. The path below us wound through acres of silent bamboo whose trunks glowed silver under a full moon I hadn't noticed before, and whose leaves sounded like surf in the breeze. I would have bet everything I owned that though the path down the mountain would take us into Portersville, the one up through the strange red gate, would take us . . . somewhere entirely different, somewhere I was meant to go.

I know it sounds dumb put like that. But it was like I was one of those iron filings used to show us how magnets worked in science class back in middle school. Something was tugging me up through that gate. I could feel it pulling at my heart, my mind, all the little iron filings of my soul bending and straining to get there. My parents, Tyler, the whole barn fiasco had been blown out of my head and forgotten. In its place was one desire, one *need*. I had to go up that path.

"It looks . . . Asian?" I asked.

"Japanese," said Emily.

We looked from the gate to each other.

"It's a *torii*," she said. "A kind of ritual path marker, I think."

I gaped at her.

"How do you know that?"

She shrugged and, even here, in the middle of all this weirdness, looked embarrassed. Our earlier conversation about being half Japanese was the first time I could remember discussing it with her in years.

"We've been doing world religions in social studies," she said. "I saw one in a book. But that's all I know."

I wasn't sure I believed her, and that seemed to increase both the strangeness of the thing and my need to learn more. I took a step through the arch. As I did so, two things happened. First, I saw what I hadn't noticed before. That the gateway—or *torii*, I guess—was only the first of several, of many as it turned out, each about five yards apart. The second, was that in between each gateway were a pair of torches set into the ground, one on each side of the path. As I crossed the first threshold, these torches leapt into flickering, greenish flame.

Emily gasped.

"Must be operated by some kind of motion sensor," I said, not really believing it. I stooped to the nearest torch and pulled a baffled face at Emily. I could see no mechanism, no fuse or fuel. The tiny pillar of uneven, emerald fire just sat over the ground itself, like it was burning some invisible gas.

"I don't know about this, Caleb," said Emily. She sounded freaked out.

"No kidding," I said.

I took a few steps anyway. Through the next *torii*. And the next.

The torch flames sputtered, marking the path and casting their unearthly green light onto the towering bamboo which grew all around us, but nothing else moved. It felt like no one else was alive in the world except the two of us, picking our slow, cautious way along the path, winding up the mountain side.

At times the *torii* were so closely packed in together that they became a long, red tunnel, and as we moved through it, Emily did something she hadn't done for years. She took my hand. I wasn't sure if she was comforting me or the other way around, but she didn't suggest we go back, and though we did not speak, I think she felt it too, that odd pull to climb, to know where the path would lead. It was more than strange. It felt . . . necessary, like we were *meant* to do this, though I couldn't say why.

So we climbed, rounding bend after bend, and sometimes the path became steps made of packed earth and wooden beams, and sometimes it was paved with irregular stone blocks, mossy with age, but always the torches glowed and the *torii* gates led us on. None of it, I would swear on my life, had been there the day before. None of it. Which was, of course, impossible, because if the stones were stained and worn and green with moss and lichen, then they had been there for years. Decades or more. They couldn't just have appeared there.

But I knew these hills, and I knew that path; they hadn't been there yesterday or last week or last year. Like I said, impossible.

And then, quite suddenly, just as we were getting used to the long, strange passage of red gateways, we rounded a corner and froze.

"Whoa!" I said.

In place of the *torii* ahead were a pair of waist high stone plinths, furred with vivid green moss and lichen, and on them sat two stone animals like dogs or wolves, one on each side of the path. The animals were sitting up, their bushy tails straight up behind them, and they were glaring down at us, teeth bared.

Not dogs or wolves, I realized. Foxes. Definitely.

The air was scented with something that reminded me of my grandmother's house, an exotic, complicated fragrance that felt old and foreign. Mysterious. Beyond the stone foxes, under the largest *torii* yet, was a wooden structure with a steeply sloping roof. It looked a little like an oversized doll house as big as a garden shed. It was hung with thick ropes, red and white screws of paper, and an ancient-looking bronze, barrel-shaped thing which might have been a bell.

"Is it a temple?" I asked.

"A shrine," said Emily. "Caleb, this is impossible. There's no way this has always been here. We would have seen it before. What is going on?"

"Got me," I said, taking a step up to the opening in the front and peering in. There were more of the unearthly green torches around the main structure, and by their light I saw a black metal cauldron full of what looked like ash, in which incense was burning. That was the scent I'd noticed before. In the heart of the shrine was what looked a bit like an altar, like you might see in a church, and on it was a shiny black box with brass hinges and bound with a thick rope tied into a complicated knot. It was marked with an emblem in gold: a diamond inside a circle. I looked at it for a moment, then reached up.

"What are you doing?"

"Seeing if anyone's home," I said, and pulled the rope drawing back a long beam like a medieval battering ram. I let it go and it swung into the great bronze bell with a deep BONG that resonated in the air for several seconds.

Maybe that was a bad idea, but it was a bell. Bells have to be rung, right? It's a kind of law.

"Caleb!" Emily exclaimed.

"What?" I said, more casually than I felt. "Nothing happened."

But that wasn't strictly true.

Nothing had happened at first. The sound of the bell had rung out and then faded, as you would expect, but it hadn't faded to nothing, and just when you thought it had, it started to come back, like we were hearing a recording played in reverse.

It grew till it was as loud as the bell had been when I first struck it and kept going. Emily gave me a wide-eyed look and we just stood there, not knowing what to do as the bell got louder and louder, till you could feel it vibrating in your gut and your skull. And now a wind had whipped up around the bamboo so that it leaned this way and that like we were in the heart of a storm. This was bad. I clapped my hands over my ears and shrunk to the ground, half expecting a tornado to touch down in front of us and blast the whole forest to matchsticks.

I thought the wind would blow out the torches, but they got bigger, stronger, and their color shifted and hardened, becoming man-sized pillars of light, not green now but gold and amber. They threw the building and everything round it into shadow. Everything, that is, except the shiny black box in the heart of the shrine. A line of hard yellow light had appeared in the seam between the box and its lid, as if something inside was on fire. It swelled till it was too bright to look at, and then the knotted rope sprang apart and the lid flew open, flooding the world with brilliance.

I shielded my eyes and turned into Emily's shoulder as she cringed away, but I couldn't stop looking, so I saw that in the heart of the light, something was coming out of the box.

It was just light, brilliant and the heart of the larger glow, but it was also somehow man shaped. It floated up out of the box and glided forward till it was above us. I wanted to run, but I couldn't move my legs, and I felt something stranger still, like I wasn't just seeing the figure in the light. I was sensing its thoughts, and what I was sensing was . . . confusion. Uncertainty.

Whatever the thing was, it hadn't expected us. Or not exactly.

And then I heard my name. And Emily's. Except that I didn't really hear them. They just sort of unfolded in my head, like the sound of the reverse-recorded bell, and the names were not Caleb and Emily, but *Hideki* and *Kazuko*.

The light hung between us and then, with something that felt like decision, it split in two and shot like lightning into our chests.

I was blown off my feet and landed sprawled on my back, but before the pain came, the world went black.

5

I don't know how long we lay there, but when I opened my eyes I saw the sky shaded by tree branches heavy with leaves. Not bamboo. Regular, North Carolina trees and shrubs, like willow oak, sweet gum and rhododendron. I sat up and looked around me. The shrine, the stone foxes, the line of *torii* leading up the mountain, they were all gone. In fact, we were back where I had sat with Emily on the fallen tree, the cicadas whining in the night.

Everything was exactly as it had been.

I poked Emily awake, and she sat up, holding her head and squeezing her eyes shut like someone had just smacked her with a crowbar.

"What ? Where?" she began.

"My thoughts exactly," I said.

"I had the weirdest dream," she said.

"If there were *torii* and a shrine and massive bell . . ."

"Which you rang . . ."

" . . .causing trouble as only I know how, then no, you didn't dream it because I went through the same thing."

"You had the same . . .? Not a dream."

"Experience," I said. "Yes. Bamboo, and a shrine and a storm and a weird box with something weirder inside. Yes. I was there too."

"Caleb," she said, getting up. "This is seriously, deeply odd."

"Emily," I said, "you're not wrong."

Something in the way I said it stopped her and she gave me a hard look. I forced my eyes to fasten onto hers, but it wasn't easy. I'd seen something.

"What?" she demanded.

"Okay, so the important thing is that we're alright, yeah?" I tried.

"What is it?" she asked again, suspicious and anxious at the same time. "Caleb?"

"Well," I said. "Now, you're not to freak out, Okay?"

This didn't help.

"WHAT?" she roared at me.

There was no easy way to say it.

"Well," I said, "you kinda have . . . a *tail*."

For a second her fear evaporated.

"Hilarious," she said.

"No, Em, I'm serious."

"Right, and as soon as I turn round to look . . ." she began, grinning. And then her hand found it, and her face went white. Then she was turning to see it, like a dog chasing itself, and it was impossible not to laugh.

"I HAVE A TAIL!" she cried out. "How can I have a tail?!"

"It's a nice tail," I said, helpfully.

It was too, long and bushy and orange, coming to a neat white tip. It was, I realized (and this took the wind out of my amusement), a fox's tail, like the ones on the stone statues guarding the shrine. Emily was holding it in her hands, staring at it with horror. She even gave it an experimental pull and winced, slamming a hand to where it snaked up out of the back of her jeans.

"Why did I get the tail?" she demanded, turning on me. "This is all YOUR fault, Caleb! We were here because of you. *You* followed the path. *You* rang the bell. *You* burned the barn down. But *I* get the tail? How is that fair?"

"Should we go to the emergency room?" I asked.

"Walk into a crowded hospital like *this*?" she shot back. "Kyle Richards's mom works there. And Jenny Astor's nosey cousin who tells her *everything*. Are you out of your mind? If anyone—and I mean anyone—hears a word about this, I will never be able to set foot in this town again. And you know who I'll blame for that?"

"The fox spirit thing that cursed you in the invisible Japanese shrine?" I tried.

"Guess again!"

"How is this my fault?" I shot back.

Somehow arguing about who was to blame was easier than dealing with the impossibility of what had just happened.

"This isn't a joke, right?" she said, desperation in her voice. "I mean, if it is, just tell me, okay? I won't be mad."

"A joke?"

"Like you put something in my food to knock me out and then crazy glued the tail to my back or . . ."

But she couldn't keep it up. The tail twitched in her hands. Realizing she had made it do that, she gaped at it, then sat down on the log again, her face in her hands.

"This can't be happening," she whispered.

I just nodded. It couldn't, but then I didn't know what the *this* was. She had a tail and I had . . . what? Nothing, so far as I could tell. But the thing in the box had gone into both of us. That seemed impossible to deny. So should I be looking to find that I was covered in fur or something when I got ready for bed? Great. Just what I needed: another way to stand out. I patted myself down uneasily, but I felt fine.

Actually, I felt better than fine. All my confused anger and sadness over the barn incident had burned off in the strangeness of what had happened and I felt unusually . . . *composed*. Which was weird. I've never felt *composed* in my life.

But here I was, hours from the worst trouble I'd ever been in and minutes from a surreal encounter in a place that didn't exist with a sister who had grown a fox tail and I felt . . . fine, thanks, how 'bout you?

Like I said: weird.

"What are we going to do?" Emily whined.

"Well, I'm guessing you don't want me to study your butt to see if the tail could be cut off . . ."

"No way."

"Then we should go home."

"Like it never happened?"

"Like it never happened."

"But something did," said Emily, "because I have the tail to prove it."

"I'd swear that shrine isn't usually there," I said. "Or the *torii* path. I know these woods."

"So they appeared and then disappeared? How?"

"Maybe we moved. The bamboo. The whole place felt . . . different."

"You think we stepped into some kind of hole into a parallel dimension or something?" said Emily. "Something that could be explained scientifically?"

"Honestly?" I said. "No. Science wouldn't explain why it felt like it was there for us. Specifically us. And it wouldn't explain your tail."

"So you're saying it was what? Magic?"

"I guess."

"No such thing," said Emily confidently.

"You're pretty sure of yourself for a girl with a tail," I remarked.

"What's the alternative, Caleb? I mean, seriously. This makes no sense! It's anti-sense. It's in direct contradiction of everything I've ever believed about a world I've lived in for 16 years. It can't be real. Maybe it's a drug induced hallucination, you know, weird mushrooms in the woods, maybe. And they have those little pollen-y things, those whady'call'em?"

"Spores?"

"Spores, right. And we breathed them in and they made our brains go wacky so that we . . ."

"Shared the same dream?"

"Okay, I admit that's a bit of a stretch . . ."

"And grew you a tail."

"Okay, but what if we're *still* asleep? What if we only think we're awake, when in fact this is all a dream and . . ."

She looked at me imploringly, but there was nothing to say.

"Come on," I said. Reluctantly, she got up, and we walked a ways in thoughtful silence.

"You've been reading about Japan," I said, trying to redirect the conversation.

She gave me a quick look.

"A bit," she said. "So? Something you want to know about?"

"No," I said. "To be honest I don't want to know any more than I already do . . . . . ."

"Which is nothing," Emily inserted.

"Which is *practically* nothing," I agreed, "and I'm fine with that. Let's just get through this, whatever *this* is, and then I can concentrate on being a regular American again."

"In a few weeks you'll have a fine bottle cap collection," said Emily.

"Thanks a lot," I said.

"Hey, at least you don't have a tail," said Emily miserably. Her tail swished like it was punctuation: an exclamation point, maybe.

"Maybe it will be gone by morning," I said, shrugging. "Maybe it will just shrivel up and fall off. Maybe it will turn out to be some kind of weird illusion brought on by . . ."

"Spores."

"Or something, yes. My point is that maybe we don't need to do anything. Maybe this will all look after itself or turn out to be nothing. Maybe we don't need to be freaking ourselves out."

"And if mom sees?" asked Emily, though she already seemed calmer.

"Were you planning on wandering through the house naked?"

"Hardly."

"Then she won't see," I said.

"What time is it?" she asked, checking her phone. "My battery died."

"Mine too," I said. "Must be pretty late. Mom and dad will be wigging."

"Great," she said, sour as old milk. "How are you *not* wigging?"

"Not sure," I said. "Pretty strange, huh?"

"Truly."

"Of course, I am a hardened criminal arsonist," I quipped.

"What do I do about this?" She swished her tail.

"Shove it down the leg of your jeans," I said. "We go home, we say nothing . . ."

"You get yelled at for burning the barn down . . ."

I shrugged again.

"So long as I'm in the line of fire, they won't be looking too closely at your butt," I said.

Emily frowned thoughtfully at me, impressed and a little confused, then nodded.

"OK," she said. "That makes sense."

"For a change," I said, reading her eyes. She was about to protest her innocence but I gave her a steady look and a knowing grin. "Come on, you were thinking it."

"Ok, yeah," she admitted. "I'm not used to you being all Mr. Level Headed."

"Pretty cool, huh?" I said, swaggering for home.

"Whatever."

We walked down the track through the woods all the way to the back of the Walmart parking lot and hopped the fence. And when I say hopped I mean, at least in my case, literally. I rested one hand on the top and vaulted it with eight inches to spare like it was the easiest thing in the world. This was the same fence that it had taken me three attempts over five minutes to surmount earlier.

Weird.

But then, what wasn't? I gave Emily a quick look but she was too busy squeezing her tail into her jeans to have noticed, so I said nothing.

Everything in town looked exactly as it had, but that just made us feel stranger. I could even smell the pall of smoke from the torched barn. There was more traffic than I would have expected at this time though, and a pair of cop cars sped past heading up the mountain road, probably to a wreck. At night the parkway was clogged up with long haul trucks, and there were so many steep inclines that there were loads of those emergency hard shoulders that bank up from the road for when brakes weren't enough to stop an eighteen-wheeler at speed. But then we saw huddles of people with spades and pickaxes walking fast in the same direction.

Something was going on. I was about to comment on it when I noticed the clock over the Marathon gas station on main street.

Nine forty-eight.

"That can't be right," I said. "That's less than an hour since we met."

Emily shook her head, and her hand wandered down the thigh of her jeans, as if the tail—and everything we had thought had happened—might not have been real. She found the tail and scowled, dissatisfied.

"At least mom and dad won't be freaking as much as they would if we'd been missing for hours," I said.

"Guess we'll see," said Emily.

But we didn't, because when we got home, house and store were both dark and silent. This was weird, and Emily got an anxious, hunted look that had nothing to do with her tail. She plugged her phone in and stared at it as it started to ping with half a dozen missed messages.

"Put the TV on," she said, not looking at me. "Something's happened."

"Well yeah, we were spirited off to some ancient shrine and . . ."

"Not that. Something real."

I turned the TV on. It was tuned to Action Twelve news, though the sound was off. A slick looking woman with bright red lipstick and a suit jacket was holding a microphone and speaking earnestly into the camera. Despite her careful grooming, she looked rattled, uneasy. Behind her were trees and rocky crags splashed by the strobing blue and red lights of emergency vehicles. Men in orange hard hats were moving around with tools and spools of cable.

"What's going on?" I asked.

"Turn the sound up," said Emily, who was still scrolling through her phone.

I did so, and the TV reporter's voice zoomed in.

" . . . and three others still unaccounted for," she was saying. "Townspeople have begun to arrive to assist with the search which is being coordinated by the Portersville Sheriff's office in conjunction with Southern Shale Gas, the fracking company which controls the site where the accident took place. We're waiting for more news, but what we know right now is that at approximately nine o'clock this evening, Portersville residents reported a loud bang which may well have been an explosion, apparently coming from the plant on Red Scar Mountain. Fracking was underway at that time. Southern Shale have confirmed that some kind of malfunction occurred, resulting in the collapse of the caverns around the drill site and the trapping of workers, but they say that there is no evidence that the fracking itself caused the collapse."

"Yeah, right," I said.

"Mom and dad have gone over with water and batteries from the store," said Emily. "They texted. I guess everyone is pitching in."

My attention had gone back to the TV where Tyler's dad, Mayor of Portersville, was making a speech about the rescue crews doing all they could, and it was probably best if no one came out, clogging up the roads and getting in the way of the professionals. I frowned at him. He was big and bland and handsome like his son, with the same toothpaste commercial good looks and the same hard eyes which tended to sneer.

I hung my head, but as I did so, the lights of Dad's pick up splashed through the living room window.

"They're home already," I said. "Does that mean it's over?"

Emily said nothing but went to open the front door. I just stood where I was. It seemed to take an age for them to come into the house. I braced myself for tears or yelling, but nothing happened. Mom gave me a slack, weary smile, and Dad nodded and looked at his hands.

"I'm sorry I took off," I said. "I was just . . ."

But Mom was already waving the remark away.

"It's fine, Caleb," she said.

I stared at her. This was not like her.

"And I'm sorry about the barn . . ." I continued, but she raised her hands in a stopping gesture.

"I'm really tired," she said. "We'll talk tomorrow."

"Did they find the missing workers?" Emily asked.

Dad shook his head.

"There's too much structural instability around the well head," he said, trying to make it sound like it was no big deal in that restrained, British way he slid into when things looked bleak. "A cavern where geological survey equipment was stationed has collapsed. Two men and a woman are trapped inside but there's no way to reach them. The entrance is completely blocked and they need to get heavy equipment in to move it. That has to be moved into place first. There's just nothing for regular folks to do right now."

I glanced at Emily and had to swallow down a wild impulse to laugh. *Regular folk, huh? Show 'em your tail, Em!* Then I saw the scale of the thing in my parents' faces, in their quiet anxiety, and I felt, not for the first time today, stupid and ashamed.

"Right," I said. "If there's anything we can do to help . . . . . ."

"Go to bed," said Mom. "We'll see where things are tomorrow."

"Right," I said again, not wanting the day to end like this, and suddenly certain that the next day would not be better.

6

Elsewhere

Lying flat on his back, Harry Peterson opened his eyes slowly then, when he realized that had made no difference, closed them again and focused on the pain instead. Most of it was in his right thigh and shoulder where the stone from the cavern roof had hit him. He tried rolling over, but his leg sent a lance of agony up from his knee as soon as he put pressure on it, so he relaxed.

Sprained at very least. Maybe broken.

He spat a little grit from the corner of his mouth and wiped his face with his left hand, rubbing away the coarse particles of sand and fractured stone. They were sharp as glass, and he winced, conscious also that some of it was stuck to him with a wet stickiness.

Blood.

He didn't really remember what had happened, but the rock fall must have caught him across the scalp and he had gone down hard.

Concussed, probably, which wasn't something you messed around with. Good thing he had been wearing his hard hat, though it had slipped off as he collapsed. Without it he would almost certainly be . . .

Best not to think about that.

Harry moved his hand back and forth in front of his eyes but could see nothing. It had been dark down here before the cave-in, so that was hardly surprising. Without moving his injured leg, he fanned the fingers of his right hand and began sweeping them cautiously around the rock floor.

Nothing.

He tried again, reaching a little wider this time, but round only loose hunks of stone. He took a long, steadying breath of the warm, dusty air.

The key is not to panic.

Then he repeated the motion with his other hand. Something cool and hard rolled away from his grasp.

His flashlight!

He reached for it, stretching till the action started to pull his body round, in spite of the rising pain in his leg, and his fingertips brushed against the long barrel of the Maglite. Slowly, carefully so he wouldn't push it away, he curled his fingers round it, managed to stretch half an inch more, then as much again, and pulled the flashlight toward him.

Come on, he thought, as he felt for the on button. *Please be working. Please be working . . .*

There was a click and the cave was suddenly splashed with hard, blue-white light, so bright that Harry winced away from it. His shoulder groaned in protest, but he felt sure that was just bruising. Not as bad as his leg, and not nearly as bad as the gash on the back of his head which he was trying not to think about.

He leaned forward and managed to get his arms to slide back so he could prop himself up on his elbows, then he swung the beam of the Maglite round the cave. His feet were pointing toward the way they had come in. The entrance was gone now, filled up with rubble and what looked to be a single hunk of rock, big as an old Buick. The seismograph he had come to check with the rest of his team had been completely pulverized, which was almost funny when you thought about it. The equipment that was supposed to warn them about earthquakes had been destroyed in an earthquake.

Hilarious.

Would this close the plant, he wondered? In the short term, for sure, and it would certainly give the environmentalists more to shout about. Harry scowled into the gloom. He needed this job. It wasn't like Portersville gave people a lot of employment opportunities these days, and with his wife pregnant again they couldn't afford to lose another pay check.

"A man needs to work," he whispered to no one.

Of course, what he really needed right now, was to survive till the search and rescue team found him. He had a small emergency pack with a couple of protein bars and a couple of bottles of water, but they wouldn't last long.

How long have I been out? he wondered. He had no idea. It could have been minutes or hours. Was he delirious, concussed? That remark about needing to work wasn't a great sign.

At least there was only one way in, so the workers would know where to get to work on the blockage. Maybe they were already out there with drills and excavators. He listened hopefully but caught nothing beyond the echo of his own breathing. The team had separated to check the equipment and had been at least fifty yards apart when the quake hit. There was no sign of Vivian Singh or Julio Rodriguez in here with him, no way of knowing if they were lying under the rubble, if they were trapped in another chamber, or if they had made it out untouched.

Keep calm, he told himself. *The worst has already happened. Now you just have to keep your head till they find you.*

"Hello?" he called. "Is anybody there? Viv? Julio?"

The echoes were deafening in the confined space, but there was no other sound.

"Hello?" he roared again, more desperate than hopeful. "I'm in here!"

And then there was something, a small, careful noise, not from the rubble filled passageway beyond his feet, but somewhere behind his head where there should have been nothing but solid rock.

He twisted round in spite of the pain in his leg, and as he did so he thought the same phrase again: *The worst has already happened.*

But it hadn't, and as the flashlight picked up the shape coming toward him from the deep recess of the cave, Harry Peterson began to scream.

7

My parents didn't open the inconvenience store the next day, which must have been some kind of record. When Em and I got up, they had already left, leaving a note on the kitchen table saying we should go to school as usual and they'd see us in the evening when they got back from the rescue site. That was what the mayor had called it: not the accident site, the rescue site. More positive, see? He was good at stuff like that.

So I ate my Wheaties and tried not to stare at the bulge under my sister's back pack, because no, her foxy tail hadn't fallen off over night or turned out to be a shared hallucination. It trailed from her bath robe, pointed sadly at the floor, and when she saw me looking at it she gave me the patented Emily death glare I so knew and loathed. I said nothing and got ready for school.

It was technically autumn, but it was still hot and muggy out so that when the wind stopped completely it was literally seconds before you started to feel like you needed a shower. I wore shorts and a tee shirt, because knowing I would never be cool meant that I didn't have to stress about fashion. I grabbed my book bag and waited, enjoying the last moments of AC before stepping out into the closest North Carolina could get to the Amazon rain forest. After a couple of minutes, I checked my phone.

"Em!" I shouted. "Come on. We're gonna be late. And don't forget your swimsuit."

Wednesdays were practice days for the East Portersville Dolphins and Em was on the varsity team. I thought they should have been called the Otters or something. Not a lot of dolphins in the Smokies.

"You go ahead," she called back from upstairs. "I'll be right behind you."

She had that bright, fake voice she sometimes used around her friends. I never liked it, but at least this time I understood.

"It's fine," I called back. "I'll wait."

There was a leaden silence then Em's door cannoned open and she stuck her head over the top of the stairs.

"I said go, Caleb!" she said, not so much lovingly grateful as sort of pissed.

"I know you are feeling self-conscious about the tail," I replied, "but it will be fine. Mom and dad didn't notice it last night, and if you keep it out of sight . . ."

"I said I'm fine!" she said. Yelled, really. She was getting pink in the face.

"And I said I didn't mind waiting. Moral support and such."

And then the thing she had been holding back broke through in a furious rush.

"I don't want to walk with you, ok?" she shot out. "Take the hint. I have enough to worry about without being seen with the doofus who burned the barn down. Not today, OK, Caleb? Unlike you, I actually have friends at this school. I'd like to keep them!"

And then she was ducking back into her room and slamming the door.

"Fine!" I roared back. Not the best repost in the world but delivered with suitable scorn. "Please yourself. You always do!"

And I took off on my own, which felt like what Mrs. Springer my English teacher would call "a loaded metaphor." As I walked, I muttered to myself about my idiot sister and her still more idiotic friends, all of whom would dump her in a heartbeat if they got a glimpse of what was curling out of her jeans. After all the two of us had been through, she didn't want to arrive at school with her little brother, her own flesh and blood, because her friends in their designer shades, strappy sandals and carefully coordinated summer dresses would think I wasn't cool enough. Classic Em.

I stopped in my tracks.

Moron, I thought. *Cretin. Idiot.*

Of course, she was pissed. Of course, she was miserable. She could hide the fox tail most of the day, but after classes finished she was going to have to quit the swim team. The thing she loved most in the world. The East Portersville Dolphins didn't have tails.

I thought about going back, telling her I understood, but I kept walking. Whatever her reasons, she clearly needed her space and it wasn't like there was anything I could do to help. Plus, whatever was going on in her head, she had called me a doofus, and though she's called me way worse, it felt mean. Or rather it felt *meant*, which amounted to the same thing.

So I completed the walk to school alone, wondering vaguely about what she had yelled right after calling me a doofus.

Unlike you, I actually have friends . . .

Not wrong, and hardly a surprise, but I found myself thinking about it. I was used to being the loser who never got picked for sports and I didn't really object to it. I mean, I cared, because no one likes to be considered useless, among the last against the wall when the captains have chosen the kids they actually want and are now trying to pick the ones who will do least damage, but I also got it because I knew I was pretty useless. But not having friends at all . . .?

That was hard.

There was Joey Fergusson (born Josephine, though you called them that at your considerable peril) but I wasn't sure they were a friend exactly. They were more someone who was a bit like me because they were sort of broody and Goth or Emo (I wasn't cool enough to know the difference), and thought most of what our classmates were into was deeply lame. They were also figuring stuff out about themselves which put them way outside what Portersville was used to. Maybe I should hang with Joey more. Friends had to have things in common, right? Was it enough that no one else wanted to be your friend? Could you form a clique of people rejected by all the other cliques? I wasn't sure.

It was an odd thing to be wondering about, today of all days. The accident at the fracking site had become national news overnight, and there were vans with satellite dishes and radio antennae all over town. Helicopters fizzed overhead like we were in a war zone or a movie.

The school was buzzing with talk of it all, and there were announcements in home room about news updates that would be made throughout the day, the availability of grief counsellors, statements of solidarity and community. I couldn't decide if the students were feeling mostly a sense of trauma or just excited curiosity. A freshman girl was the daughter of one of the missing men, but I didn't know her, and she hadn't come into school today.

Other people claimed less direct connections:

"My aunt used to date an engineer who got out just before the cave collapsed."

"My dad works for the fracking company and he was right there where it happened just three days ago and if he'd stayed there. . ."

"We live across the street from one of the guys on the rescue team and *he* said . . ."

With a population of 6,732, (though maybe the sign writer had his paint out ready to make a change), it made sense that there was a sense of connection to what the TV folks were now calling the Red Scar Tragedy, but it was strange to see how badly people in Portersville wanted to make those connections. I saw a girl in the hallway crying, though I guess that could have been about anything, and I saw huddled groups having stunned, anxious conversations in low, halting voices. But for some, it was as if the disaster was shining a spotlight on our little town and they couldn't wait to bask in it, all the ordinary details of the place we lived in made suddenly dramatic and significant. I didn't know what to think of that, but it took people's attention away from the black- ened remains of the old barn, so I was, in a shameful sort of way, glad of it.

As it turned out, I was also wrong, as became clear the moment I saw Tyler in the cafeteria. He was the centre of an eager audience of students keen to get the inside scoop from the mayor's son, and looked, it had to be said, a little taller and shinier than usual, as if the spotlight on his dad had somehow filtered onto him as well. He glowered at me, so that the little ring of attentive listeners fractured and turned to see what could so have riled the great man's first born. Their faces curdled when they saw me. Bobby Davenham, who was eating a tangerine, spat a seed at me, but it fell short.

"And what are you doing to help, Smith?" he sneered.

"What?" I asked, genuinely confused.

"Maybe you hadn't noticed but Portersville suffered a tragedy yesterday in addition to the one you caused."

"The accident," I said quickly, trying to salvage the situation. "Yes. I know."

I glanced around the cafeteria and my eyes fell on DeMarcus, the quarterback hopeful whose pass I had dropped. He had a sandwich halfway to his mouth. His eyes met mine, then slid away.

"Kind of a big deal for our community," said Tyler, making it clear that that "our" didn't include me. "Everyone is helping out. But I didn't see you there last night."

"My parents were there," I said. "They took supplies from the store . . ."

"Made a pretty penny off them too, I'll bet," said Tyler.

"What? No, they were donating them . . ."

"Yeah," he said. "Sure they were. Maybe they can take some of what they made and put it toward the rescue costs, if they're not sending it all home to China."

"They aren't from . . ." I began.

"Maybe they should be paying into the Barn Rebuild Campaign," Tyler persisted. "Seems fair. My dad launched it this morning in between coordinating the Red Scar worker recovery plan."

"Right," I said, having nowhere else to go. "Great. Good job him."

Tyler took a sudden, menacing step toward me.

"You trying to be funny, Jap boy?" he snarled.

"What? No!" I said, involuntarily backing into the wall. "I was agreeing with you!"

He poked me in the chest.

"Good," he said. "Keep it up."

And he turned away, smirking. Bobby Davenham took this moment to fling the remains of his tangerine at me.

What happened next was . . . unexpected.

It should have hit me in the face, a spongy wet mush slap in the kisser, and any other day it would have. But today . . .

Today, I caught it. That might not sound like much, but that's because you've never seen me try to catch anything. Also, I had to catch it twice, because it came apart in mid-air. The first piece was the heavier one because it still had a few segments of the uneaten fruit in it, while the second was just peel, so it came slower. I caught the first one before it hit me in the face, then caught the second as it came at my chest. I caught them in the same hand, my left. I'm right-handed. And in the same motion, I detached a segment of the tangerine and popped it in my mouth.

"Thanks," I said.

Bobby stared, open mouthed. Tyler looked uncertain, and then someone sitting alone at a table behind him began to clap. It was Joey and they were grinning.

Tyler turned his fury on them, then muttered, "Freaks" and stalked away, his slightly baffled entourage trailing after him.

I went over to Joey, conscious of DeMarcus a couple of tables over, carefully focused on his sandwich.

"Hey," I said.

"Pretty deft, Smith," they said. "Hell of a moment to find some hand eye coordination. It will go down forever in the annals of, well, me."

"Didn't make you any new friends among the future mayor's inner circle," I observed.

"That ship sailed some time ago," they replied, dry as the Mojave. "Sailed, hit an iceberg and sank with the loss of all hands. I'm over the mourning period."

They said this absolutely deadpan, like a news reader recounting the movement of the stock market.

"You are so weird," I said, unable to keep it in, but grinning.

"This we knew," they said. "Wanna sit, finish Bobby's ballistic tangerine?"

I did, dragging over a plastic chair.

"So what do you think of this fracking thing?" I asked.

"You mean the fact that there was an accident or the fact that the accident was entirely predictable when you consider that the industry is based around blasting mega jets of high-pressure water until the bed rock fractures? I mean, it's right there in the name. 'Fracking'. But people are surprised. '*How could this happen?*' they say. 'All we did was shoot mega jets of high-pressure water into the bed rock . . .'"

"I meant the accident," I inserted. Joey could get on a roll that was tough to stop. Not, ironically, unlike jets of high-pressure water. "Weird, right?"

"Weird?" they said. "How so?"

I caught myself.

"Not weird exactly," I said, back pedalling. "Just, you know. Stressful. Sad."

"For the people who are missing and their families, for sure," they said. "Not for the people who want to make it somehow about themselves, but yeah. And I guess *that's* weird, but you meant something else."

"What? No," I said, not so much back pedalling now as doing a kind of private reverse tour de France. "Wrong choice of word."

Joey's eyes narrowed, unconvinced.

"Something going on with you," they said. "I mean, apart from your scorched earth campaign regarding the history of Portersville."

I sighed.

"You heard about that, huh?" I said.

"Dude," they replied. "There are tribes in the Brazilian rain forest who have no contact with so-called first world civilization who heard about that. When I saw the news choppers this morning, I just assumed they'd come to catch you in your next great art installation."

"Art installation?"

"Yeah, you know, a bold political statement about the unspoken historical roots of this crummy little town. The barn had it coming."

"I don't always know when you are kidding," I said, baffled into honesty.

"I get that a lot," said Joey. "But you didn't answer my question."

"Which was?"

"What's going on with you? You seem . . ."

"Weird?"

They shrugged.

"No weirder than usual, but definitely different."

I looked away.

"Nope," I said. "All normal here."

"Well now I know you're lying," said Joey. "But that's cool. You'll tell me when you're ready."

I laughed, like this was all a private joke between pals, but they just watched me and nodded thoughtfully.

"So you wanna tell me about the barn thing?" Joey asked.

"Nothing to tell," I said. "The auto light switch broke, caused some kind of electrical fire."

"And the rest, as they say, is history," Joey inserted. "Or not, because you burned it down. So that's the story you're sticking to, huh, Smith?"

"Do I need a lawyer?" I said, trying to play along.

Joey got up.

"You might before all this is done," they said. "People really liked that barn."

"No idea why," I said, still going for light.

"Because whatever it stood for, it wasn't people like us," they said. "See you around, Smith."

And they left.

I watched them go, then realized someone was standing over me. It was DeMarcus. He was looking awkward.

"Hey," I said, cautious.

"Hey," he said, not looking at me. There was a fractional pause.

"Can I help you with something?" I asked.

"No," he replied. "I'm good."

"Ok," I said, not sure where this was going. "I'm sorry I dropped your pass."

He glanced away again, his eyes flashing round the cafeteria as if he wanted to know who might see him talking to me, but then he looked directly at me.

"No biggie," he said. "But I wanted to say . . . I mean, my sister said . . ."

He stalled again. DeMarcus was a tall, confident person, the kind of easy presence that made people like him. I don't think I'd ever seen him look so uncomfortable.

"Your sister . . ." I prompted.

"Tyler's an ass," he said abruptly. "Don't let him get to you."

"Oh," I said, so astonished that that was all I could manage. "Right. Thanks. I try not to."

"Cool," he said. "Cool. Oh, and you should try out for the team again."

I stared at him.

"You remember what I was like yesterday, right?" I said.

"Yeah, I remember, but I also just saw you catch that tangerine," he replied. He smiled suddenly, a bright, wide smile which I had never been on the receiving end of before. "There's a second round of trials tomorrow after school."

"Right," I said. "Thanks. Maybe."

He left, and for a second I just sat there in stunned silence, but then everyone's phones were buzzing.

News alert.

I pulled up the headline and blinked.

It made no sense. I read it again, then scrolled quickly through the story, but it still made no sense though the facts were clear. Early this morning the rescue workers had begun using heavy drilling and earth moving equipment to clear the blockage caused by the collapse of the cavern where the missing workers had been stationed. The rescue operation had now cleared enough to be able to get inside, but the missing workers were nowhere to be found.

No bodies, no nothing. They were just gone.

8

No one knew how to react. It was a relief that the workers hadn't been found dead, but their vanishing into thin air raised questions that were almost as unsettling. Pictures on the TV showed the half-cleared cavern and rescuers in hard hats milling around looking bewildered and a bit lost. The mayor made his calming speeches, but he looked rattled and out of his depth when the out-of-town journalists—who were a lot less respectful than the *Portersville Chronicle* and *Action News Twelve* folks—started pushing for explanations.

"We were pretty sure they were in there, but I guess that wasn't right," he said.

"You guess?" echoed one of the carefully groomed and hard-faced reporters.

"Right," said the mayor, rallying. "So now we'll have to look for other areas of collapse that we hadn't noticed."

"There were cave-ins that you didn't notice?" said the reporter, more pointedly this time.

"It's a possibility we are looking into," the mayor replied, looking shifty.

"Let's hope you're more observant this time around," said the reporter.

Something flashed through Tyler J. Miller the second's face, something annoyed and ugly like an animal escaping a cage. There was a flurry of camera flashes and then the mayor was ducking behind his aide who ended the press conference.

"So weird," said a voice at my elbow. I had been watching the news bulletin in the AV room and had thought I was alone. I turned to find Madison Haynes standing no more than six feet behind me, like a blond angel who had floated noiselessly in and was just hovering, buoyed up on her own astral perfection. She looked taken aback to see me but managed a smile.

"Oh," she said. "Hey."

"Hey," I said.

"Sorry. I didn't mean to disturb you. But it's just so strange. How can they not be there, right? It's so strange."

"Pretty strange," I agreed.

Come on words, where are you?

"You're the kid who burned the barn down, right?"

It was like being slapped upside the head with a gold bar.

"You heard about that, huh?" I said, not having learned from Joey.

"Yeah," said Madison. "People were pretty upset about that. Not me though."

This unexpected ray of sunshine was the lifeline I needed.

"No?" I replied. "How come?"

"I don't know," she said, with a little dimpled smile that would have made nations weep. "I'm not that into old stuff."

"Right," I said. "Old stuff. Who needs it, am I right?"

"Totally," she said, and then cocked her head on one side. "And Emily Smith is your big sister?"

I hadn't expected this shift in direction but saw no point denying it.

"She is," I said. "One year older than me. Why do you . . .?"

"She's so pretty!"

"She is?"

"Exotic. And cool."

"I never really thought about it," I said, not wanting to think too much about '*exotic*'.

"She's on the swim team, right?"

"At the moment she is, yeah," I said, wondering if that was still true.

Madison gave me a twinkly look that made my legs weak, a look I've never had from anyone before, least of all Madison freaking Haynes, and added. "And I hear you are trying out for football."

45

I gave a spluttering sort of cough and then tried to recover my cool, something I have never had, ever.

"Did you?" I managed. I could feel my ears turning pink and the world around us had begun to feel oddly muffled.

"From Ayisha," she clarified. "DeMarcus said."

"Right," I agreed. "Quite a guy that DeMarcus."

"So you're not trying out?" she asked, momentarily—if bewilderingly—crestfallen.

"Well, I kind of went yesterday but . . . you didn't see me there?"

She shook her head.

"Maybe you had gone before I arrived," she said.

I hadn't, but I'd take it. Anything was better than her having seen just how awful that had gone.

"That must be it," I said.

"But I'll look for you tomorrow night," she said.

"Will you?" I said, peering at her as if she might burst into hysterical laughter at any moment and her friends would pop out from behind the desks and yell "April Fool!" even though it was September. I'd had dreams like this.

"Right. OK then. I guess . . . I'll see you there."

She gave me another heart melting smile and then turned and walked out. For a long moment I just stared after her, feeling hot and stupid and somehow floaty, and then I began to consider what Madison had actually said, rather than just basking in the fact that she had spoken to me at all, and blessed me with her smile and had seemed sort of possibly interested in talking to me again at some point. It was all very strange, about as strange in fact as vanishing fracking crews, mysterious impossible shrines, magic fox tails, and me trying out for the football team, and somewhere, deep inside me, I felt this odd prickling certainty that they were all somehow related.

A familiar bing-bong came from an overhead speaker, the sound used to introduce general announcements.

"Caleb Smith, please report to the principal's office immediately. That's Caleb Smith to report to the principal."

I sat up, eyes wide. Suddenly anyone left in the cafeteria was eyeing me, mixtures of contempt and curiosity on their faces. I kept my head down and got out, walking fast.

The stares continued through the corridors, and it suddenly seemed a very long way to the principal's office. Not that I wanted to get there quickly. My mind raced in circles but no clear ideas emerged. I was getting pink again, but not in the floaty way I had with Madison. Now it was like being a bug in the sink when the plug is pulled out: I was flailing, spiralling round and round the drain, powerless to do anything. My punishment for yesterday's disasters had been decided upon, and there was nothing I could do about it but accept the sentence: suspension or expulsion. I felt dizzy. Fifteen years of staying below the radar, now this. For a decade and a half, I had managed to go unnoticed, but I would make up for it today. Hell, it was only the fracking accident keeping me off the front page of the *Portersville Chronicle*!

I opened the principal's door and was surprised to find not just Mr. Grealish, the principal, heavy set sweating through his shirt, but my home room teacher, Miss Malinski, two men in suits, and the sheriff in his tan uniform, pistol at his waist, and . . .

"Emily?"

She just nodded and looked down. She was wearing jeans again, in spite of the heat and I knew why. She looked pale, anxious.

"Have a seat, Mr. Smith," said the principle.

"Why is my sister here?" I demanded. I figured I had nothing to lose at this point, and that made me defiant. "She's not involved in this. You shouldn't punish her for what I did."

"You misunderstand the nature of this meeting," said the principal with a quick smile, though it didn't quite reach his eyes and he looked nervous and unsure. The two men in suits were quiet, serious, and I suddenly wondered who was in charge here. "These gentleman are from Southern Shale Gas," he said, reading my look. "The fracking company. They'd like to ask you and your sister a question."

I scowled, perplexed, and glanced at Emily inquiringly. She kept her eyes down, but I thought I saw the smallest shrug of her shoulders. She didn't know what was going on either.

"We were wondering," said one of the suits, a big guy who looked like he'd rather be outside in camo and an orange wind breaker, "if these symbols meant anything to you." His name badge read 'J. Ashworth.'

He produced a tablet computer and typed on it.

"Check your school email accounts," he said.

What is going on?

I pulled out my phone, found a new message and opened it. There were a series of attached pictures. I scrolled through. They were all images of the same thing. It looked like a slip of paper, white with a black border, covered in a set of complex characters in red which looked like it had been made with some kind of stamp, and others in black hand written over the top. The paper had been torn precisely in half.

The characters were Japanese.

Or at least I thought so. They could have been Chinese. I didn't know the difference.

I looked up, blank faced, not sure what they wanted from me or why.

"I can't read this," I said.

"Do you know what it is?" said the other guy in the suit. He was pale, his reddish hair cut short. He was the only person in the room who looked comfortable in his formal clothes. I thought he might be a lawyer, someone employed by the fracking company to protect them, though from what, I had no clue. He had a predatory stillness about him that put me on my guard.

I shook my head.

"You're what, Japanese, right, Smith?" said the sheriff. That was Mark Halpern's dad. He came in the store from time to time and always made my dad nervous, like he was looking for some violation of local ordinance in the way we shelved our cookies or something.

"No, sir," I said. "I'm American."

"Ok," he said, smirking out of the corner of his mouth. "You know what I mean. Where are you from?"

"Here," I said. "Portersville. Never been anywhere else."

Miss Malinski tried to smooth things over.

"I think Sheriff Halpern means . . ." she began but I cut her off.

"I know what he means," I said.

"Where are your parents from?" Halpern persisted, less amused now.

"My dad is from England, near Manchester. Mom is from here, like us," I said, nodding at Emily.

"You're being unhelpful, Caleb," said Halpern. "I'm sure you don't mean to be, but let's put the political correctness aside for a moment, shall we?"

"I'm not being politically . . ."

"Mom is Japanese-American," said Emily, speaking suddenly and decisively. "She is a US citizen and was born here in North Carolina, but her parents were first generation immigrants from Japan."

"And do these markings look like Japanese to you, young lady?" said the first suit.

Emily bit her lip.

"They could be. I'm not sure. Why do you ask?" she asked. "What has this to do with anything?"

There was a silence, as if they hadn't decided how much to reveal, but at length, the one I thought was a lawyer spoke up. I wasn't surprised to find that he was in charge, though he didn't swagger like the others.

"It was found in the cavern," he said simply. "The cavern where the missing workers should have been. We thought perhaps it was just a label, a logo from a tool or something, but we have no record of it in our system. We thought perhaps you could help."

"I've never seen anything like it before," I said, pleased to be able to be honest. "And I can't read it."

"You think your mom could?" asked the bigger of the suit guys. Ashworth.

I shook my head. Emily clarified.

"She's not what you'd call 'in touch' with the culture of her ancestors," she said.

It was an odd way to phrase it, and I gave her a quick look, but she gave nothing away.

"Your grandmother lives locally too, right?" said Ashworth.

"You think she climbed into a cave and abducted three grown men?" I said. "She's like eighty years old."

"We were wondering if this paper was some kind of slogan," said Sheriff Halpern. "A political statement, maybe. Some foreign environmentalist thing."

"I don't know," said Emily. "I can't read it."

She sounded like she was starting to get annoyed. Or ashamed. Something. Then her face clouded as she put two and two together, and when she spoke again her voice was a little harder, shriller.

"Wait, are you saying you think that the accident was some kind of terrorist act?"

Another loaded pause. Ashworth's eyes slid to the lawyer-type—who wasn't wearing a name badge—to determine what could or should be said.

"We are exploring all possible avenues at this time," he said. "Have either of you been up to the cavern any time recently?" he asked blandly.

"No," said Emily.

"Not since the fracking site was set up," I added. "Sometimes I go walking in the woods but I haven't been near there for a couple of years, not since that colony of cedar waxwings were nesting there."

"Waxwings?" said Ashworth, baffled.

"Birds," Emily inserted. "He goes bird watching."

Halpern gave me a distasteful look, as if I'd confessed to collecting the kind of magazine Mom refused to stock in the store.

"And you've not been up there for two years?" he said.

"That's right," I said.

"You sure about that?" said Halpern. "There are security cameras, you know. We can check."

"So what are you asking for?" Emily snapped. For a second everyone stared at her, then she said, "If Caleb says he wasn't there, he wasn't there."

"If you have any insights into the symbols," said Halpern, "if you remember anything which might be relevant, our contact information is in the email my colleague sent you. Now, we need to get back. The situation on the mountain is . . . delicate. We need to find those men quickly and, frankly, we don't know where to look. Hence our exploration of other possibilities, however unlikely."

This was supposed to be a concession of sorts, and he managed a kind of smile. When Em and I said nothing in response, he added a parting remark, and now he was all business again.

"Expect us to follow up if we don't hear from you."

9

Spokesmen for Southern Shale were now insinuating that the missing workers may have gone AWOL before the quake and subsequent cave-in, a pretty sketchy strategy which the surviving family members were not happy about.

"You think Harry took off for a weekend in Vegas or something without telling me?" one of the missing men's furious wife barked at the Action 12 reporter. "Why don't you ask why Southern Shale doesn't want to spend money on a proper search for the men and women who put money in their pockets?"

She wasn't the only outraged voice. An ugly climate was building in town, dividing friends and families, often according to which of them worked for the fracking company and which didn't. My mom and dad adopted their usual strategy: keep your heads down and don't get drawn in, even when people start rowing about it in the snacks aisle.

The only thing keeping me sane was the prospect of the second round of football try-outs, which was, of itself, pretty strange. I was feeling good about the test to come, though why was anybody's guess given the way things had gone last time, especially since Madison had promised to come and watch. Maybe it was just that football, in comparison to everything else in my life, seemed so regular, so ordinary, but I was weirdly confident.

Physically I felt strong, graceful even. Since vaulting the fence the night of the barn burning, I'd had a handful of moments like the one when Bobby had flung his half-eaten tangerine at me. I'd caught a falling coffee cup shunted off the kitchen table by my Mom's elbow, diving and grabbing it before it hit the floor. A customer in the store accidentally nudged a stack of unshelved magazines and I crossed two aisles to steady them so precisely that she didn't even notice. Generally I was the one causing the mayhem everywhere I looked. Now I was the nimble saviour.

Deft, Joey had called me. They were right. I felt it. All my usual clumsiness had been replaced by this curious spatial awareness, like I was doing everything in slow motion and had time to consider the effects of very movement I made, weigh up the consequences and precisely execute the action in the blink of an eye. I felt changed, like I'd grown out of my fumbling, awkward adolescence and had become a strong and agile adult. I'd make the football team. I could feel it in my bones.

I told my dad while he was fiddling with one of his model trains, and he took a cautious don't-get-your-hopes-up-too-high tone, though he was clearly glad that I was giving it another shot, and when I hinted that there may be a girl involved, he got genuinely happy, albeit in that supremely understated English way of his.

"Yeah?" he said. "Good on ya, mate."

Trust me, this, from him, was the equivalent of a marching band with baton twirlers, none of which they have in Manchester.

Emily was broody and solitary, resentful of my mood and, frankly, a bit disdainful of my chances. I didn't care, and that really stuck in her craw.

"You gonna come watch?" I asked.

"I have homework," she said.

"I'm sure your friends will be there," I replied.

"And the more I'm with them, the more likely they are to see that I have a tail," she snapped. "So no, I won't be volunteering to be somewhere I can be stared at."

"Makes a change," I said.

"Right, popularity makes me shallow and attention seeking, whereas you wanting to show off for Madison Haynes is just good competitive maleness. Got it."

And she stormed out.

"Your sister doing alright?" Dad asked, catching the end of this little performance. "Doesn't seem herself."

"We choose the people we want to be," I said, a remark that was so completely unexpected that he just stared at me as I headed out to claim my destiny.

Now, given that this is, you know, *me*, you could be forgiven for assuming that the previous few pages were an ironic prelude to disaster. But for once you'd be wrong. The football try-outs, or at least my part in them, were a stunning success. I was implausibly good: fast, lithe, smart in my play, positively elegant in my jumping, catching and dodging. I was, the gob-smacked coach observed, not so much a surprise as a revelation. After the drills, DeMarcus had picked me quickly and we squared up against Tyler with the bizarre sense of an army with a secret weapon, like a company of out-numbered medieval knights who had been gifted a fully functional Sherman tank just before the battle started. I wasn't sure why DeMarcus was as confident in my abilities as I was, but I was determined to prove him right, and did.

I sprinted, I dived, I weaved, faked and caught. I played quite literally the game of my life, and we won. The spectators roared with delight and, after one play where I jumped higher than seemed physically possible and came down with the ball for a touchdown, they actually chanted my name.

"CALEB! CALEB! CALEB!"

It was astounding.

The moment the game was over Madison ran out onto the field and threw her arms round my neck. It was just in congratulations, but it also felt like she was staking her claim on me.

Madison Haynes, letting the other girls of the school know that they would have to go through her to get to me.

Let that sink in for a moment.

My floaty feelings were back and then some. In a high wind I might have drifted away. So *this* was what it was like to be popular, to be in the centre of things and have people want to be around you. Like I said, astounding.

Tyler was pissed, and—predictably—mean.

"So you caught a few passes, Smith," he said. "Big deal. Better hope you can do it every time you suit up, because trust me, if you can't, they'll turn on you like rabid dogs. Personally, I can't wait to see them tear your freak self apart."

But that was ok. What was a little harder to take was what happened when I noticed that there was a figure sitting by herself in the bleachers.

Emily. I drifted over to her, grinning but ready to accept her apologies and congratulations with grace.

"You came," I said.

"What the hell was that?" she demanded.

"What?" I shot back, amazed. "My try out? Awesome is what it was."

"It wasn't you, Caleb. You've changed and it's not right."

I stared at her.

"Are you for real?" I said. "Are you so fragile that you can't support me when I finally do something right just because things aren't going well for you?"

"*Not going well?*" she echoed. "My body has been changed by supernatural forces, and I think you have to accept the fact that so has yours!"

I gaped at her.

"You just can't let me have this, can you?" I retorted.

"You know it's true, Caleb," she said, leaning forward. "Something has happened to us, and you can't ignore it just because you like what you got from it."

"Why not?" I yelled at her. "If I'm better for whatever happened, who cares? Maybe I like being like this."

She sat back and nodded before saying quietly,

"So, you knew. You pretended you didn't, but you did. Whatever happened to us at that shrine has changed us in ways we can't possibly predict."

"So? What do you want to do about it? It's not like somebody gave us gifts we can just return. And why would we?"

"Because gifts have a price, Caleb. If we're going to consider a fox tail a gift. Sometime soon, we're going to pay for whatever this is."

"Why do you have to do this?" I gasped. "Why do you have to ruin the one good thing I have?"

"Because I'm not convinced it's good, or not entirely." She paused, suddenly conscious of the people around us. None of them were close enough to hear, but she had a kind of hunted look on her face, like there was something important she needed to say but thought it too risky to reveal here.

"What?" I demanded, trying to imply that I didn't really care.

She grabbed my wrist and got up abruptly. Then she started dragging me down to the field and round the back of the bleachers. I resisted at first, feeling awkward and stupid, but I knew Em. She wouldn't quit till she had said her piece. I went with her, rolling my eyes and shrugging at my teammates as if to say *family, eh? Whatya gonna do?*

She didn't speak till we were alone under the shade of the bleachers, then she released my wrist but held my eyes with hers.

"Tell me you don't think those slips of paper from the cave are relevant to what's happening here," she said.

Now I was genuinely confused.

"The paper things with the writing on them?" I said.

"The *Japanese* writing on them," said Emily pointedly, drawing out her phone, pulling up the images and shoving the phone into my hand. "I think that what happened at the fracking site is connected to us. To you and me. I don't know how that can be possible, but I think it's true, and in your heart of hearts, you know I'm right."

She waited for me to say something, but I stared fixedly at the phone, scanning the news headlines.

"That show you just put on?" Emily persisted, "Come on, Caleb. I've known you all your life and I've never seen you do anything like what you were doing out there. I have a tail. Something that called us by our Japanese names is making all this happen, and it's also responsible for the disappearance of three people. We have to do something," she said.

"Such as?" I replied, quiet now, resigned to the fact that she was right but with absolutely no idea what we were supposed to do about it.

"I don't know. Maybe we can research Japanese . . . stuff."

I grinned at that.

"There might be a lot of Japanese *stuff*," I observed. "Not sure we are qualified to even ask the right questions."

"So maybe we ask someone else," said Emily, her eyes brightening with what was clearly an idea.

"Like who? Mom? I don't know that she knows more than we do and she sure as hell won't want to discuss it. '*Japan is just where my ancestors came from,*'" I said. "Remember? She always says that. '*It has nothing to do with who we are. We're American, Caleb.*'"

"So, we don't ask her," said Emily. "We ask someone else."

I considered her face but she just stared back at me, waiting for the penny to drop. At last, it did. But I shook my head emphatically.

"No way," I said. "Absolutely not. Mom would kill us."

"It's our only choice," she replied. "

"I'm serious, Caleb. We should go see *Bāchan*."

Bāchan, you'll recall, is what we called our grandmother on Mom's side.

"And I'm serious too, Emily," I said. "Mom will kill us. Literally. With a meat cleaver."

See, we didn't spend time with our grandmother. She and my mom had had some falling out years ago. She came over for Christmas dinner, birthdays and such, but she didn't say much and we *never* went to her place anymore.

"How is *Bāchan* going to help?" I asked.

"Maybe she can tell us what's going on," Emily replied. "Mom won't. Dad can't."

"This is crazy."

"Yep, but it's not All American Crazy, is it? It's Japanese crazy. So *Bāchan*'s our best bet. Plus, she's the one person we can talk to who won't tell anyone else."

"Or if she does, no one will listen."

"That too."

"Okay," I said. "We talk to our wacky grandmother and hope mom never finds out."

"And if she has some ancient Japanese spell for transferring my tail onto someone else, you don't hesitate to drop your pants, got it?"

I grinned.

"Something tells me that's not how it works."

"When do we go?" Emily wondered.

"No time like the present."

Bāchan AKA Granny Watanabe (as opposed to dad's mom, hilariously known as Granny Smith), lived in the smallest house in town, a shotgun shack on the edge of what had once been rice fields down by the creek. It was a forty-minute walk from school, mostly off road, so we kept our eyes down for copperheads in the fading light, walking in silence.

"I'm sorry for what I said before," I said at last, glad of the darkness.

"Me too," she answered.

And that was that.

"That's *Bāchan*'s house," said Emily. "There's a light on in back. She's gonna be pretty surprised to see us."

"Even before you show her what's growing out of your pants."

"Let's play that by ear, shall we?" said Emily. "Not sure I wanna tell anyone about that just yet."

We moved to the porch, opened the screen door, and knocked.

"*Obāchan!*" called Emily. "It's us, Caleb and Emily."

Bāchan means grandmother. I'm not sure what the O in front of it that we sometimes use means. I think it's more polite.

The door opened but no one was waiting inside. I guess it might have just been well oiled and swung back when I rapped on it with my knuckles, or maybe it was one of those doors that gets sucked open when the AC blows or someone opens another door inside.

Maybe.

Emily and I looked at each other, then I moved through the entry way and into the little house. *Bāchan* was sitting in a rocking chair, looking— as always—like a big kindly prune in clothes. Half her face was lit by a table lamp with one of those old-fashioned incandescent bulbs, low wattage, so that even though the room was small, its amber light barely made it beyond her chair, and the corners were in shadow. She considered us with her hard black eyes and nodded fractionally.

"Come in," she said. "Sit down. There is much to discuss."

10

I looked at Emily and I could see in her face that she wanted answers fast, so I did as *Bachan* asked, taking one of the two available armchairs. The house was divided into three sections: this front sitting room, the kitchen/dining room behind it, and the bath/bedroom behind that. You passed through each to get to the next. It had always felt weird to me, because the house was so small and there was no hallway, so you walked right into someone's life, you know? It felt rude. I can't say I missed the place once Mom decided she didn't want us coming over here.

It felt stuffy too, though *Bachan* was wrapped in one of the ancient kimonos she wore as a house coat, all dark browns and shabby greens, like she was cold. That's an old person thing, I guess. It can be a hundred degrees outside but you still see them dressed like they're going seal hunting in the arctic. The three of us sat perched on overstuffed chairs which filled half the room looking at each other in tense and musty silence.

"Where's Snowball?" I asked, trying to break into things gently.

Bachan gave me an odd look.

"Snowball?" she said, shaping the words like they came from a foreign language.

"Your cat," I replied, my heart sinking. If *Bachan* had forgotten she had a cat—albeit a nasty, smelly cat which had lost its tail in an accident years ago—it seemed likely that I had overestimated how much help she was likely to be.

"Oh," she said, and grinned alarmingly. "Out mousing," she said. "Will bring me voles and birds later. Anyway, tell me what happened."

"How do you know something happened?" I asked.

She licked her lips and her eyes fixed on me in the gloom.

"I felt it," she said.

Which was as much as I was going to get, apparently. Emily nodded, like it made sense that your grandmother should sense it when you grew a tail, and launched into the story. *Bāchan* watched her, motionless except for when she lifted a tea cup without a handle to her lips and sipped some pale milky liquid. She showed no surprise or disbelief as Emily recounted what had happened on the mountain, even when Emily got to her feet to show her the final humiliating truth.

"But when we woke up," she said, "I had this!"

She plucked the tail from her jeans and turned round so that we could see it, bristling in the heat. Even here, in this strange little room with my odd little grandmother looking at us with her beetle-black eyes, I had to fight down a giggle.

"And that's all?" *Bāchan* said, her voice sandpaper dry and cool as cucumber.

"All?" Emily repeated, aghast. "Isn't it enough?"

"And what can you do?" asked *Bāchan*, sipping her milk, her movements small and slow.

"Do?" Emily parroted.

"You have . . . abilities?" asked *Bāchan*, licking her lips. "Things you could not do before?"

"Well," said Emily, her panic starting to sneak back in, "I have this TAIL."

"What does it do?" asked *Bāchan*, and her eyes were narrow now, like a cat watching a bug.

"Do?" Emily said again, sounding stupid and exasperated. "It doesn't *do* anything. It's a tail. I can swish it a bit but . . . I don't think that's the issue, do you?"

"And you, boy?" asked *Bāchan*.

I frowned at her calling me *boy*, but before I could say anything I was distracted by a sound, like something wobbling in the corner of the room. I shot a glance that way and saw an old wooden box about a foot square sitting in the darkness.

"Well?" *Bāchan* pressed.

"Not much," I said. "I feel fine. Better than fine actually. Sort of poised and strong . . ."

Again the low rattle from the corner, and this time I was quick enough to just about make out the tremble of the box in the shadows.

"You have a mouse or something . . ." I began.

"Pay that no mind," said *Bāchan*, and her voice had a sharpness I had never heard before. I looked at her, half expecting to see someone else, but it was still her. "Let me see your tail again, my dear," she said to Emily, and now the edge in her voice had gone and she sounded sickly sweet and pitying. Emily gave her an uncertain smile but did not flinch away as *Bāchan* inspected the fox tail, though she was careful not to touch it. As my grandmother leaned forward her kimono shifted. I stared.

Where her foot should have been—typically wearing socks and ancient sandals—I saw . . .

A paw.

There was no other word for it. It was grey, covered in short, trim fur and looked for all the world like it belonged to a large cat.

As quickly as I saw it, she adjusted the kimono and it was gone again, but I was on my feet and staring by now, speechless with horror.

"What?" said Emily, reading my face.

Bāchan glanced at me with her usual kindly face, but in that instant the box in the corner rattled again and I saw her turn to it. Her eyes were suddenly yellow, her lips pulled back from bright, sharp teeth and she began to hiss. It was an awful, menacing snarl of a sound that promised serious injury to come, and Emily spun round in horror.

"I think we should leave," I managed to say, but as Emily nodded furiously, *"Bāchan"* turned her yellow cat's eyes on me and then flicked one hand, a gesture that slammed the door even though it was yards away. Another twitch of her bony fingers, and the lock snapped into place, and then the fingers were thickening. Grey fur spread over them like moss while the nails lengthened and curved like sickle blades. The monster shrugged out of *Bāchan*'s drab kimono and under it she wore something trimmed with gold and red thread over her furry body. Her head swelled, her ears pricked and long whiskers sprouted round a wedge-shaped nose and lethal looking mouth. In seconds she was a cat.

A cat in clothes. A cat bigger than the largest mountain lion. A cat standing on its hind legs, its tail lashing back and forth, in a room barely big enough to swing a . . . well, you know.

Emily shrieked and went for the door. I looked wildly at the windows, but they were latched and shuttered.

"Through the back!" I shouted, making for the door into the kitchen.

The cat creature waved a massive paw and a display cabinet full of old cups and plates slid across the room to bar my way. I stopped and turned just in time to see the other paw slashing at my face, claws out like knives. I ducked away, though what had been "*Bāchan's*" forearm still caught me across the chest and sent me flying.

Whatever the thing which had looked like my frail old grandmother was, it was seriously strong. I looked desperately round for something I could use as a weapon, but it was *Bāchan's* house, so unless I could come up with a lethal uses for doilies, I was dead meat.

Emily, who was taller than me and had seen me go down, turned on the cat creature with the kind of fury no regular person would ever want to see, but the monster just hissed and spread its immense claws, ready to cut her down.

It also levitated. For real. Just a few inches at first, but it floated up and hung there in mid-air, all four paws ready to slash.

"Stay back!" I shouted at Emily. The hiss had reminded me of something.

I lunged to the corner of the room where the rattling box had been, the thing which had apparently bothered the monster into revealing its disguise. There was something in that box it didn't like. Maybe something it was afraid of.

That was good enough for me.

I sprawled headlong into the corner, reached for the box and, feeling the cat's eyes on my back, fumbled with the catch till I felt it snap open. The lid popped off, and I peered hopefully inside to see what terrible creature or extraordinary weapon was going to save us from the shape-shifting nightmare living in my grandmother's house.

It was a teapot.

Small, cast iron, black. I had seen it here before. The possibility that it would now save our lives seemed a bit on the slim side.

And then it grew legs.

They popped out of the sides, little claw feet apparently made of the same stuff as the teapot, but alive. As I stared, a pair of eyes, one on each side of the spout opened, and the lid snapped like jaws. I snatched my hand away and rolled back into the corner as the little teapot leapt out of the box, half turtle, half puppy—though still, you know, *a teapot*—its lid chittering like a manic squirrel. From my spot, scrunched into the corner, I watched it, and a single thought came loud and clear through my brain.

We are SO going to die.

11

There was a broom propped against the wall, one of those old-fashioned ones whose head was made of stiff grass bound tight together. As the cat-monster glowered at the animated teapot, I flung myself across the room, my new-found grace helping me snatch up the broom and turn on the cat in a single easy movement. I would have felt pretty good about myself if I'd come up with a sword or spear or something. I brandished the broom, swinging it till the air hummed, but it was still just a broom.

The cat turned back to me, yellow eyes narrowed, its great jaws drooling and spitting.

I swung the broom hard at its head, but it batted my attack away with one paw as another scythed at my face. I gave the broom handle an improbable spin, parrying the clawed assault, then reversed my grip and jabbed the cat-thing in in its gut with the butt end. It winced but came on, slashing and snapping, and I realized the real horror about it being able to hang in the air unassisted: it could use all four paws to fight.

Or hold. Its forepaws—what I still thought of as its hands—snagged my wrists with the needle-sharp tips of its claws and pinned me against the wall. When I kicked out, its lower claws bit into my legs and held me fast. I was still clutching the broom handle in both hands, but the strength of the monster was pushing it up under my chin. I was going to be throttled by my own weapon. If the cat didn't choose to tear my throat out with its teeth first.

Up close the monster stank, an animal rankness but edged with something considerably fouler, something like decay; like death. Its eyes were mad and fixed. With horror I felt the rough wetness of its sandpapery tongue on my neck and I tried in vain to shrink away, revolted. It was enjoying itself. It was going to kill me, not out of panic or self-defense, but because it wanted to. It was savouring the moment.

There was a rush of movement and a cry of rage: Em had flown at the cat thing, a ceramic lamp lifted high over her head. She brought it crashing down onto the creature's skull. The lamp shattered, and for a second the cat closed its eyes. Then it was alert again, snarling and hissing an even greater rage than before. It released my right arm just long enough to swing at Emily, its paw expanding as the hooks of its claws extended. I didn't see what happened, but Em was thrown back against the wall and into a heap of boxes.

She didn't get up.

"No!" I roared, fighting to get free, though my hands and legs were still held tight. I twisted and struggled, then stabbed my head forward hard, right into the great cat's face. The monster looked momentarily dazed, but I couldn't get free, and it was soon focused again. It became still, deliberate, and its snarl became something satisfied which was almost, horribly, like a purr. It bared its teeth and cocked its head, ready to bite into the soft part of my throat.

Dimly, as if from far away, I heard the shrill chittering of the animated teapot which had, it seemed been upended by Emily when she fell. Now it was on its feet (!) again, and charging at the cat, its lid snapping. For a moment, even in the face of certain death, it was almost funny. My sister was out of it, I was about to have my head severed by the jaws of a giant floating cat in clothes, and my only hope was a magic teapot . . .

The effect of the charging kettle on the cat was bizarre. The monster turned to stare at it, hissing and yowling. The noise was still angry but there was an uncertain note there too, a hint, almost, of panic. It turned back to me, to finish the job, but it couldn't seem to ignore the teapot which was now nipping at its feet and tail, rising from the floor a few inches on its impossible little legs. The cat winced away as if scalded, forgetting me in its dread of being touched by the kettle's biting lid, and in a second I was free. I collapsed in a heap as the wild-eyed cat bounced around the little room, harried by the vengeful teapot, flinging its paws in ways that sent furniture flying. Books and chairs and old photograph frames hurtled at the teapot, but it wouldn't stop its yipping pursuit, and at last the cat had had enough.

It pointed one paw at the front door which burst open as if caught by a tornado, then it streaked out, its paws not touching the floor, and vanished into the night.

In the surreal stillness which followed, I stared after it, horror, incredulity and relief fighting for space in my stunned head. Then I saw Emily stir. She sat up slowly, holding her head, eyes half closed.

"Em!" I shouted. "You ok?"

She nodded slowly.

"The world makes a lot less sense than it did a little while ago," she replied, feeling her head gingerly, "but yeah, I think I'm ok."

We stared at each other, breathing hard.

"Did that just happen?" she asked.

"Afraid so."

"OK," she said, trying to process it. "OK. Well, at least it's over."

Except that she still had a fox tail and there was a teapot bustling around the room, looking pleased with itself. Our eyes fell on it as it hopped back into its box and went to sleep. Or rather, it retracted its legs and became a teapot again. I watched it for a while, even picked it up and considered filling it with water just to see what would happen, but in the end I just set it back in the wooden box, closed the lid and latched it with something like relief.

"So, not over then," I said.

We closed the doors, peering out into the street for any sign that the creature might come back, listening for the sounds of panic which could suggest that someone else had seen it, but there was nothing. At last, our breathing returning to normal, we sat in *Bāchan's* ancient armchairs and considered each other.

"You think our grandmother was always a cat-monster-thing?" asked Emily.

I shook my head.

"Doubt it," I said. "Whatever that thing was, I don't think it knew us at all."

"No," she answered. She said it sadly, and I thought I knew why.

"Better search the place," I said. "Just in case."

She didn't ask what we were searching for. She knew.

We went through into the kitchen/dining room where we had used to have supper sometimes when we were little, before my mom decided that it would be better for us not to spend so much time with her mother. Nothing seemed out of the ordinary, so we went all the way into the back room where my grandmother slept. I don't think I'd ever been in there before.

It was strange, though not the supernatural strange which we should have been getting used to by now. It was foreign strange. Japanese strange. The floor was covered in a kind of pale matting which Emily said was *tatami*, and there was only a little coffee table thing where you would expect the bed to be, and a heavy wooden chest in the corner. It turned out that the bed—actually a rolled-up futon—was kept in a cupboard, so the only place still to look was the chest, which had been latched closed like the box holding the teapot. That made me cautious. I didn't want to find myself surrounded by an army of animated dinnerware brandishing steak knives, but Emily got on with it, flipping the hasps and throwing the lid back.

Bāchan was lying on her side, her knees drawn up to her chest and her eyes closed. For a moment it was as if all the air was drawn out of the room and time stopped. After the madness of the battle, the thrill of still being alive at the end of it, reality crashed in on us.

"Oh no!" gasped Emily. "*Bāchan?*"

For several long seconds, nothing happened, and then, as if the world had begun to breathe again, the old woman's eyes opened.

"She's alive!" I gasped. "Help me get her out."

That wasn't as easy as it sounded. Lifting old people—even tiny ones—is hard work, and I think that on any other occasion we would have been at it half the night but today I was strong. It hadn't helped against the cat monster, but it helped now.

Bāchan was scared, which you couldn't really blame her for, but she looked at us with kind, serious eyes so like herself and so unlike the cat-thing which had looked like her that it was hard to believe we had been deceived by it even for a second. I felt bad about that, if you want to know the truth, like we had let her down.

But she led us into the kitchen and we sat together and she made green tea, which I hadn't had in years and didn't really like, but I drank it anyway. I told her about the teapot which had saved our lives (and there's a phrase which may have never been said before) and she just nodded, like it was to be expected.

"Did you hear what I said, *Bāchan?*" I remarked. "Your teapot came alive."

"Old things," she said with a shrug. "Sometimes that happens."

"No, *Bāchan*," I said. "It really doesn't."

"Your mother should have told you," said *Bāchan*, scowling at her steaming cup. "Should have told you many things."

"I think she wanted us to be like . . ." I began, but Emily cut me off.

"What things?" she said.

Bāchan shook her head. "I think it is not my place to say," she said.

Our grandmother was born in Japan and lived there till she was in her twenties. She spoke excellent English but she had a strong accent and sometimes got words wrong and often took time to put a phrase together. I waited to see if she was hunting for the words, but she sat quite still, satisfied that she had said all she needed to. All she could.

"You think mom is going to explain why I have a fox tail?" Emily pressed.

Bāchan shook her head.

"Then I think it *is* your place to say," said Emily.

Emily could be pretty intense when she wanted to be. *Bāchan* looked at her, then set her cup down and moved to a photograph in a frame on the kitchen cabinet. There was a little incense burner in front of it and a tiny wooden model of some kind of shrine or temple. She lifted the picture down and smiled as she handed it to us.

"My father-in-law" she said. "He died many years ago. Your mom never knew him."

Bāchan nodded again, smiling her faraway smile like she was remembering things that made her happy and sad at the same time.

"His name was Watanabe Raiko and his son was my husband, Hirokuni. Raiko thought that his children should stay close to the land he had walked all his life, but after he died, Hirokuni thought it would be better to live here in America. He had a farm in California. When the war came, that was taken from him and he was interred in a camp. He was released after the war ended, of course, but by then he had lost everything."

I looked at the picture but didn't understand why she was telling us about her father-in-law or her husband who had died when Mom was very small. Emily said she remembered him a little, but I didn't.

"He decided to move east and settled here in Portersville because the mountains reminded him of his home in Yamanashi." She looked distant, wistful but maintained the same mild smile.

"Your mom is very American," said *Bāchan*, smiling not unkindly. "Or she wants to be. She thinks the past is best forgotten. Look forward. Build a future. She didn't want you growing up with a lot of talk of dead people and old habits. It is . . . understandable."

"Okay," I said, "but what does any of this have to do with what just happened here?"

Bāchan frowned again and was quiet for a long time.

"Your mom also didn't want me to tell you things which sound . . . crazy." Her voice was very quiet and each word came out slowly, like she was still trying to decide if she should speak at all.

"Crazy how?" asked Emily.

"My father-in-law—your great grandfather—was a very unusual man," said *Bāchan*. She studied her finger ends and I could tell she was being careful, like she was afraid to say more.

"In what way unusual?" I asked.

"I don't know that I should say," she replied.

"*Bāchan*," I said, "we just got attacked by a cat in clothes. I think we can handle it."

"Not a cat," said *Bāchan* with a certainty that surprised me. "A *bakeneko*. A goblin cat. They can change their appearance but they are always, in certain respects, cats."

"A goblin cat," I said. It wasn't really a question. I just wanted to see if I could say the words without screaming with laughter or, I suppose, madness.

"A monster cat," said *Bāchan*, trying the phrase, but not liking it. "A demon cat. English is . . ."

She made a face. *Wrong*, it said. *Inadequate*.

Emily and I looked at each other. The idea that our *Bāchan* was an expert on Japanese monsters was almost as bizarre as the fact that there *were* Japanese monsters.

"Okay," I said forcing myself to stay calm. "So Raiko, our great grand-father was . . . what?"

"A Shinto priest," she said. "And a warrior of remarkable gifts. But there's something else." Here she looked apologetically at Emily. "He married a beautiful woman called Mayumi." She hesitated and looked down.

"What?" Emily asked. "Mayumi. She sounds nice. She was nice, right? Nice and normal?"

"Mayumi was a *kitsune*," said *Bāchan*.

"I don't know what that means," I said.

Bāchan nodded.

"A fox," she said.

"WHAT?" Emily shot back. "Our ancestors were *animals?*"

It was a mark of how strange our lives had gotten that her tone was charged more with outrage than disbelief.

"Not all your ancestors," said *Bāchan*. "Just her. And the *kitsune* is no ordinary animal. Mayumi was a shape changer. When she was young she was probably a fox most of the time, but then she met my father-in-law and decided to stay a woman forever. For him."

She smiled and Emily's furious shock evaporated as she processed the idea.

"That's so romantic!" she exclaimed.

"Can we get back to the part about her being a fox before we do the Lifetime TV version?" I asked.

"My father-in-law had been a powerful demon queller early in life and had made enemies," said *Bāchan*. "I think he was older than he looked."

"How much older?" said Emily, sensing something. "Like he was in college when his wife was in high-school or . . .?"

"Centuries," said *Bāchan*.

"Excellent, "said Emily, putting her face in her hands.

"A demon queller?" I said.

Bāchan gave me a blank look.

"I don't know what *quell* means," I said.

She looked surprised and confused.

"This is not an ordinary word?" she asked. "A demon fighter, controller. Someone who… beats demons down."

"Ok," I said, as if this was now all clear and we weren't talking about demons.

Bāchan hesitated. "Long after Raiko settled down with Mayumi, after my husband was born, something came looking for him."

I didn't like the sound of that, not the way she said it.

"What?" I asked.

"I do not know," said *Bāchan*. "If he knew, my husband would not tell me. He said it was something terrible which his father had fought before.

He fought it again and defeated it, but not before it . . ." She faltered and looked down.

"What?" asked Emily.

I don't know how I knew, but I did. I felt it as I had felt the need to go along the bamboo path through the *torii* gates.

"It killed our great grandmother," I said.

Bāchan looked at me and nodded slowly.

"Yes. The enemy, whoever or whatever it was, tricked Raiko into some wild goose chase leaving his wife alone. Mayumi had lost her ability to change, so when the fight came to her, she was powerless. Her death changed my father-in-law. After years of saying we must all stay in Japan, he changed his mind and told my husband to leave at once. The thing which had killed my mother-in-law would not rest until it had destroyed our whole family. My husband got word that his father died a few weeks later, but I do not know how."

"But Raiko killed the monster, right?" I pressed. "Before he died, I mean."

She tipped her head on one side and made an uncertain noise.

"Defeated," she said. "Not killed."

"Oh," said Emily. "I don't like the sound of that at all."

"My husband—Raiko's heir—died many years ago. I think the thing Raiko defeated has been searching for me, for my children and grandchildren for many years," said *Bāchan* seriously. "Tonight, I think, it found us."

"What?" I sputtered. "The accident at the fracking site is somehow about us?"

Emily stared at me, then looked to *Bāchan* for reassurance.

"That's not what you mean, right, *Bāchan*? You can't think it's still hunting us after all these years?"

But *Bāchan* said nothing and Emily gaped.

"You *do* think that!" she said. "You really do! You think your father-in-law's old enemy was this cat-goblin thing, the . . .neo . . .?"

"*Bakeneko*," said *Bāchan*. "No. That may be allied with the thing he defeated, but it is only a servant or warrior. The thing itself will be far more terrible."

That sure killed the conversation. If there was something worse than the cat-goblin out there, something that had it in for our family . . .

"We gotta get out of here!" I said.

"Right there with ya, little brother," said Emily, getting to her feet. She sounded defiant, but her face was bloodless and sweating. She was at least as scared as me.

"No," said *Bāchan*, also rising and looking suddenly fierce. "You have been chosen by Raiko! You are his heirs! You possess his spirit and he has given you his gifts! You must stay and fight the evil in his name!"

"His gifts?" Emily shot back. "If a fox tail is a gift, I want to exchange it."

"Yeah, no offense, *Bāchan*," I agreed, "but we are not remotely the hero types. I'm sorry, but it's the truth. People have gone missing and the cops are involved. If we go telling them about ancient Japanese monsters, they're gonna throw us in jail. Or an asylum. And even if they did believe us, I don't know anything about Japan and, to tell you the truth, I don't want to. We nearly got killed by a cat in a dress which you say is only a servant of the Big Bad and you think we can fight it? That's just not going to happen. We're *way* out of our league here and believe me when I say that if your father-in-law could see me, he wouldn't expect me to achieve anything but total disaster. If something is coming after us, we're gonna have to take off. I'm sorry, but Raiko's gonna have to find another warrior."

"You are the last son of Raiko, the demon queller!" *Bāchan* exclaimed. "You are Watanabe Hideki!"

"No," I said, shaking my head sadly but with absolute certainty. "I'm Caleb Smith, and I don't do this kind of thing."

12

See? I told you I was a loser's loser. But what would you have done? And think long and hard about that question before you jump in with some tale about how heroic you'd be, how much you'd risk for a little glory. It's all nonsense. Think you'd run into a burning building, wrestle an ornery gator or sprint across a battle field? That's just movie stuff. Sure, in a story it sounds like fun, like it's not a big deal, because you can't feel the heat of the fire, you can't smell the gator's breath or hear the bullets zipping through the air, but when you're in it, when you're *really* there, it's different. And I'll tell you something else, fire and gators and bullets are all part of regular everyday reality, so you can think about them and figure out your chances because you know exactly what you are dealing with. But when you've just been inches from death at the hands—well, *paws*—of something whose existence you hadn't believed in ten minutes earlier, that's a whole other ballgame, one where you don't know the rules and the ball explodes. My regular life sucked, but it was better than this alternative I found myself in.

When we got home we found my mother waiting on the doorstep of the inconvenience store like a person-shaped storm cloud. She was dressed, as usual in a matching skirt and crisp jacket, what she insisted was "professionally appropriate" though the look might be better suited to selling designer shoes and jewellery rather than energy drinks and Slim Jims.

"Where have you been?" she demanded, lightning in her eyes.

"We had a meeting after school," said Emily.

Technically true.

"And Em waited for me to finish the football try-outs," I added.

"How did that go?" asked my dad, from behind the counter.

Mom gave him a killer look, and his smile fell like a stalling biplane. He started studying the cash register like it was the most interesting thing he'd ever seen.

"The Sheriff was just here," she said, turning her laser gaze back on us.

Emily and I looked at each other and made showy shrugs of bafflement.

"He said he had already spoken to you," she said, watching for our response.

"That's right," I said brightly. "Helping them with their enquiries. But we didn't."

"Because we didn't know what this was," said Emily, whipping out her phone and flashing the image of the torn paper at her.

"Yes," mom said, turning quickly away. "They showed it to me, as well. I told them I couldn't read it."

Emily shot me a curious look. She didn't have to tell me that mom was being . . . economical with the truth.

"You can't?" Emily pressed.

"You know I don't read Japanese," she said, face and voice tight. "I was born here, like you."

"But it is Japanese," said Emily. "Not, I don't know, Chinese or something?"

Mom looked away, caught out. I met Dad's eye and shrugged.

"Don't you have homework?" Mom asked.

"I've done it," said Emily. "You know what it is, that paper thing?"

"I said already," said mom, turning on her and getting frosty, "I can't read it."

"That's not what I asked," said Emily.

"Leave it, Em," I said.

"I'm just asking what that paper is, because you know, don't you, Mom?" she pressed.

Mom hesitated, lips pursed into the thinnest of lines, and for a second, though it made no sense, I was sure my sister was right.

"You are being disrespectful," Mom said. "Go to your room."

"Are you kidding?" Emily shot back.

"You heard your mother," said Dad.

Emily gave me a look.

"Way to back me up, Caleb," she muttered as she stomped out.

I said nothing. After all, we were supposed to be done with all this. We'd said no to *Bāchan*. We should leave it to the authorities. Keep our heads down. Stay out of it.

I made the JV football team. Coach Pickens implied that if I could demonstrate that my last try out hadn't been a fluke, he'd be considering me for Varsity. Our first game wasn't for two weeks, he said, but there was training and practice and plays to learn. 'A lot of work', he said, grinning, like that was a special prize all by itself.

And I was pretty happy about it for about an hour, and then I started to remember that I had never really been interested in sport and this was, as the coach had said, going to be a lot of work. On the other hand, it might not be bad to fill my time in ways that kept my mind off *ancient Japanese monsters . . .*

Emily had no such option. She had quit the swim team, citing scheduling conflicts which everyone took to mean that my parents were forcing her to work in the store. In fact, she spent most of her spare time hiding out in her room, barely leaving the house except to go to school, and never seeing her friends. It was weird. I was used to Em being everything I wasn't: part of a group of annoyingly giggly girls who talked about boys and clothes and music incessantly, sharing every (carefully lit) moment of their lives on Instagram and TikTok, and bubbling through life like chatty little corks on a frothy pink river. Now she lived like a hermit in a cave. She added a bolt to her door and forgot to shower.

And then, two days later, she emerged, eyes wide, her usually glossy hair tangled, wearing a stained sweatshirt and a knee length skirt, but grinning in my doorway. I looked up from my computer and considered her.

"Er . . . hey," I said cautiously. "What's up?"

She said nothing, but slowly pirouetted on the spot, a gradual 360 degree turn with her arms over her head like a somewhat moth-eaten ballerina.

I gave her a baffled frown, but then it hit me.

"Your tail!" I gasped.

"Gone," she said, grinning like the cat which had eaten the canary and washed it down with a pint of full cream milk.

"How?" I exclaimed, leaping to me feet. "Did you cut it off?"

She shook her head.

"Eww," she said. "No. I made it go away."

I returned to my doubtful frown.

"You made it go away?" I parroted.

"With the power of my mind," she said, like a TV magician.

"O . . . K . . ." I said. "And how does that work, exactly?"

"Not sure," she said, "but it does. Wanna see?"

"Wanna see you bring back the tail you've been trying to get rid of for days?" I asked. "Why would you . . .?"

"Because I'm in control," she said. "It's all about control."

"OK, but what's the point of . . ."

But she wasn't listening. She raised her hands till they were a couple of inches from the side of her head, fingers splayed and slightly curved as if she was cradling an invisible helmet, then closed her eyes. For a moment she just stood there and then . . .

Then something bad happened. She was there, and then her clothes were in a little heap on the floor, and sitting in the middle of them, eyes shut and nose in the air, was a fox.

Not a girl with a fox tail. An *actual fox*, lithe and cute and feral looking, russet on top, white underneath, its long brush of a tail snaking out behind it like, you know, a *FOX*!

Its eyes opened, then widened, and its lower jaw dropped open, revealing sharp little teeth, but my attention was still on its eyes. They looked scared and confused. They looked, more to the point, like Emily. Fox-Emily looked at itself, its paws, its tail, and then looked up at me and yelped.

"Change back!" I said. But the wild-eyed creature looked paralyzed with fear. "Em! Change back!"

But it was all too clear that she couldn't.

13

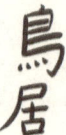

Elsewhere

Blake Wilde and Davey Kott, high school seniors who had only narrowly survived their junior year, were drinking beer purchased for them by Blake's older brother on the old footbridge. Eighty feet below them the Great Bear River ran through the rocky gorge. This was a favourite spot of theirs after dark. No one ever came up here, partly because it was too far from the water to fish, and partly because the path on the far side of the bridge from town didn't really go anywhere except up, connecting with various hiking trails neither boy had ever been on. And they were boys, though they drank beer and *were* big enough to pass for men.

Blake cracked open another Pabst Blue Ribbon and took a long, showy slug. This, he thought, was the life. Which was probably as well, because his current prospects didn't include much else. His grades were so lousy he had almost been held back a year. Davey who was currently staring vaguely at his phone, had a part time job in a sort of informal apprenticeship at Steve Merchen's body shop, and would probably get a full-time position there when he graduated, but Blake had nothing, as his dad kept reminding him. His dad drove long haul trucks: not a bad gig in that it kept him out of Portersville, but the hours were brutal and the money was only so-so. Blake had his eye on greater things.

"You should hear my new guitar, man," he said between mouthfuls. "With the gain cranked up, that thing shreds."

"Where you get it?" asked Davey, who was starting to slur.

"Pawnshop," said Blake, fiddling with the shark tooth on the silver chain round his neck. "Got me a deal. Gonna start a band," said Blake, not for the first time, "get a record deal and make a fortune. This town won't know what hit it. You gotta have vision, you know? Belief. That's why I'm gonna be something and you're not."

Davey nodded vaguely, as if agreeing, though he had no belief in himself and less in Blake whose guitar playing he had heard before. Blake applied the same rules to his music that he did to the rest of his life: all attitude, no skill. A lot of flash and big talk, no real product. Davey didn't say so, because Blake was his oldest friend, though he sometimes thought that was just an accident of history. If they met now for the first time, like, if they had grown up in different places and just bumped into each other, he doubted they'd get along. When he was being honest with himself, Davey thought Blake Wilde was kind of an ass.

Davey scowled at his phone which had died suddenly, though he was sure he'd had plenty of battery.

"What you gonna play in this band?" he asked to fill the silence. It was a warm night and the trees around them rang with the drone of frogs, crickets and cicadas.

"Metal, man!" said Blake, as if this was obvious. "Scorching speed metal."

"Gotta be a good guitarist to play that stuff," Davey mused. "Fast."

"I am good," said Blake, getting unsteadily to his feet. "I'm great!" He shouted this last into the night. "Woo! Yeah, baby. Rock and roll!"

Behind them, something mewed as if in response. A cat, grey and with a long tail which it lashed as the two boys turned to look at it, was sitting on the wall of the bridge.

"My mom wants a cat," said Davey vaguely.

"Cats are dumb," said Blake.

He drained his beer can and hurled it at the cat, which squawked and jumped out of the way. The can clunked on the wall and dropped into the darkness over the bridge. It took a surprisingly long time to fall, and it hit the water below without so much as a splash. Blake leaned over the rail to see if he could see it bobbing on the current, but it was too dark.

"We should heave the cat over," he said, grinning maliciously. "See if it survives the fall. See if it can swim."

77

He turned around to see if the cat was still in sight, and only then did he see the light. It was orange and shifting, like a flame, but small.

A candle or lantern.

It was over on the far side of the bridge, not the town side, the mountain side, and now that he looked at it he thought he could see something else: a shadowy figure. The light, whatever it was, was being held by someone who was coming slowly toward where Blake and Davey were drinking.

Blake straightened up, the cat forgotten. He didn't care what anyone thought of him drinking, but he could do without a warning to his folks or another suspension from school.

"Hey," he said quietly to Davey. "Check it out."

Davey made an exaggerated and unsteady turn, his head lolling, his beer-addled senses trying to figure out what he was looking at, and then he went still. It was a girl. A girl in fancy clothes with some kind of parasol and an old-fashioned lantern.

"Woah," said Davey. "Cute." He struggled to his feet and smoothed his wrinkled clothes, trying to look nonchalant.

"Oriental chick," said Blake, muscling him out of the way. "Sweet. Watch and learn, Davey boy. Watch and learn." He took a few swaggering steps towards the approaching girl, smiling smugly. "Hey, baby," he cooed. "Nice dress."

In fact it wasn't a dress exactly. It was a deep crimson kimono, overlaid with pale flowers and trimmed with silver embroidery which managed to be both restrained and dazzling. Davey swallowed and took a step back, instantly recognizing that he was out of his depth, but Blake had no such qualms.

"What's that, an umbrella?" he said stupidly. "You think it's gonna rain?" The parasol was bashfully tilted to obscure the woman's face, but Blake could fix that. "Come on, baby," he said, extending his hand to hers. "Let's have a look at you."

The woman was shy but unresistant as he took the hand holding the parasol and pushed it up till the light of her antique lantern lit her face.

Or would have, if she'd had one. Where eyes, nose and mouth should have been, there was only pale blankness, smooth and featureless as an egg.

Blake shrieked and tried to get away but in the same instant the woman—if that's what she was—seized him by the wrist and held him in an iron grip. He fought to get away, stabbing with his elbows since he couldn't swing his fists, but she had him in a crushing bear hug, her empty face pressed against his cheek. Arms pinned to his sides, Blake roared his terrified madness.

Davey didn't hesitate to ditch his friend. His eyes went wide and he broke into a stumbling run, pounding his erratic way along the bridge toward town as Blake's screams tore the night to shreds. He kept running, gibbering incoherently, off the bridge and on into town, as Blake's cries faded away.

"Not possible," Davey gasped as he ran. "Not possible. Not possible."

He was flagging now, the beer and horror taking its toll on his legs. He glanced behind him in case the thing he couldn't name was coming after him, but there was only the warm Carolina night, the trees and the whining bugs, like everything was ordinary, normal. He pulled out his phone, but it was still dead.

"No, no, no" he muttered, forcing himself to keep running, though he was weaving now, clumsy with tiredness.

He rounded a corner onto the main drag into town and saw the lights of a gas station up ahead. Davey focused on it, trying not to think what might be happening to Blake back at the bridge, blundering across the forecourt with its pumps, and bursting into the brightly lit shop beyond. There was an old white guy Davey didn't know behind the counter. He barely glanced up as Davey stumbled in, his eyes down on a scratch ticket.

"Call the cops," Davey managed. "My phone . . . there's something back on the bridge. Oh man. It got Blake!"

"What?" said the old guy, "What are you talking about? What do you mean 'something'?"

"Like a girl but not," said Davey, swallowing.

"You're not making sense," said the shop keeper.

"It looked like a woman but then her face went all . . ."

He shook his head, unable to complete the sentence.

The old guy frowned, then said,

"Was it like this?"

And he passed his hand over his face which promptly vanished, becoming as smooth and featureless as an egg.

Davey screamed.

14

"Hi *Bāchan*," I said, pushing past her and into her little house. I had one arm looped through the handles of a picnic basket, inside of which was my big sister, and there's another of those sentences that might never have been said before. Here I am, I thought wildly, like Little Red Riding Hood going to see my grandmother, but I'd brought the big bad wolf with me in a basket . . .

It was crazy. But it was so completely and utterly crazy that there was nowhere else I could go. *Bāchan* was the only person who wouldn't completely flip out if I tried to explain what had happened, or I hoped as much. Even so, I set the basket on her little coffee table and opened it without a word, *Bāchan* peering round me expectantly.

The fox that had been my big sister sniffed the air and blinked.

Bāchan made one of those slow Japanese noises of surprise and wonder and looked at me.

"*Kazuko-chan?*" she said.

"Yes," I said. "It's Emily. She managed to lose the tail, but when she tried to show me that she could bring it back . . . Now she's stuck."

"I see," said *Bāchan*, as if I had just told her that a power outage was caused by downed trees.

"Can she understand us?" I asked. "It still seems like her, not like a real fox, you know."

"When did this happen?"

"About an hour ago," I said.

"Then yes, probably, in a way," said my grandmother. "But the longer she is like this, the harder it will be for her to remember what it is to be human."

"She won't be able to change back?" I gasped, staring at her.

"She won't want to," she replied calmly, stroking the little animal with a wrinkled hand. "We are memory. When we forget what we were, we become something else. It is the way of things."

"This is not the way of things!" I exclaimed. "She's my sister. She's supposed to be swimming and trying on clothes and making dumb jokes about my parents and studying for exams and . . . not hunting for chickens, or whatever foxes do all day."

"Does your mother know?"

"God, no," I exclaimed, suddenly struck by the full horror of how I would explain this if we couldn't fix it.

"I cannot turn her back," said *Bāchan* simply.

"What? You must! You're the only one who understands . . ."

But she was shaking her head solemnly, her eyes closed.

"This requires power," she said. "I do not have it. Something needs to show her what she is, show her the way to become herself."

"Like what? Should we go back to the shrine? That's where all this started."

Again she shook her head.

"The shrine appeared when it needed you," she replied. "It is not there now."

"But this is that Raiko guy's fault! He made her like this!"

"He activated what was already there in both of you," she replied with that same eerie composure, as if she was puzzling over a crossword. "We need someone else to teach her mastery of her gift."

"Her gift? She's a cartoon character!"

"Silence," she said, waving a hand and wandering into the back room with little, halting steps like her knees were tied together with string. She stopped then, head tilted up as if listening to something far off, and for a long moment was completely still. Then she rummaged through a drawer in an end table, pulled out a notebook and leafed through it, holding it so close to her face that it almost touched her nose. She gave a satisfied grunt, and then she was coming back, purposeful, picking up a little hand bag and her keys.

"We are going out," she said. "Call for a taxi to this address," she said, handing me the notebook open to a page with a couple of lines of spidery writing. "Bring the basket."

Ten minutes later we were sitting in the back of an Uber driven by a kid called Warren who had graduated from East Portersville the previous year.

"What's in the basket?" he said cheerfully.

"Biscuits," I said, stupidly.

The basket gave a rustling wobble in my lap. I steadied it hastily.

"Smells kind of rank," said Warren, wrinkling his nose.

"I didn't say they were good biscuits," I replied.

"You hear about Blake Wilde?" he said, switching direction, and glancing at us in the rear-view mirror.

I shook my head. Blake was senior: cool in his way, but also dangerous —wild by name and by nature, I remember someone saying once. Always wore a shark's tooth on a chain round his neck. I tried to avoid him exactly as I would avoid a shark.

"What about him?" I asked.

"Missing," said Warren gleefully. "Presumed... well, no one knows, but nothing good. The cops have his buddy in custody. Davey Kott. You remember him?"

I shook my head again, feeling a low level stirring of anxiety. Warren's eyes kept flashing to the mirror. I was sure he was watching *Bachan*.

"Apparently," said Warren, "they found Davey staggering down main-street last night babbling about a monster dressed in Japanese clothes."

He let that little detail hang in the air, watching us in the mirror. My mouth had gone dry. I licked my lips and said,

"He was probably drunk."

"Who, Davey or Blake?"

I shrugged, feeling the color rise in my face.

"Either," I said. "Both."

I had hoped Warren would laugh or nod, but he said nothing, his eyes flicking between the road ahead and our faces in the mirror.

"I expect Blake will turn up," I said, trying to sound optimistic.

"I expect so too," said Warren. I smiled but he added "One way or another. OK, this is you."

"What do you mean?" I demanded, defensive.

"I mean, this is your stop," he replied. "You can get out. And don't forget your cookies. I don't want them stinking up the car."

I peered out of the car window and my heart sank. I had been expecting some kind of sacred space: a temple or shrine, maybe a grave-yard I didn't know about. Not . . . this.

"You sure this is the right place?" I said.

"I just take people to the addresses they give me," said Warren philo-sophically. "Whether that's where they need to be . . . that's on them."

We got out and he spoke through the open window.

"Y'all keep your eyes open for Japanese monsters, ya hear?" he said, grinning.

I opened my mouth to say something but he was already pulling away. I turned to *Bāchan*.

"You heard what he said?" I asked. "About the kid from school going missing, about the...?"

"Japanese monster," she inserted. "Yes, I heard."

"And?" I almost shouted.

"One thing at a time," she said, walking away.

The cab had dropped us at an inauspicious looking strip mall on the west side of town. Most of the stores had been abandoned, and there was a massive sign advertising, somewhat hopefully, "Great Retail Space!" but the place was deserted. There were a few cars parked outside of a dollar store, and there was one of those big boxes whose makeshift banners said that it was being temporarily rented out to sell Halloween costumes, but the central lot felt like it should have tumble weeds blowing across it. A couple of buildings over from the costume place was a squat looking structure with a sign in faded red lettering: *Hibachi Prince Asian Steakhouse and Sushi*.

"You've got to be kidding," I said, but *Bāchan* was already hobbling over, her purse clasped primly to her chest.

I had noted how squat the building looked on the outside, but I hadn't anticipated how miserable that would make the place on the inside. It was low ceilinged, low rent and loaded with low expectations. It was also deserted, except for an East Asian guy who gave us a glower as we came in and snarled, "Closed. Come back later."

I say he was East Asian—Chinese or Japanese, probably—but he had one decidedly uncharacteristic feature; his nose looked like a piece of broom handle glued to the middle of his face. It was so improbably big that for a second, I wondered if he'd bought it at the costume shop down the block. When *Bāchan* responded in what I took to be polite Japanese, he whirled round to consider us properly. It was a good thing the place was empty: that nose of his could have wiped out half his clientele. Now that I got a better look at it I could see that it was less like a broom handle and more like something between a banana and a cucumber, and it curved up slightly near the tip. High school for this guy would have been a nightmare.

He stared at us in response to *Bāchan*'s greeting, then bowed fractionally and muttered,

"*Irasshaimase.*"

He gestured vaguely to the empty tables, which I took to mean sit where you like. We did so, but before I could look at the menu he snatched it out my hand with lightning speed and tossed it onto a neighboring table.

"OK," I said.

"He will choose something for us," said *Bāchan*, as if this was quite normal. She bowed and smiled.

"What is happening?" I said.

But the restauranter—I didn't know if he was waiter or chef—was staring fixedly at the basket I had set beside my chair, his massive nose tilted up, sniffing. *Bāchan*'s smile dried up and she watched him, not moving a muscle. He gave another interrogative sniff, this time as he stooped to the basket like a cook inspecting suspicious meat. His eyes got big, and I actually saw the hair on the back of his neck stand on end.

He growled, a low, guttural sound like a wary dog scenting an intruder. Instantly, it was clear: he knew.

Without taking my eyes off the man, I whispered to *Bāchan*. "What is he? Some kind of dog?"

Bāchan half smiled. "Not quite," she said. "This is Mr. Saito. He is a *tengu.*"

At the sound of that word, he shot her a quick, predatory look full of warning.

"This is my grandson, Hideki," she said. "He has a right to know things, including what you are."

"*Soshite, kore wa onna ga, desho,*" he replied.

"What did that mean?" I asked, still speaking under my breath.

"He said, 'And this is the girl,'" she replied.

I stared at her.

"He knows who we are?" I said.

"You are the heirs of Raiko," she replied with something caught between pride (in her family) and disdain (for my idiocy). "Of course, he knows who you are. And you will need him moving forward."

I considered the *tengu*—whatever that was—taking in more than his big nose. He was a sinewy, strong-looking guy, tall for a Japanese man. His hair was long, streaked with iron grey, and tied back into a kind of man bun, though on him it looked kind of cool, which I wouldn't have thought was possible. His eyes were black and sharp, their brows arched and bushy. With the nose he should have looked absurd, but there was a wildness to the man that you couldn't help but respect.

He looked me up and down critically, then delivered a stream of caustic Japanese to *Bāchan*—or I assume so. She responded in kind, quiet at first, but then when he interrupted, louder, more forceful. They were arguing and I was a spectator.

"Hello?" I said. "If you're going to discuss me and my sister, it would be more polite if you spoke in a language I understood."

The *tengu* gave me a fierce look, and I took a step back, certain that I'd given the kind of offense that might get my throat torn out. With his teeth. But as I was ready to run for the door, he bowed sharply, lowering his eyes to the floor.

"*Gomen nasai*," he said. "I apologize for my rudeness."

His voice was still guttural and stiff, but his English was excellent, and he spoke with what I had once heard described as *gravitas*: a kind of weighted dignity.

"No prob," I said, feeling like I'd shown up to a black-tie dinner in shorts and a tee shirt. "So, you think you can fix my sister?"

"Fix?" he said, those great eyebrows tightening like flexing mice.

"Bring her back," I clarified.

He glanced at *Bāchan* as if wondering why she had brought the village idiot to his restaurant.

"She does not need to be fixed," he said. "She needs to decide what she wants to be."

"A girl," I said. "A high school student."

He shrugged, noncommittal.

"That is up to her," he said.

"Hmmm, get her life back," I said, "or enrol in a good flea and tick program: tough call."

"If it is such an easy decision," he replied, returning his attention to the basket and cautiously raising the lid, "why has she not made it?"

"Because she doesn't know how to!" I said. "If you can't help, just say so. But spare me the mystical mumbo jumbo, ok? If you can help, let's get on with it, yeah? Time's a-wastin'. That's why we came to you: so you can change her back. Right, *Bachan*? That's why we came to this dump?"

He straightened up. In fact he seemed to grow a little, so that he loomed over me, his dark, hard eyes full of rage. His nostrils flared and he inhaled my scent critically before pronouncing his verdict.

"You are rude," he said. "And you are no heir to Raiko. You should leave."

15

I stood outside, fuming, the hot sun bouncing off the empty concrete of the parking lot while *Bāchan* made my apologies to dog-guy. We'd trekked out here for nothing but insults and scepticism from a man with a nose like a banana, and my sister was still likely to chase the cars and freak out when the mail arrived. Awesome. It wasn't like I had wanted to get involved with all this mystical nonsense in the first place . . .

"You didn't bring *Kazuko's* clothes."

It was *Bāchan*. She had half-emerged from the restaurant but was holding the door open as if she didn't actually intend to leave.

"Neither did you," I said. Not my most mature come-back, I'll admit.

"I thought they were in the basket."

"I didn't think foxes cared much about clothes!" I protested.

"Not usually," *Bāchan* agreed, serene as a mountain pond, "but teenage girls do, particularly when they have none."

"You changed her back?" I exclaimed, turning to go back inside, but *Bāchan* blocked my way.

"She changed herself back with Mr. Saito's help," she said, "but she is unhappy about being naked, a situation for which she blames you."

"Me?" I gasped, though I was also smart enough to shrink away from the restaurant door. Going in now was more than my life was worth. "What did I . . . ?"

"There is a store at the end of the mall. Buy her some things to wear."

"I can't . . ." I sputtered. "I don't know how to . . ."

"Here is money," said *Bāchan*, thrusting some notes into my hand. "Go. And be quick."

I would have argued, but she walked back inside and closed the door, so—very reluctantly—I trudged down to the low-end department store which was having its closing down sale. Whole ranks of shelves were empty and what remained looked like it had been tossed aside when the shop succumbed to the zombie apocalypse. There was only one register open and the woman tending it viewed my purchases suspiciously. There were a pair of flip flops, neon green shorts, a bright yellow shirt sporting unidentifiable cartoon characters, and some underwear I had nudged gingerly into my cart without much close examination. I had no idea if any of it was the right size, and when I tried to think about it, my brain shut down in protest.

I returned to the restaurant red faced and sweating.

Emily was sitting at a table covered with an array of dishes full of food I couldn't name, sipping a glass of water and looking stunned. She was wearing some kind of loose cotton robe with big sleaves patterned in blue and white bamboo. One hand had it clutched closed at her throat. She managed a smile as she saw me enter with my shopping bag, though the smile burned off like morning dew when I dumped the contents onto the table.

She held the shorts up between finger and thumb like they might contaminate her, and she stared at the T shirt in appalled fascination.

"You thought I'd wear this?" she said.

"There wasn't a lot of choice," I replied.

"Think I'll stick to the *yukata*, thanks."

"The what?"

She pulled at the cotton robe which could have been a kind of kimono. *Bāchan* came over with the *tengu*.

"You don't know what a *yukata* is?" she said.

"One of those?" I said, nodding at what Emily was wearing. *Bāchan* exchanged a knowing look with the *tengu* who raised his considerable eyebrows and snorted scornfully.

"Just give me the underwear," snapped Emily.

I shoved it across the table, but she yelped.

"Caleb! What size do you think I am?"

She pushed them back at me, her face hot and pink as she turned away.

"What?" I protested. "Too big? Too small? How should I know what . .
.?"

"Stop talking!" Emily snapped, eyes shut and hands up. "Give me the
flip flops."

My one achievement, I guess.

"Such gratitude," I shot back. "I feel so appreciated."

"Kazuko has been through a difficult experience," said *Bāchan*.

"Not my fault," I said. "And her name's Emily."

Another glance between *Bāchan* and the *tengu*, but they decided to let
that one go.

"Sit," said the *tengu*. "Eat."

"I'm not hungry," I said. Feeling misunderstood was making me
petulant.

"Sit," said *Bāchan*. "Eat."

"Oh, I see," I sneered. "Everything is my fault so y'all get to tell me
what to do . . ."

"Sit," said Emily. "Eat." I glared at her. "Seriously," she added. "The
food's amazing."

I gave the various dishes a surly look. I didn't know what any of it was,
but it did look fantastic which, in the circumstances, was annoying. I
looked for a fork so that I could stab something meaningfully, but there
were only . . .

"Chopsticks?" said Emily, sliding a packet across the table to me. She
had taken pity on me and was trying to be nice. "I've seen you eat with
them before. You could use the practice."

So not *that* nice.

I pulled the chopsticks out, separated them with a brisk snap which
was supposed to show how I totally knew what I was doing and then tried
to spear a little square of . . . something, nestled with beautiful artistry in a
bed of . . . something else. It flew off the plate. I tried again, but my
attempt at a pincer action made me look like a crab which had just had an
unfortunate encounter with a boat propeller. More food on the table,
none in my mouth. Attempt three flicked blobs of sauce down my front
but still didn't actually get me anything to eat.

"*Bāchan*," said Emily with a sad little sigh, "do you think you could get
my brother a fork before he starves to death?"

I stared at her resentfully, as she picked up slices of . . . something,
presumably food, and popped them delicately into her mouth.

"What?" she asked.

"When did you learn to do that?" I demanded.

"Last summer," she said, shrugging. "Mandy and Simone got on a ramen noodle kick. I got tired of getting all the crap and none of the benefits."

"All the crap?" I said, taking a piece of whatever she was eating in my fingers and popping it in my mouth before she could object. I chewed, swallowed and still didn't know what it was, but it was good: light and crispy on the outside, hot and fluffy inside. "Hey," I said, "is that . . .?"

"Sweet potato tempura," she said. "I mean the crap we get because we don't exactly blend into the Portersville background."

I gazed at her with a mixture of admiration and suspicion.

"You know way more about Japan than you've been letting on," I said.

She shrugged. "Maybe a bit," she said. "Try the miso shiro with the konyaku."

"The what with the what?"

"The soup with those bean things."

"Does mom know that you've been secretly studying up on the Land of the Rising Sun?"

She shook her head.

"No chance," she said. "I brought a manga home one day—one of those Japanese comic books . . ."

"I know what a manga is," I said, though in truth I'd never read one.

"She burned it," said Emily. "It wasn't even in Japanese. And it was a library book."

"What's with that?" I said. "I mean, I get the whole fitting-in thing, the More-American-than-the-Americans thing, but to this extent? I don't get it."

"I think I'm starting to," said Em, shooting *Bāchan* a furtive look. Our grandmother was deep in conference with the *tengu*.

I stared at her, mouth open.

"You think Mom knows about his stuff?" I gasped. "Magic and shape-shifting foxes and god knows what all?"

"I think she wanted to put some things behind her," said Emily. "Things about where her family came from. I've always thought that, though I didn't know what they were. Now I'm starting to wonder if . . ."

" . . .*Bāchan* gave her the whole 'Heir of Raiko' thing and she freaked?" I said, completing the thought for her. "Oh my God, you're right. Wow. But why would she run from it? Cool, demon-slayer ancestor sounds pretty great to me."

"You remember the *bakeneko?*" said Emily, giving me a hard look. "The killer goblin cat which we only survived because our grandmother happened to have a magic teapot? You remember the way we took off out of there swearing we'd never have anything to do with all that hero madness?"

"There is that, I guess," I conceded. "But mom didn't know monsters were gonna come hunting for us!"

"You sure about that, Caleb?" she replied. "Because I'm not."

"We could ask *Bāchan,*" I suggested, watching the old woman I had known all my life without—it seemed—ever really knowing who she was.

"You know what they used to write on maps when they had no idea what was there?" said Emily with a bleak smile. "'Voyager beware; here be dragons.'"

"Japanese dragons," I mused. "Are there Japanese dragons? I don't even know that."

"If I had to choose between a dragon and mom after she finds out who we've been hanging out with . . ."

"Yeah," I agreed. "Tough call. So how did you get back to being . . . you? I mean how did you stop being a fox?"

"He said things to me," said Emily, suddenly dreamy, a faraway look in her eye, "things I didn't understand but still made sense. It was like . . . like I was lost in a thick fog and then he showed up carrying a lantern. I followed him out." She continued, still miles away so that her voice seemed to come through bad speakers. "Everything looked different and smelled different. Really different. It was like I could *see* the smells. In color. But the really strange part was that it didn't feel weird at all. It felt normal, like I was remembering."

"Remembering?" I said. "Remembering what?"

"What I was," she said, and then she seemed to remember who she was talking to, and she got this freaked out, hunted look, like she was embarrassed and a little afraid. I swallowed and looked away, because suddenly I was too.

"Finished?" said the *tengu,* appearing beside the table. He was wearing an apron with a pocket in which sat a heavy cleaver and carrying a basket of onions which he set on the table.

Emily nodded then seemed to remember something and, articulating the words slowly and carefully, said,

"*Gochisosama deshita.*"

She gave *Bāchan* an inquiring glance, and the old lady nodded, smiling fractionally. The *tengu* turned on me.

"What she said," I remarked.

His eyes narrowed and he muttered under his breath as he set to clearing the table.

"What?" I protested. "I don't speak Japanese."

"I can't help you," he said, bustling with the plates and dishes.

"No one asked you to!" I replied, getting hot in the face again.

As the *tengu* moved toward the kitchen with his stack of dishes, he threw *Bāchan* a glance.

"I did," she said, acknowledging his point.

"To change Emily back," I said. "Not to teach us Japanese."

"I didn't ask him to teach you Japanese," she clarified. "I asked him to train you, so you could use your gifts."

"I came to get Emily fixed," I retorted. "That's all."

"Fixed?" said the tengu with immense disdain.

"Cured, then," I said.

"You understand nothing," he shot back. "She has not been fixed or cured. She is a *kitsune*, a fox and a human intertwined. I helped her recover her human shape but she is still a fox and always will be."

"She needs to learn how to control the change," *Bāchan* inserted. "As you, Hideki, need to learn your physical abilities, your combat skills. You are in danger. Something is looking for you. We believe it has tracked you in order to take revenge for something Raiko did many years ago."

"It followed us from Japan?" said Emily. "But our family left there almost a hundred years ago. You said so yourself. Something has been hunting us for a century?"

She sounded freaked.

"So it would seem," said the tengu.

"And what are *you* doing here?" I demanded of the cook. "Hell of a coincidence, you setting up shop here, exactly where some cat-monster-thing from the old country shows up! And what *is* a *tengu* anyway?"

"I am a being of the mountains," said the *tengu*, solemnly. "I am bound to the wilderness, which is harder to find in Japan than it once was. I was drawn to this place long ago but for what purpose, I cannot say."

Bāchan gave him a look, as if she thought he was holding something back.

"You knew we were here," I said, staring down the guy with the cartoon character nose. "You were charged to protect us or something, right? Given some protective mission which you chose to ignore or dodge when the going got tough."

For a moment *Bāchan* looked genuinely angry. At me! I was sure I had said no more than she was thinking, but all her kindly old lady aura burned off and her face clouded, eyes flashing, her jaw locked.

"You see?" said the *tengu*. "He perceives nothing. And if the girl were a true *kitsune*, she would have needed no help in returning to her human form. These are not the children of Raiko. They are . . . *Americans*. Their blood is impure, contaminated by their father's line, and by the ideas which come from this place. They are only half Japanese and I can do nothing with halves."

And there it was.

Half.

Emily got up, and her former rage was back.

"Speaking as *'the girl'*," she said, her voice hard and brittle as ice, "I turned into a fox! You're saying I don't have magic in my veins?"

"You have some," he said. "Not enough. If your family had married into another old Japanese family, then perhaps. But your parents are . . ." he shrugged. "Mixed. Diluted. Inadequate."

"What kind of medieval bullshit is that?" Emily demanded. "Half? I am me! One hundred per cent. I'm not half anything. And neither is Caleb."

"That's right!" I said, and I could feel it crackling in my skin again now, an old, confused anger that didn't understand itself but wanted to lash out, to scream, to smash things. Suddenly, though I was looking at the *tengu*, I saw other faces, sneering and dismissive, lining up back through the years, faces like Tyler and his buddies calling me "weirdo Jap," and for a mad second I totally understood why my mother had burned Emily's manga, though it was an understanding that only fired my rage like blowing oxygen into a furnace.

I flamed white hot.

Or at least that's how it felt. What I actually did was grab an onion from the basket on the table and throw it with all my strength at the *tengu*.

Not the most sophisticated of arguments, I grant you, but I was in the moment.

The *tengu* was standing maybe twenty feet away. But somehow, before the onion reached him, he managed to set the dishes on a table, sweep the cleaver from his apron pouch and slice the incoming vegetable in two. It was impossible, or would have been for any normal person, but he did it with such precision, such economy of movement that he made it look easy.

So I pitched another at him. It wasn't just that he had it coming. It was that the ease with which he had countered my attack made me lose it. The frustration, the sense of powerlessness . . . It was too much. So I threw another onion, and he cut it *twice* in mid-air, first into halves then, in two swift slashes, into quarters before it hit the floor. I threw another, and another, each toss increasingly wild and inaccurate, none of them troubling him, and then he did something I couldn't possibly have anticipated.

He threw the cleaver at me.

16

He threw it hard. The cleaver came at me, turning end over end right at my throat. Emily screamed, but the sound seemed to come from a long way away. I saw the steel flash through the air and, without thinking, I swept up the palms of both hands, like I was clashing a pair of cymbals, catching the cleaver between the flat of my hands. I stopped it two inches from my face. If I'd had a nose like the guy who threw it, I'd have nicked the end off.

For a moment, there was a stunned silence. Then Emily started.

"What the hell was that?" she roared. "You could have killed him! What if you'd hit him?"

"Then I would know he wasn't the heir of Raiko," said the *tengu* dispassionately.

I took a second to process this.

"Wait," I replied. "So you are saying that we *are* the . . ."

"I am saying," said the *tengu* solemnly, "that I will train you to use your gifts for your own self defense, and to honor your *Bāchan's* wishes. But," he added quickly, seeing the flash of triumph in my face, "I am not hopeful. You know nothing. You understand less. You are . . ."

"Yeah, you said all that already," I remarked, suddenly quite cheerful. "But deep down, you know that's not entirely true. Right, *sensei?*"

I flashed a grin at Emily. *Sensei* was one of the half dozen words I knew. I mean, come on; everyone has seen *Karate Kid*.

The *tengu* turned away, muttering unhappily but the battle, for the moment at least, was won.

"So, I have a question," I said, feeling chipper for once. "Some Japanese big bad which had it in for our great grandfather has come looking for us. What does that have to do with the fracking accident?"

"Nothing," said the *tengu*. "Coincidence."

"And if this cat thingy . . ." I persisted.

"*Bakeneko*," Emily inserted.

"Right," I said, "that. If that knew where *Bāchan* lived, and it's going after Raiko's heirs, why hasn't it come for us yet?"

"Because your blood line is not strong enough for the *yōkai* to have sensed you," said the *tengu*.

"This again?" I said, giving him my steeliest stare.

"What are *yōkai*?" asked Emily.

"Monsters," said *Bāchan*. "Supernatural beings. Not human, or not human any more, and not ghosts. Almost any other supernatural creatures which are not gods can be *yōkai*."

"Including shape-shifting foxes?" Emily said.

Bāchan looked hesitant but the *tengu* was emphatic.

"Yes," he said. "*Kitsune, tanuki, kappa, oni.* Many others. All different, but all *yōkai*."

"So I am a monster," she said.

"The words don't translate," said the *tengu*, unmoved by my sister's concern. He saw *Bāchan*'s face and relented a little. "Not all *yōkai* are evil. Some are merely tricksters. Some are even benign in the right circumstances."

"Damned with faint praise," I said to Emily, grinning. "See Em? In the right circumstances, you might not be evil."

"I'm not convinced that the fracking accident is irrelevant," said Emily, deliberately changing the subject. "It happened right around the time the shrine appeared in the woods. And there was the . . ." she glanced around, then remembered and glared at me. "You didn't bring my phone?"

"What were you going to do, bark into it?"

"Show them the image of the paper from the cave," she said.

I unlocked my cell and showed the screen to *Bāchan* and the *tengu*. Both frowned, first at the image, then at each other.

"This is an *ofuda*," said the *tengu*.

"A kind of charm or payer," said *Bāchan*. "You can buy them at shrines and temples. For good luck or protection."

She exchanged a few rapid words in Japanese with the *tengu* and he nodded seriously.

"They are sometimes used as seals, fastened to doors and windows to keep bad fortune, evil spirits, or monsters out."

"What would one be doing up in the old cave?" asked Emily.

The *tengu* scowled, seemingly annoyed at not being able to answer, and *Bāchan* shook her head.

"Perhaps the cave was where my husband took refuge," she said. "A fortress or safe place. He needed to keep something out."

The *tengu* shrugged expressively.

"Still just a coincidence," he said. "Hirokuni has been dead many years. If the *ofuda* seal was once important, I do not see how it could still be. The *bakeneko* has not been stalking Portersville for decades. We would have heard of it before. It has just arrived, so the *ofuda* is not relevant."

"And the missing workers?" I said.

"Industrial accidents happen all the time," said the *tengu*. "There are casualties. This happens when people plunder the earth for profit. When they see something they want, they are not careful enough about how they get it. The missing workers are not my problem. You are."

I frowned.

"And Blake Wilde, the senior whose friend says . . ."

"His friend is a liar," said the *tengu*. "Probably a murderer as well. You need to put such things out of your minds and focus on what you need to learn."

"Well, we can't keep trekking all the way out here," said Emily. "If we're going to meet regularly . . ."

"I will come to you," said the *tengu*.

At the prospect of some big-nosed Japanese mystic showing up at the inconvenience store and telling my parents he'd come to train the heirs of Raiko, Emily and I exchanged looks of alarm.

"We will work something out," said *Bāchan*, her usual unreadable self.

"OK," I said, "but be, you know, discrete."

Bāchan said nothing on our way back into town. Emily had, very reluctantly, put on the clothes I had bought her, but she would—she announced—be changing the moment we got home, something she was keen to do without being spotted. When we reached the inconvenience store, I was sent on ahead to make sure my parents' attention was else-where. We had agreed, on *Bāchan*'s emphatic advice, to tell them nothing. Yet.

Emily needn't have worried. The moment I stepped into the store, I had my parents' undivided attention. The reason? A letter addressed to them which was sitting on the counter by a rack of gum and candy. They had been summoned to a meeting at school the following day to discuss my conduct with regard to the "loss of a cherished local monument" and my "future at East Portersville High School." My parents didn't say much, but their faces spoke volumes.

"Ok," I said. "Well, I guess something like this was to be expected."

Mom's eyebrows about flew off her head. "You don't sound very upset," she observed.

"Would that help?" I said.

"Caleb, don't cheek your mother," said Dad, loyally.

"I'm serious!" I said. "I did something wrong, something bad happened as a result, and I'm going to be punished for it. What else do you want? It's not like I did it on purpose."

I think what bothered them most was that I was calm, unlike my usual self. I didn't know if that was because I had awakened the spirit of Raiko in my (mixed) blood, or because someone had just thrown a meat cleaver at me, but in the grand scheme of things, this seemed . . . do-able.

"Don't you feel anything?" asked Mom, aghast.

"For an empty barn?" I said.

"For *us*!" she exclaimed, letting it out in the kind of breathless cry that made me realize she had wanted to say this days ago.

"For you?" I said, genuinely confused for a moment.

"All your life we've done everything we could to help you fit in," she replied. "And you didn't always make it easy, Caleb, believe me. Now this. Can't you see our shame, our humiliation?"

For a moment I just looked at her.

"I'm sorry, mom," I said, "to be such a disappointment to you. Now, if you don't mind, I have football practice."

Mom looked like I'd slapped her, but Dad just shook his head.

"No, son," he said. "You don't. You've been cut from the team . . ." he flipped open the letter's second page and read, "since you are unable to attend the scheduled training sessions."

"What are you talking about?" I said, snatching the paper from him. "Training is after school and I am . . . in detention!" I concluded lamely, my eyes burning into the letter like lasers. "For six weeks."

"After which, Coach Pickens will consult with the principal as to your suitability to play."

"That's not fair!" I exclaimed. "What has the barn thing got to do with football?"

"It's the way things are," said Dad.

"Perfect," I said. "That's just great. The one time I wasn't going to be a joke and a loser in this school, and it's gone. Excellent. And, as ever, thanks for your emotional support."

And I stormed out.

Unfair? Perhaps. Well, yes, probably. And I guess I had no one else to blame for the barn thing, but it's how I felt, and everyone wanted me to be honest, right? This was me being honest. I went to my room and locked myself in. The heir of Raiko, the mighty demon queller, had been grounded.

And this was, alas, only the beginning. We didn't speak that night or at all the next day, not until our meeting with the principal, at which point, things kind of went downhill.

My dad wore jeans and a button-down shirt, but my mom wore a black business suit, like she was going to court. As we walked through the school gate and went to sign in at the office, I could see people staring down from the classroom windows, like we were the delegation from Mars.

"You should have just worn regular clothes," I muttered.

"If you respect the process, it will respect you," said Mom.

I gave her a disbelieving stare.

"Have you watched the news, like, ever?" I asked. "You shouldn't let people push you around so much."

That was rich coming from me, who got pushed around more than a Walmart shopping cart, but I was about to get suspended or worse, and was feeling defiant.

The gathering in the principal's office felt less like a meeting and more like a firing squad. The principal sat sombre faced and shiny headed (Grealish was bald as a turkey vulture) and Miss Malinski, my home room teacher who sat next to him looking slightly pained, as if she had eaten bad shrimp for breakfast. The full scale of my sins were recounted—again —and there was a lengthy eulogy on the age and beauty (!) of a building seated at the heart of the Portersville community, its value beyond rubies.

I shifted in my seat. I was getting immune to the massive guilt I was supposed to feel over what had been, after all, an accident—it wasn't like I'd rented a flame thrower from the Home Depot and targeted whatever I thought would wound the town to its very soul—but the talk about value made me uneasy. Surely, the building had been insured? Could they possibly imagine that sticking my folks with the bill would achieve anything other than ruining them?

For the first time since the night it had happened, I felt genuinely panicked. We had a little money put by in college funds but I didn't think there was much in the way of real savings. The inconvenience store was hardly Macy's. And it wasn't just the money. My parents' quiet nods and respectful apologies made me unexpectedly, desperately sad. For a long moment, I hung my head, then I looked up, and something of my former certainty returned.

"Look," I said, interrupting the principal. "I know I'm just a kid, legally speaking, and am therefore my parents' responsibility, but this really has nothing to do with them and they shouldn't be punished for what I did. Hell, they've already been punished by being made to sit here."

"Caleb!" said Mom, exactly as she always did when I said 'Hell.'

"I mean it, Mom," I said. "I wasn't acting out or reacting to anything at home. I may have been dodging some racist bullshit from some of the students, but I was just hiding out. I didn't mean for the stupid barn to burn down, ok?"

But they weren't really listening to me anymore. At the word 'racist' the teachers had sat up, all attention. Miss Malinski looked suddenly anxious, as if the phosphorescent shrimp in her gut had done a few back flips, but the sick look in her face was also pitying. Grealish, on the other hand, looked stern.

"I'm sure you don't mean to suggest that you have been the recipient of racially motivated abuse," he said, managing a sort of smile as if this was too preposterous to say aloud.

"Are you for real?" I asked, genuinely surprised.

"We don't tolerate racism at this school," said Grealish, as if he were running for office and thought there might be news cameras somewhere.

"Well, that's all right then," I said, dry as the Gobi desert. "So long as you don't *tolerate* it."

"Caleb, there's no need to make this all *political*," said my mom, the last word raising, as it always did in her mouth, a ripple of distaste. "I'm sure that's not what my son meant," she added, smiling at the principal.

"Of course, that's what I meant!" I said.

"Perhaps you misunderstood . . ." Grealish began, but I cut him off, turning to my mom pointedly.

"You remember the stew leftovers you gave me for lunch last week?" I said.

"Caleb what has that to do with . . .?"

"I never got to eat it," I said, pushing through, driven now by anger. "Know why? Because some idiot's dog had gone missing, and his buddies thought they should check my lunch box to see if it was in there."

Mom looked bewildered. "Why would they think . . .?" she began, but I interrupted again.

"Because that's what we 'Japs' do!" I said, my voice rising. "We eat dogs and cats and other things that *real people* treat as pets. You didn't know that? I'm a computer nerd who doesn't speak English, Emily is one of those mysterious and sexy Orientals, and you're that Lucy Liu look-alike whose store is a front for heroin smuggling."

"Lucy Liu?" said my mother, still more confused.

"Michelle Yeoh," I went on. "Awkwafina. They're all the same, right?"

Mom turned to my dad. "What is he talking about?" she said. "Who are these people?"

"Actresses," he said. "Caleb is just making a point."

"What point?" she replied, confusion giving way to annoyance. "I don't accept his point. I'm not some actress. I am not Japanese. I am an American. I do not experience racism in this country."

"You remember during the pandemic when someone put a brick through the store window?" I fired back.

"That was just vandalism. It wasn't racial."

"Mom, come *on!*" I exclaimed. "You don't experience racism in this country? You experience it every day! Every time people count their change in front of you. Every time they assume you can't speak English or use a fork. Every time they ignore you because they think you're not one of them. But it's more than that. Because not being one of them means you aren't actually a person, not a real one, anyway. Maybe you ignore it. Maybe you work through it. But you can't say you don't see it."

"I *do* say that!" she said, getting to her feet. "I won't listen to any more of this. I am sorry, Principal Grealish, for my son's behaviour. Ignore his excuses. We will cooperate with whatever punishment you think is appropriate."

She made for the door and Dad, looking shocked—even alarmed— went after her. I nearly went too, but I knew that unless I apologized for everything I had just said, unless I denied any of it was true, it would make no difference. When Mom was fired up, she wasn't open to what I called 'reasoned discussion' and she called 'defiance'. And I knew that I'd touched a nerve, one Em and I were generally smart enough to avoid. She wouldn't be getting over this any time soon.

I looked up, realizing that the principal was talking.

" . . . which just leaves us to assign the nature of your detention," he was saying, his face carefully impassive. "I see from your transcript that you have never taken any of Mr. Watkins' woodworking classes."

I blinked. Then shook my head.

What was he talking about?

Woodworking? Those classes had been huge thirty years ago when the school fed directly into Portersville's thriving furniture industry, but now they were hobby classes for a handful of arty types who wanted to be serious craftsmen. Their stuff got displayed at open days and such, and it was impressive, but I didn't know any of the students who took them, and I was pretty sure Mr. Watkins had retired years back. His classes now were really after school clubs.

"Mr. Watkins has been charged with supplying skilled student carpenters and related labour . . ."

"Excuse me, sir?" I cut in. "I'm no good at stuff like that. It's just not my thing."

"Whether it's your *thing* or not is irrelevant," said Grealish. "It's how you will be spending your detention and working off your debt to the school."

"I just mean, I have no experience with stuff like that," I said. "Tools. Wood. I wouldn't know where to start."

"Which is why you'll have a teacher," he replied.

My defiance flared again at the absurdity of the thing.

"What's the point of carving wooden ducks or making peg boards . . .?" I began.

"You won't be carving ducks," he said abruptly, his face going very slightly red as if it was taking considerable effort not to scream at me. "You will be rebuilding the barn."

I gaped at him.

"The barn?" I stammered.

"The one you burned down," he agreed. "Yes. Actions have consequences, Mr. Smith. Actions have consequences. Report to the site after school tomorrow afternoon. Don't be late."

17

Going home that afternoon was like stepping into a deep freeze. I told my family how I would be spending my detention and I tried to say that I was sorry for the fight in the principal's office, but Mom said everything was fine. I replied that it obviously wasn't but that I hadn't meant to upset her, and she told me to eat my lasagne so I could get on with my homework. I gave up and excused myself, saying I had to go to the library.

"You know how lame that sounded, right?" my sister whispered, catching me before I head out. "You don't have the internet anymore? Library, my tailless behind."

I shrugged.

"They bought it," I said.

"So where are you really going?" she asked.

"Just . . . out," I said. "I need to be . . . away."

"Very specific," said Emily.

"I'm going to the woods," I said. "Happy?"

"You're going looking for the shrine."

"Maybe," I said. "If it's there . . . I have questions."

"Yeah, me too," said Emily. "Like how my loser brother got the interest of Madison freaking Haynes."

This was unexpected, and I blushed with secret delight, though that only heightened Emily's astonishment.

"That right there," she exclaimed, pointing at my hot pink face, "is what I'm talking about. How did the barn-burning doofus, the football dropping, monument to uncoolness snag one of the most popular girls in school?"

"Just lucky I guess," I said.

"Lucky?" she sneered. "Did you pull some weirdo demon-fighting Japanese mojo on her, depriving her of the use of her common sense?"

"Your support is touching," I said. "Now, if you don't mind, I'm going out."

"To see Maddie?" she cooed, making little kissing noises.

"Oh my God, Emily, no!" I said. "I told you; I'm going to the shrine."

"Don't tell her about it," said Emily, suddenly earnest.

"Madison?" I said, derailed for a moment. "I wasn't going to."

"You sure?"

"Of course not!" I scoffed. "Why would I?"

"Because it makes you special, and you're not used to being special."

"Whereas you . . ." I began.

"Relatively speaking," she shrugged, "yeah. You know that. And that's why you should listen to me. I'm used to being popular."

"Yeah, you're quite the A-list celebrity," I remarked, beginning to get annoyed.

"I'm just saying," she continued, lowering her voice and banishing all trace of her playful grin, "be careful. I know you are going to want to tell people about all this, but it's a bad idea, and though it may seem like it will make people like you more, it really won't."

"I told you," I said, "I'm not going to tell anyone."

"I know how much you like Madison," she said. "I've known for years. The way you get that puppy look whenever you see her, the way you forget everyone is around when she happens to walk by, the poem you wrote when you were in sixth grade . . ."

"I told you never to mention that again!" I hissed, my blush returning.

"I just mean that I know that you've liked her for a long time and that you can't quite believe she's interested in you—which, to be fair, no one can—and that you want to impress her before your new found notoriety wears off and she remembers that you're just that strange little kid who lives over the convenience store on the edge of town and dreams of having a bottle cap collection. All those things might make you tell her something you will regret. Seriously, Caleb. This mythic monster hunter stuff might make you seem cool, but if anyone finds out for real, they will freak out. I mean, seriously. Don't do it."

"I know!" I yelled. "Don't treat me like I'm a kid."

She nodded, considered me for a moment, then lifted my chin so I met her eyes.

"You really like her?" she asked.

"You know I do. You just said . . ."

"I mean you like her? Not just you think she's cute or some kind of out-of-your-league prize to shoot for. You really like her."

"Yes," I said.

"OK," she said. "So you need to be super careful. I don't want you to get your heart broken."

This remark was so unlike anything my sister had ever said to me before that I just stood there with my mouth open. To add to the strangeness, she gave me a little peck on the cheek, and left.

I walked up to the shrine in the mountains, or rather, I walked up to where it had been. There was no sign of it, except for a weathered slab of stone which I wouldn't have given a second glance if I hadn't been on the alert for trace evidence of the experience I had shared with Emily only a week earlier. I wasn't even sure the stone was connected to the shrine, but on one side it had been carefully carved with a symbol I was sure I had seen before: a diamond enclosed in a circle. I thought I had seen the same motif on the lacquered box at the heart of the shrine.

I touched it, tracing its lines with my fingertips, even tried shutting my eyes and calling on the spirit of Raiko, but nothing happened. Whatever wisdom or insight I had hoped to find up here in the woods, was denied me, and I trudged home feeling stupid, abandoned and vulnerable. The trees hummed with the shrill, scratchy whine of the cicadas, and on one tree I saw the empty, golf ball sized husk of one of the insects in its pupal form: dry, brown and neatly split along the spine where the mature flying bug had emerged, like something out of one of the *Alien* movies. It was strange to think that one of the gossamer winged insects singing shrilly all around me was once this hulking beetle thing; that a silent creature of the ground, a crawling, burrowing thing, could become an animal of air and sound. I wondered if it remembered what it had been, and if it felt the same as it always had.

I don't know if it was the strangeness of these thoughts but I started to get the oddest sense that I was being watched from deep in the forest, and not by cicadas. That's not an uncommon sensation in woods as full of life as ours, but this felt different, eerie and I found myself moving quickly, keen to get back to the lights of town and home.

News of my detention got around fast. Caleb the Carpenter. It was a joke but, like a lot of things in my life right now, it was the kind of joke that was only funny to people who weren't me.

"Me Caleb, me bang in nails with my head," said Bobby Davenham, miming at his desk from the back of our American history class. "Me build new barn to sleep in with cows. Nicer than my house."

"The old barn never had cows in it," said Joey, not looking up from their book.

"Did someone ask you, *Josephine*?" said Bobby.

I turned to face him but DeMarcus spoke up first.

"You want to give it a rest, Bobby?" he said.

"Oooh," said Tyler, delighted. "DeMarcus joins the loser team. Maybe you should do a bit of barn-building too," he suggested. "Leave football to the real athletes."

"Sounds about right," said Bobby.

He said it smugly, like there was another meaning under the words, and DeMarcus's face clouded.

"What's that supposed to mean?" he demanded.

Bobby just shrugged and grinned till DeMarcus turned back to his book, frowning. I wasn't sure what had just happened, and when I looked inquiringly at DeMarcus he pretended not to see me. I tried to catch up with him after class, but he just said, "Not now, Caleb," and took off.

So I wandered out to where the old barn had been and stood around in the steaming heat which came up off the grass like the earth was cooking. I hadn't been back since what Mom called "the incident" and I braced myself, half expecting to find a blackened frame of still smouldering timbers. In fact the site had been mostly cleared, the remains bulldozed into a corner of the grounds where it now provided a suitably unnerving perch for a pair of black vultures. One corner of the barn had survived with surprisingly little scorching, and a panel or two from the front which had hung over the door had been salvaged. The rest was toast.

I looked at the vultures and they looked back at me with their hard, shiny little eyes as if to say, "Your handiwork, huh? Nice going."

"Not much to work with, is there?" said a voice at my back.

I spun round and there was an old guy in shirt sleeves and a student, big and beefy. He was the one who had spoken. They were both white, both smiling, albeit cautiously.

"You must be Caleb," said the old guy.

"I must," I confessed, wishing it wasn't true. "Mr. Watkins?"

"Right and correct," said the old guy, offering his hand. I was surprised by that, and a tiny bit grateful. I took it and shook it. The student followed suit. He looked familiar though I couldn't say where I knew him from.

"Sorry about this," I said.

"Not at all," said Watkins breezily. "Accidental, the way I heard it, and we like a challenge, don't we Daren?"

The tall boy grinned and nodded.

"You really going to rebuild it?" I asked.

"*We* are going to rebuild it," the teacher replied. "With some help."

"From . . .?"

"A few other students," said Watkins, ticking off the options on his fingers, "maybe some parents, the Southside lumber yard—who are giving us a significant discount on materials—and an architectural consultant."

"You can really rebuild it?" I asked, unaccountably relieved.

"Not exactly," said Watkins. "We can replace it, but there's not enough of the original to rebuild and, to be honest, I'm not sure we'd want to."

"How do you mean?"

"Well, the barn was interesting because it was old," said the boy, "not because it was particularly well made."

"We're going to make it better," said Watkins, beaming in a mischievous way that took decades off him. He put a finger to his lips. "Our little secret. The original was roughly thrown up and nailed together. It had to be repaired every few years because the craftsmanship was so shoddy. Ironic for a town which prides itself on its woodworking, or used to."

"And this time?" I asked.

"This time it will be better," he said, the light of conviction flaring in his eyes. "A work of art which will stand for hundreds of years, assuming no one burns it down. No offense intended."

"None taken," I said. His enthusiasm was infectious, if baffling. "OK, so you're not just going to nail it up. What will make it the new version so special?"

"To begin with," said Watkins with a conspiratorial wink, "no nails."

"No nails?" I parroted stupidly.

"Or bolts," said Watkins.

"Or screws," said Daren.

"No glue or girders either," said Watkins, thoroughly enjoying himself.

"What will hold it up?" I asked.

"Craftsmanship!" he exclaimed. "Good old-fashioned joinery. Precise, hand-tooled timber work. A thing of beauty."

"You can do that?" I asked, genuinely impressed.

"With the right tools, the right skills, and a little old school expertise," said Watkins, "yes."

"That's amazing," I admitted. "You must know a lot about woodworking."

"You know," said Watkins, "I rather think I do, but for a project of this size, I'm bringing in a real master. I met him years ago when he was doing some construction work for a garden exhibit over in Raleigh. I'd never seen carpentry like it! The most intricate of joints, all hand carved with ancient tools that were sharpened daily. And, speak of the devil," he said, turning and waving extravagantly, "here he is. Over here, Mr. Saito!"

I spun around, mouth open.

Walking toward us, a tool box in one strong hand and a roll of charts in the other, eyebrows huddled down on his forehead, and his ridiculous nose sticking out in front of him like the carrot on a snow man, was the *tengu*.

I said nothing, waiting to see how he would greet me, but he focused entirely on Mr. Watkins, bowing to him fractionally, and muttering a few words in Japanese which the old teacher clearly appreciated even if he didn't understand them. His bow to Daren was smaller, shallower, but the one he gave me was little more than a nod.

Ok, I thought. *Playing it like that, huh?*

So I said nothing, following everyone else's lead as Mr. Watkins invited the *tengu*—sorry, Mr. Saito—to walk us through the joinery techniques we would be using, and the tools we would use to make them. The tool box contained a selection of chisels, hammers and planes, all rough looking, but sharp as razors, so that the *tengu* could run them along the surface of a beam and strip a long, curling ribbon of wood as thin as tissue paper. He also had a selection of lumber samples into which he had already cut various mortises, dovetails and other more complex joints. They were amazingly precise, the pieces of lumber slotting together perfectly, and then staying seated without movement. Some were as intricate as three-dimensional jigsaw puzzle pieces.

"This is the *yonmai-kama-tsugi*," said the tengu, almost to himself, illustrating a four-way connection. "And this," he said showing a joint where two horizontal beams slotted into a vertical corner strut and were held in place with wooden pins, "is a *toshi-chigai-hozo-soshi-hanasen-shikuchi*. Don't worry. You do not need to remember the names."

There was a relieved chuckle from the group, but they were also mesmerized by the work. Against my better judgment, I was impressed too. It was—and I can't believe I'm saying this about carpentry—cool.

By this time the rest of the club had arrived. I didn't know them, but they clearly knew enough about me to give me the odd glance when Mr. Watkins talked about the unique opportunity that had come to us through the tragic loss of the barn. If anyone thought it was odd that the strange half-Japanese kid who had torched the original structure was now being assisted by a mysterious Japanese man none of them had seen before, they didn't say so. I kept a low profile, letting the rest of them ask quiet, respectful questions, as the *tengu* walked them through the plans for the barn.

"The building is simple in design," he said, "but we must study the dimensions and determine a work sequence before the lumber arrives. This is what we will do this week. And we can practice using the tools. But we will stop now."

I was amazed to see that we had been there two hours. The *tengu* showed how the tools should be packed up, and as everything was locked away in the grounds keeper's shed, Mr. Watkins pronounced the first meeting a great success and the rest of the carpentry club began to drift away. I stalled. Only when everyone was gone did the *tengu* speak to me directly. He looked around the empty school grounds. We were screened by the gym on one side and by some pine trees on another, but it wasn't exactly maximum security.

"Take up the roll of charts," he said, without preamble, "and follow me."

I did so. He led me into the stand of trees beside the barn site, following an overgrown path into a thin clearing, no bigger than a couple of parked cars side by side. There was a burned patch in the middle where kids had come to hang out, probably drink beer or smoke weed. It felt unnaturally quiet and, in the late afternoon light, it had a golden caste to it which made it feel special, sacred.

The chart roll was heavier than I expected, and I realized that there was something inside the cardboard tube. When he nodded to it, I upended the tube and gradually withdrew a long wooden object, thicker than a broom handle, but not by much, and slightly curved. It was about a yard long and featureless, or very nearly, so that I didn't immediately notice the crack running about a foot from one end, and the bamboo peg which sat a few inches above the seam. The *tengu* held out both hands, palms up, and I presented him with the wooden object. He took it with a kind of quiet ceremony, rotated it till the slight curve of the ends arced toward the ground, grasped what I now saw was the handle end, bowed to it, and—with an elegant, sweeping motion—drew out . . .

A sword.

18

A sword.

The word doesn't do it justice, but that's what it was. It had no hilt, no hangings or decoration, but it was bright and elegant and, in its way, beautiful.

"This is for you," said Mr. Saito. "You will learn how to take care of it, and how to wield it."

"Cool," I said.

He gave me a doubtful look, as if all this was against his better judgment and he was already regretting it.

"I mean, yes," I said quickly. "I'll learn."

He hesitated, then slowly offered it to me, blade up, handle toward me.

"Do not touch the metal," he said. "The oils in your skin will damage the polish."

I nodded, but I wasn't really listening. All my attention was on the sword, something I hadn't known I had wanted till about thirty seconds ago, and now never wanted to put down.

"Oh yeah," I said, swinging it. "That's what I'm talking about."

"You weren't talking about anything," said the *tengu*, baffled and getting annoyed.

"Figure of speech," I said dreamily.

"Don't wave it around like that."

"It's light," I said. "I thought it would be . . ."

"Heavy," he concluded, as if correcting. "No. Hold it like this, with your hands positioned here."

I made an overhead cutting swash, pretty sure I looked like Luke Skywalker, and he tutted, catching my arm and moving behind me.

"No, no, no," he said irritably. "It is not a club. Or a poker. It is designed to slice. The movement of the blade should be sweeping. Not like that. It is also not a saw. Look. Like this," he said, tightening his grip on my arms and moving them in a slow, smooth arc. "You see why you need to train? You have some strength and some speed, but you have no skill."

I didn't care. It felt glorious in my hands. Natural.

"Spread your legs further," he added. "Balance yourself and feel the earth through your feet. Extend your arms to reflect the angle of the blade. Always keep the edge open to your adversary . . ."

And so it went on, for an hour or more until the sun was completely lost in the trees whose shadows had dipped the clearing into the beginnings of darkness.

"Take the *katana* home and study this book," he said, handing me a slim volume no larger than a pocket diary. "It will teach you the parts of the sword, the process of its forging and how to clean the blade without damaging it. Get used to the feel of the sword in your hands but do not cut things with it or show other people. Except your sister. You must learn to treat it as a part of you, a part which must be treated with respect. The dog which is mistreated will bite its master when it gets chance. We will practise when we have a private place."

I couldn't wait to get started, and left the circle of trees reluctantly, walking home with the cardboard tube under my arm, a tube concealing a legitimately cool Japanese sword. The day was getting better.

The evening, however, proved different. Maybe it was that sense of having taken a step to being a little closer to being Raiko's heir, to being somehow special, but the prospect of going back to the inconvenience store, to my disapproving parents and the demoralizing ordinariness of my life, drained the joy out of me. Perhaps now that I had the sword I could find the woodland shrine, connect to the ancestral spirit which had spoken to Em and me there. Maybe that was why I hadn't been able to find it the other night: because I hadn't been suitably armed, wasn't a warrior.

Maybe I should try again, take the sword with me. Maybe this time . . .

I stood in front of the house, the store front occupying the entire lower front of the building, suddenly sure that I didn't want to go in. It was getting dark now, autumn showing itself in that if not in the persistent summer heat, but the lights were still on and would be for another couple of hours. The plate glass windows were lit with a bright, flat light with a very slight blue-green tint from the fluorescents. There were adverts for lottery cards and slushies, beer, milk and toilet paper (half off!). Out front was a display rack of browning bananas. Dad had ordered too many again. He would be inside now, manning the register, while Mom cooked or did the books. It all felt small and a little sad.

I turned toward the mountain road, but as I took my first step, I caught movement out of the corner of my eye. There was something in the shadows at the far corner of the store front, something small, half hidden by the bushes Mom had been telling Dad to prune for weeks. I stared hard into the darkness, trying to identify what I thought I had seen but there was no sign . . .

And then there it was again! A careful shifting right by the window sill. I remained motionless, watching, my breath held and now I could see what it was. A grey cat was squatting on its haunches, half under the bushes, its eyes fixed on the store window. As I watched, it reared up on its hind legs and put its forepaws on the glass, first one, then the other. Its eyes narrowed with concentration, and in a movement that somehow was and was not strictly feline, it stood up. Vertically. Its whole body seemed to flex, to elongate and it became a small cat-shaped person.

Bakeneko!

It showed no awareness of me, so fixed was its attention on whatever was inside.

Or whoever.

Dad! I thought. *Mom!*

And with that thought came another realization: the cat was getting bigger. It was already the size of a Labrador. It walked its front paws up the window as it grew, morphing from pet to monster.

"Hey!" I shouted, fumbling for the sheathed sword in the cardboard tube.

The cat turned like a striking snake, its yellow eyes finding me, its mouth opening with a hiss. It fixed me with a look of intense ferocity and hatred, and I remembered how close it had come to killing me at our last meeting. I dragged the sword from its scabbard and held it between us. The cat's bright eyes seemed to contract with thought and then it pivoted to face me, still standing on its hind legs, still big as a large dog and growing. Claws slid from its paws like switch blades, and it lowered its head, fangs bared.

You have a sword, I told myself. *You have a sword.*

But I didn't know how to use it. I was stronger than I had been, faster. But, as the *tengu* had been quick to point out, I had no skill.

Fake it.

I held the sword like he had shown me, spreading my feet and canting the blade at a diagonal angle across my body: what I hoped looked like a fighting stance.

But the cat was getting bigger all the time, and it struck me that I didn't know if there was a limit to how large it could get. The last time I had seen it, it had been *Bāchan*'s size, but maybe that was because it had just been pretending to be her. If I let it grow, would I find myself facing a cat the size of a horse?

I swallowed. The *bakeneko* was almost my height. There was no time to think. I raised the sword above my head, yelled for all I was worth, and ran at the cat.

In the same instant, the door of the inconvenience store opened and Dad leaned out.

"Caleb?" he said. "What are you . . .?"

But I was committed to my charge.

"Get inside and lock the door!" I bellowed over my shoulder, but when I refocused on my attack, the cat was gone.

In fact, it was still there, but it had become a regular sized cat again, and as I blundered into the bushes, hacking wildly, it shot, yowling, between my legs, and took off into the night. I sprawled hard into the shrubbery, getting a face full of privet. I fell face forward, the sword clattering on the sidewalk under me and only narrowly avoiding my neck.

For a moment, I lay there in the bushes, considering my options, none of which seemed good, avoiding my Dad's baffled gaze. I must have looked like an idiot, or—worse—a cat hating maniac.

"Caleb," he said, using that soft, understated English tone he always adopted when tackling something awkward. "What are you doing?"

"Sorry," I muttered, getting hold of a thin branch and trying to pull myself up. "I can explain," a monumental lie which I knew only made my situation worse the moment I said it.

Dad just stared.

"I hope you weren't going to hurt that cat," he said.

"Probably not," I said truthfully.

"Not like you," he said. "I thought you were an animal lover."

"I am!" I protested.

Just, you know, not a shape changing supernatural creature lover, I thought wildly. *Apart from my sister, of course.*

I tried to give him a reassuring smile but realized that he was looking past me, and that there was something new in his face. He looked pale, rattled.

"What is that?" he said.

"It's a sword," I said, thinking fast. "Not a real one. Just a kind of replica. I got it from a pawn shop . . ."

"Not that," he said, looking past me into the shrubbery. "*That.*"

I followed his gaze, sitting up. I was still holding the thin stick-like branch.

Except that it wasn't a branch. It was the remains of an arm, dried and shrunken to skin and bone, with only the sinew holding it in place.

Because with a rush of horror I saw that it wasn't just an arm. There was a hand with stiff fingers. Appalled, I flung it from me, but I couldn't look away. There was a shoulder, a ribcage in a stained tee shirt, a skull with hair and a necklace.

A necklace with a shark's tooth.

In other words, there was most of the upper half of a dried-up corpse. I scuttled away from it, retching, but through my revulsion I had just enough functioning brain to know that I had found the remains of Blake Wilde.

An ambulance came for the body, and with it, Sheriff Halpern, notebook at the ready.

"And you just found it there under the bushes?" he said, for the third time.

"That's right," I said. "I spotted it in the light from the store as I was about to go in."

"And you were on your way home from school at nine o'clock at night?" he replied.

"I had some after school stuff," I said, not looking at my parents or Emily.

"Which can be verified by the staff?" said Halpern.

"Yes," I said, thinking privately that I'd need to fill in the hour or so I had spent alone with the *tengu*.

"How did the boy die?" my father asked. He hadn't said it, but I knew from the way he avoided looking at me, that he was afraid the cop would say something along the lines of "slashed to death with a long blade . . ." The kind of long blade I had stashed under my bed, wrapped in old clothes.

"Hard to say," said the Sheriff, glancing at the ambulance. "Large animal attack, possibly. Seems to have been dead several days, assuming it's who we think it is."

"Blake Wilde," said Emily.

"We can't confirm that at this time," said Halpern, retreating into professional-speak.

"But he only went missing a few days ago," said Emily. "The body looked . . . old. Desiccated."

"The coroner says that's exsanguination," said Halpern, brandishing the word as if it might shut us up.

"He had his blood drained?" I said. "What kind of animal would do that?"

"Extensive blood loss is common when there are a lot of deep wounds," said Halpern, looking uncomfortable. "A bear or mountain lion . . ."

"There are no cougars in North Carolina," I said.

"Bobcat, then," said Halpern. "Maybe coyotes."

"Here?" said Emily. "Outside the store? And no one saw . . ."

"The animal injuries may have been post mortem," said Halpern, who was getting flustered now. "There's a cut on the neck which looks clean enough to have been made by a blade, but animal claws can be pretty sharp."

Now Dad's eyes flashed toward me, just for a second.

"But you're sure he'd been dead some time?" I said, spelling it out.

"Yes," said the Sheriff. "We assume the body was dragged here by an animal or animals sometime after death. It's . . . incomplete."

He didn't need to say that it was missing its left arm and everything below the waist. That cheery little detail was burned into my memory.

"We'll look for the rest closer to where he was last seen," he said. He realized he had said too much and, annoyed with himself, added hastily, "Assuming it is who we think it is. You are on the edge of town here," he added, as if this was significant of more than just being close to the woods. "Not much between you and the gorge. Or the mountains."

No, I thought. *There isn't.*

I had to figure out how to use that sword, and fast.

19

Elsewhere

Jed Ashworth was unhappy: with the failure of the search to find the missing workers and with the company's vague "explanations" about what must have happened. He had only known Valerie Singh for a few months, but Julio Rodriguez had worked with him for the best part of two years, and he'd known Harry Peterson since college. They were his people. The idea that they might have deliberately sabotaged the project—which is what Southern Shale was insinuating to the media—was absurd. And crazy. It didn't explain the disappearing bodies.

"Knew they were going to get caught," said Chris Collington, "so they took off. Probably half way to Mexico even as we speak."

Ashworth had gazed at him, incredulous, and Collington had shrugged and looked away, so that Jed couldn't read his face. Did the Southern Shale rep. really believe it, or was he just trying out the party line to see how it sounded? It was impossible to say. Either way, it was wrong. Jed wasn't a man who paraded his morality, and he did his best not to judge, but slandering the memory of his co-workers was wrong. He was sure of it.

And it *felt* wrong, and not just ethically. It felt wrong like when you slipped your right foot into your left shoe, like when you have to navigate a room in pitch blackness even though you've seen it a hundred times in daylight or like when you walk into the kitchen and catch the smell of something rank, a foulness that shouldn't be there. Something stank, and he wasn't just going to open a window and hope it went away.

He turned on his flashlight and stepped over the caution tape at the mouth of the cave. The police had wanted to treat the area as a crime scene, but Collington had had a word with the mayor who had spoken to the sheriff . . .

Typical small town ass-covering. And the mayor had supported the expansion of the Sheriff's department, a new cruiser and a pair of holding cells into the bargain.

Meanwhile, of course, the fracking plant stood silent, all that hard and costly drilling work wasted until they could turn the water back on and start filling their gas tanks. Jed didn't believe Peterson and co had been crazed environmentalist activists or saboteurs, and he didn't want their memory slandered, but he also wanted this whole episode closed so they could get on with the job.

Harry Peterson would have understood that, he told himself, and if the others wouldn't . . .? Well, no one forced them into this line of work. They knew the risks. Their disappearance was sad, sure, but the company had a lot of people who needed to put food on the table.

Or, in Jed's case, boost his stock portfolio. A few more years with Southern Shale and he might seriously start looking for a place in the Caribbean. Costa Rica, maybe. Perhaps he could land a consultancy gig in one of those central American countries who were just dipping their toes into the waters of fracking. There was serious money to be made in those jungle mountains. But first, he had to get the Red Scar pumps up and running, and that meant assuring Collington and the rest that the cave was stable enough to restart the process, missing workers or no missing workers.

That ripple of unease went through him again, that tremor that something was off or out of place, but he suppressed it. Life didn't always work out like you wanted it to, didn't always feel right, especially in business; a man had to make tough choices.

He moved the beam of his mag light over the debris which the earth movers had carved their way through. There were a few boulders the size of cars, but most of it was smaller, slabs and hunks of granite like overstuffed armchairs, and rough heaps of still smaller pieces, pushed together like irregular basketballs. You could see the sharp striations on the stone floor where the bulldozer blades had scored it. Jed had watched the whole process in person, craning his neck to see as the rescue team in hard hats explored the paths made by the diggers and dozers. He had seesawed between hope and despair, alert for the first cry saying they had found someone, or what had once been someone. But there had been nothing.

It made no sense. But it was time to get the seismographs set up again. Make sure the rock strata was sound and they could get back to work.

What Harry would have wanted, he thought again, as if reiterating the thought would make it feel more true.

He climbed over a shelf of stone, flashlight lancing into the darkness. The shelf was long and flat as the counter of a bar, and Jed slid along it on his butt for a few feet before clambering down the other side. He was in the cave proper now, and it sounded different, each grunt he made, each clumsy footfall echoing slightly. He swept the light around, eyes peeled for bats. He didn't like bats. Jed had spent a lot of time in quarries and caves, at well heads and drill shafts, but he had never quite got used to bats. He kept still for a moment and half closed his eyes, listening. Sometimes you could catch the high-pitched chirruping as they whirled and dived for insects . . .

Nothing.

And then . . . not nothing.

Somewhere there round the corner made by a great jagged outcrop, somewhere his light couldn't reach, he had heard . . .

Voices?

He wasn't sure but . . . there it was again: a low, rasping whisper which sounded like speech, but if there were words in it, he didn't understand them. Jed frowned, suddenly uneasy and not sure why. The hairs on the back of his neck pricked up and he thought again about how things sometimes just felt wrong.

He forced himself to move, quietly, and with his flashlight turned down to his feet, so that he wouldn't give himself away. If it was Vivian, Julio and Harry, he would have things to say, though it might be good to see what they were doing before they realized he was there.

This was a good, rational thought, one he forced to the front of his mind like a lantern, even though he didn't really think it would be them. He put one hand on the stone so that it took some of the weight off his feet, and he took another pair of slow, careful steps.

He could hear them again now, clearer than ever: voices, or rather one voice, though what was being spoken was still just meaningless sound.

A foreign language, and nothing he was used to, like Spanish.

Not Rodriguez, then. Not Singh or Peters either.

Jed licked his lips, suddenly conscious that his heart was racing.

Feels wrong . . .

And then he was round the great crag and he could see a figure, upright but hunched, a figure wrapped in a long close-fitting dress or robe, and with some kind of scarf or kerchief over her head. An old woman, he was sure of it.

Quickly he raised the flashlight and saw, in the strange, leaping shadows, who she was talking to. Or rather what. The woman was talking to her cat. It slunk beside her, tail down and back arched, hissing as it realized he was there. The old woman looked up, startled by the light, instantly shading her eyes against the brilliance, and Jed relaxed.

After all that heart-in-his-mouth stuff, it was just some crazy old woman out with her pet! He almost laughed with relief but took a stern tone.

"Excuse me!" he said. "You can't be here. This is a dangerous and restricted area. I'm going to have to ask you to leave. Now."

The old woman stared back at him, saying nothing. The cat crept behind her and peered out, the shine of its eyes unnervingly bright.

"Hello?" he said. "You speak English?"

He wasn't sure why he said that but there was something foreign in her wrinkled face. One of the Cherokee from up on the Tennessee border? Or an Asian. He couldn't always tell the difference.

The old woman was clutching some kind of purse and wearing a straight gown of some drab fabric, one side wrapped around the other and closed with a kind of broad sash around her waist.

Kimono.

The word popped into is head, and though it felt right, it only increased his confusion and alarm. He thought of the Smith kids at the school who had denied knowing anything about the paper slip they had found, their parents who ran the convenience store over by the derelict Walmart. Wasn't there some elderly relative in town too, a grandmother?

"If you don't leave now," he announced, "I'm going to have to call this in."

Still nothing from the old woman. She stood very still, staring back at him, her eyes glittering like black glass, and then she was speaking, but the words were strange and muttered. They were also not for him. He wasn't sure how he knew, but Jed was certain that the old crone was talking to her cat.

For some reason, this bothered him. His flesh crept, and the back of his neck tingled again. The cave suddenly felt unnaturally cold.

"OK," he said, speaking louder than he meant to. "Have it your way."

He pulled his cell phone from his pocket and dialled 911. As soon as he was connected, he started talking. That seemed important.

Show you're in control, and you get control, he thought. *No reason to be scared.*

He didn't know why he thought that. Of course he wasn't scared. Of a mad old woman and her cat? That was nuts.

"Yeah, this is Jed Ashworth," he said. "I'm up at the cave site on Red Scar Mountain, and we have a perimeter breach. There's an elderly Asian woman inside the restricted search area. I have tried to explain the situation but she is being non-compliant with instructions for her to leave the area. I don't want to make a scene, but maybe you could send someone over."

That sounded right, he thought: the right tone, measured and professional but very slightly casual, like he was doing stuff by the book but didn't think it was a big deal. Yeah, that seemed right. He was especially pleased with words like 'perimeter breach' and 'non-compliant.'

"Sure thing, Mr. Ashworth," said the operator. "So, you've spoken to her already?"

"I have," he replied. "Several times, but I can't get a response."

"Is she unconscious?"

"No Ma'am," he said. "Standing here big as life. Just not talking. She might not speak English."

"Ok," said the operator. "We'll have someone right over."

"Might want to send someone from animal control too," he added, pleased with himself now. "She has a cat."

He hung up and turned to the old woman but she was just looking at him, her face curiously shadowed by the head scarf so that her mood was unreadable.

"You might want to move on before they get here," said Jed.

No response.

"You speak English?" he said again.

Nothing.

"*¿Hablas inglés?*" he tried, straining to the full extent of his foreign language fluency.

Still just the black-eyed stare from her and the yellow one from her motionless cat. It was giving him the willies. He noted the way the old woman clutched her purse.

"What's in the bag?" he asked, suspicious.

Still no response, though he thought he saw some muscle flex in her jaw. A smile?

More like a grin, and in the cold and the dark and the silence, Jed Ashworth was suddenly sure he wanted to be somewhere else. He had called it in, done his duty. Let someone else deal with the lunatic old biddy. He was out of here.

He turned his back on woman and cat, and headed for the cave entrance, calling over his shoulder as he walked away.

"I wouldn't stick around if I was you, 'less you wanna spend a night in the sheriff's shiny new cells."

He didn't like having the woman behind him and speeded up, conscious that his haste was spoiling his look of easy nonchalance, but not caring. He had barely reached the great rock shelf that he had had to shimmy across when a figure in the tan uniform of a sheriff's deputy appeared in his flashlight.

"How'd you get here so fast?" he gasped. "I literally *just* called the operator!"

The woman smiled. She was young, pretty in spite of the uniform. He didn't know her.

"I was in the area," she said.

"You got a cage for the cat?" he said. "I told them there was a cat."

There was the tiniest hesitation, and then the deputy raised her right hand. It was holding a long trap made of steel wire, which was odd, because Jed would have sworn her hands had been empty moments before.

Trick of the light, he thought.

"Where is the woman?" said the deputy.

"Back there," said Jed, jerking his head without actually turning round. He wasn't sure why but he didn't want to look back into the cave. "You'll handle it from here?" he asked, hoping the deputy couldn't hear the hint of desperation in his voice.

"Sure," she said, "no problem. It's just an old lady, right?"

"Yeah," said Jed breezily. "Not sure she's all there though. Might not know where she is. Might not speak English either." And then, because he had to get it out, he added, "Kind of weird."

The word hung in the air for a moment and the deputy frowned.

"Weird how?" she asked.

"I don't know," Jed replied, wishing he'd said nothing. "Just weird."

"Weird . . ." said the deputy lifting her hand, "like *this?*"

She swept her finger tips across her face and it wasn't there anymore. Where there had been eyes, nose and mouth, there was only a smooth whiteness like pottery.

Jed took a step backwards, and then the thing with no face was coming toward him and there was nowhere for him to go except back into the cave. So he staggered that way, a gasping, stumbling run, his head empty of thought as panic took hold. He blundered round the rocky crag, his flashlight bouncing around the cave walls, and there was the old woman, still and patient as before, her cat uncannily reared up on its hind legs. It seemed to be growing.

"You have to get out of here!" Jed managed. "There's something coming . . ."

"Yes," said the old woman, shrugging out of her scarf so that he could see her terrible smile. "Most helpful."

And then she was moving toward him with long, rapid strides, still hunched over, but with her awful face stuck out in front of her. One claw-like hand reached into her purse and the Mag light flashed along the blade of a long butcher's knife. "Fear," she said, licking her grinning lips, "does wonders for the flavour."

20

The police were back first thing. Specifically, Sheriff Halpern and a younger white deputy I didn't know. When they arrived I was up in my room reading the clumsily written book on Japanese swords which the *tengu* had given me. I was studying the various blade types: the *odachi*, some of which were twice as long as my *katana*, the shorter *wazikashi* and the knife-like *tanto*. I was engrossed, but the strobing lights outside sent me into a fumbling panic. I hid both book and sword under the bed and scattered some smelly clothes in there as a deterrent to anyone who might go poking around. I might not know how to wield a sword but I was a master at weaponizing socks.

My parents were polite, but on edge.

"We told you everything we could about the body," said Dad. "I don't see how we can help further."

"We are here about a different, but related matter," said Halpern.

"Ok," said Dad. "What?"

Halpern turned to specifically address Mom.

"We are here to let you know that we've taken your mother into custody," he said, "in connection with the disappearance of Jed Ashworth from Southern Shale, the fracking company, and possibly of the other missing workers."

"You've arrested my grandmother?!" I exclaimed, incredulous. "She's like a thousand years old! What do you think she did, bore him to death with tales of life before the wheel?"

"What makes you think he's dead?" said Halpern, quite serious.

Emily gave me her death stare.

"Caleb," she said, "stop talking." She turned to the sheriff and managed a smile. "This must be some kind of mistake. Why was she taken in?"

"Before disappearing, Mr. Ashworth made a 911 call from the cave on Red Scar Mountain last night," he replied. "He reported the presence of . . ." here he consulted his notes, "an elderly Asian female with a cat."

"A cat?" I said.

Emily gave me another death stare, and I shut up.

"Not a lot of elderly Asian women in Portersville," said the young deputy with an apologetic nod. Halpern gave him a look not unlike Emily's and he wilted a little.

"Sounds like Mr. Ashworth conversed with the woman in question for some time before calling emergency services," said Halpern. "She refused to respond to his instructions."

"Wait," said Emily, "you arrested her because of a recording made by a man no one can find?"

"In the light of where Blake Wilde's body was found," said Halpern, "I'm sure you can see why we'd be looking at your family."

So, they weren't being coy about the identity of the desiccated corpse. The morning paper was full of the story.

"Coincidence," I said.

"Circumstantial evidence," Emily amended.

"And CCTV footage," said Halpern, with the merest hint of triumph, as if he'd been holding this card back, waiting for the right time to play it. "There are security cameras at the cave."

We stared at him.

"Mr. Ashworth went in," said Halpern, "and did not come out. This woman, however, did."

He fished in an inside pocket and produced a grainy black and white image on glossy paper. It was taken from up high and the area was starkly contrasted into bright light and deep shadow. The figure in the centre of the image had her face tilted down, and her head wrapped in a scarf.

It could have been *Bāchan*.

"Hardly conclusive," I said.

"You'll note the kimono," said Halpern, playing another card. "And the cat."

The beast was clearly there, but almost entirely in silhouette.

"Could be any cat," I said. "Not necessarily Snowball."

Halpern looked up, smiling fractionally.

"That's your grandmother's cat, is it?" he said.

I felt my face flush and looked away, avoiding Emily's eyes.

"If it is *Bāchan*, maybe she was lost," she said. "Confused."

"She was in a restricted area," he replied.

"Hardly a reason to arrest her," said Emily.

"I'm sure they were just looking to get her somewhere safe," said Dad.

"They arrested her!" I said.

"Because when the patrol team reached the cave," Halpern explained, "there was no sign of Jed."

"She was there alone?" asked Emily.

"She wasn't there either," said Halpern. "We picked her up from her residence this morning."

"So you arrested her because she was an old Japanese woman?" said Emily.

"An old Japanese woman with a cat," said the younger officer, whose name badge said Williams. "As per the emergency call's description."

"This is crazy," I said.

"Your grandmother is not being helpful with our inquiries," said Halpern.

"Good," I said. More death stares, and not just from Emily.

"We thought you would come down to the sheriff's office," said Halpern to Mom, "and translate."

"Translate?" said Emily. "*Bāchan* speaks perfectly good English."

"Well, she's not saying anything now," said Halpern. "Which isn't helping her case. It's important we get her side of the story as we attempt to locate Mr. Ashworth. Or his remains."

I was about to laugh at the ridiculousness of the thing, but that last word caught me off guard. We all looked at each other.

"Mrs. Smith?" said Halpern, clearly conscious that my mother, whose face was as closed as the windows of a shuttered house, had not said anything since he had arrived.

There was a loaded silence, finally broken by my mother's terse,

"I cannot help. If my mother chooses not to speak, I cannot make her."

For a second, everyone just looked at her, then Dad spoke up.

"Come on, Jenny," he said. "We should go and see what's going on."

"You go," said Mom with brittle brightness. "I'm sure you'll be just as much use, and I have work to do here."

"Mom!" Emily exclaimed, accusingly.

"What?" Mom fired back. "This is not my business. I don't know what your grandmother has been doing, but only she has the power to make things right."

It was a strange remark, loaded—I thought—with other things, things accumulated over many years. It was also final. She turned on her heel and moved into the back of the shop, ostensibly to refill the fridge units. My father watched her with concern.

"We'll come with you," I said. "Right, Em?"

Emily nodded.

"Should I . . .?" Dad began, but Emily cut him off.

"Stay here with Mom," she said. Dad nodded, his gaze straying back to where Mom was bustling about, conspicuously hard at work.

Halpern watched the whole thing, keeping his face blank, but Williams looked baffled and surprised.

"Just what my rep needed," Emily observed as we stepped outside. "A trip in the back of a cop car."

The cruiser smelled unnaturally clean, like it had just rolled out of the show room. No burger wrappers on the seats, no soda bottles rolling around on the floor. Once belted in, I folded my arms, as if afraid of contaminating the vehicle by touching it. Or the other way round. I wasn't sure.

Emily sat in the back beside me, scrunched low in the seat, a hand in front of her face every time we slowed down, in case someone recognized her. I didn't even try. It wasn't like my 'rep' could go down much further. Hell, if Madison found out I'd been hauled in by the cops, her impression of me might go up further. I could live with being a bad boy. It wasn't like anything else had worked for me.

Halpern escorted us through the sheriff's office, down a featureless corridor to a T junction where we turned right, following the sign reading "Holding: Female" and round a corner to a cell, two walls of which were floor to ceiling bars. *Bachan* was sitting in prim silence on a plastic mattress on a raised platform. She was wearing, I was sorry to see, a drab kimono remarkably like the figure in the picture. Her face gave nothing away as we came in and her eyes stayed on Halpern.

"*Bāchan*," said Emily, as the cage door was opened. She perched quickly on the edge of the bed. "You ok?"

Bāchan was still watching Halpern, but she nodded.

"Perhaps your grandmother would like to tell us all what she was doing in the cave," said the deputy.

"I would like to go home now," she said.

"No chance," said Halpern. "I can hold you for twenty-four hours, longer if I charge you with obstruction. You should get comfy because you're not going anywhere."

"Then I would like to speak to my grandchildren," she replied, quiet but determined. "In private."

Halpern shook his head.

"I read you your rights," he said. "Whatever you say can be used in evidence. That means that if you talk, I can listen. No private audiences."

Bāchan blinked, then spoke very carefully.

"Then I will speak to Emily. The deputy and his staff may listen if they must, but Caleb should go."

"What?" I protested. "No way."

"I insist," she replied. "You are too young to hear what I have to say, and I'm sure you can find better things to do with your time."

I gaped at her in the uncomfortable silence which followed. I could feel everyone looking at me, could sense the color in my face rising again. This wasn't fair! It was stupid and humiliating and . . .

"Please, Hideki," she said.

I turned on her, ready to scream at her for getting my name wrong again, but something in her gaze stopped me. It wasn't angry or apologetic. It was . . . significant, like she was telling me something she didn't want anyone to know.

But what?

"Ok," I said, nodding. I made for the door so quickly that the deputies didn't move in time and I had to push my way through. Out I went, back along the hall, my mind racing.

Think!

I saw her face in my mind's eye, her muted voice echoing in my head as I rounded the corner.

"*Better things to do with your time . . .*"

Like what? And why just send me? The important stuff was happening back there with Emily and the sheriff . . .

Unless that was what she wanted them to think. I paused and my eye fell on the wall sign. "Holding: Female."

Light dawned. I turned the corner and found what I was looking for. "Holding: Male". And there, sitting alone in an identical cage, was a kid not much older than me. He looked ragged, drained, his face pale and eyes clenched shut.

"Davey Kott?" I said.

The boy's eyes opened wide. He immediately looked ready to run, though there was nowhere to go.

"Get away!" he gasped. "You're one of them!"

"I'm not," I said, dropping to a whisper and pressing my face against the bars. "I came to help. But I need to know what happened, and quickly."

"You won't believe me," he said, with a manic chuckle. "No one believes me. They all think I did it. Blake . . ."

His face twisted with anguish at whatever he was remembering. I instantly knew that he was holding on to sanity by the slenderest of threads.

"Davey," I said. "I believe you, but I need to know what you saw. Was it a cat?"

His face clouded with doubt, but the pain and horror melted some. He shook his head.

"A cat?" he said. "No. There was a cat. Blake wanted to toss it in the river, but this was a girl. Cute. In a kimono, but her face . . ."

He hesitated, and the madness flickered in his eyes again.

"What was it like?" I asked. "Her face."

"She was . . ." said Davey, entranced by the memory, making a vague gesture with his hand, fingers fluttering as they passed over his face, "all smooth. No eyes, no mouth, no nothing. Like an egg. Only it was her head, and just a minute before it had been . . . not possible. I ran. I didn't see what happened to Blake. I just *ran*. And then the guy at the gas station."

He stared at me, as if begging me to understand.

"What about him?" I asked.

"Same thing," said Davey. "He had a face, then he didn't. Smooth as an egg."

He started to laugh then, a wild, unhinged sound that made me take a step backwards as the sound rose to full, wall-shaking hysterics, and finally into a terrified shriek that made my hair stand on end. I turned on my heel and had just rounded the corner when I slammed into Sheriff Halpern coming in the opposite direction.

"What's going on?" he demanded. "What did you do?"

"Got turned around," I lied, heading for the front office and out into the street before he could decide to make something of it.

Emily joined me ten minutes later.

"So what did *Bāchan* have to say?" I asked.

"She gave me her recipe for *tonkatsu*," she replied, leading the way home.

"And?"

"And nothing," said Emily. "That was it. But if you want breaded pork cutlets for dinner . . ."

I grinned,

"And that's all she said?"

"Halpern was *pissed.*"

"That's pretty bad ass," I said, amazed.

"It is," she agreed. "And you?"

"I found out what scared Davey Kott off."

"Spill," she said, checking over her shoulder that there was no one in ear shot.

"He said it looked like a girl in a kimono," I said.

"Like . . . a *child?*"

"I don't think so," I decided. "He said she was cute like he might say . . ."

"Hot?" said Emily.

"I guess," I said, unaccountably embarrassed.

She rolled her eyes.

"Quite the man of the world, aren't you, Caleb?" she said.

"You want to hear this or not?"

"Go on."

I told her, even making the gesture he had made as he described the way the girl's face vanished. Emily's brows tightened.

"So a shape changer, like the *bakeneko*," she said. "Is that news?"

"Sounds different from the cat monster though," I said. "For one thing, we didn't see its face do that. It went from *Bāchan* to killer cat. And when it looked like *Bāchan*, it could talk but it didn't know us and didn't act like her. It was a copy, but it wasn't in her head or ours."

"And this other thing was in Davey's head?"

"Well, it knew what he wanted, what he and Blake both wanted."

"A hot girl," said Emily. "High school boys. Big surprise there."

"But it took on the form of the guy in the gas station too, which means it either travels really fast, and probably invisibly, or there's more than one of them."

Emily nodded thoughtfully.

"And it sounds like it was kind of messing with him," she agreed. "Freaking him out rather than hurting him. The *bakeneko* didn't do that. It tried to trick us, and when it revealed itself, it went straight into slice and dice mode. I think you're right. Whatever this thing is, it's different."

"So there's *two* shape shifting Japanese monsters stalking Portersville?" I said. "Awesome."

"Working together?" she mused aloud.

"He said there was a cat there," I said. I had forgotten that part. "But he didn't say it was involved in what happened."

"But he didn't see what happened to Blake because the faceless thing scared him off," said Emily.

"Leaving him with the cat," I said, feeling a cold little shudder in my spine.

There was a long pause while we considered what might have happened next, then Emily said.

"*Bāchan* has a cat. And those CCTV pictures from the cave . . ."

"You're not serious!" I said. "There's no way! We know these things can change shape. One of them looked like *Bāchan*. That's all."

"You sure, Caleb?" she replied seriously. "Ashworth saw an old woman and her cat."

"And Davey saw a young woman and a cat," I said. "Same thing."

"But they didn't behave the same way, did they?" she replied.

"The cat thing attacked *Bāchan*, remember?" I said. "Tied her up and stuck her in a chest."

"So she says, yeah," said Emily. "And tying her up is kind of odd when you think about it. The *bakeneko* wasn't looking to tie *us* up. It wanted us dead."

"So what, *Bāchan* is in league with whatever is terrorizing the town?"

"No!" Emily said. "Maybe. I don't know. I just think we shouldn't jump to conclusions. The truth is, we don't know *Bāchan* that well. Not really."

"Why would she . . .?"

"I don't know! Ok, Caleb? I don't know. But none of this makes any sense, and I don't know what to think or who to trust."

I scowled at her, still angry.

"Apart from you," she said.

I processed that and nodded.

"Ditto," I replied. I thought for a moment and added, "If *Bāchan* is not involved, then someone is trying to make it look like she is. Why else bring the remains of Blake Wilde to the store?"

Emily nodded.

"Someone or something," she said. "We are being implicated. Or taunted."

"Called out, you mean?" I said. "Yes. It feels like that. But why? They know where we live, why not just attack us where we are?"

"No clue," she said.

"I've met that cat thing twice but I'm still alive. Why? Both times it took off when it didn't need to, but it tore Blake Wilde to strips, and he was twice my size."

"You had the sword," said Emily.

"The second time, yeah, but a samurai warrior, I ain't. Frankly I was more likely to cut my own leg off than do the *bakeneko* any real damage. It could have killed me. I'm sure of it. So why didn't it?"

"Still no clue," said Emily. "But I think it's time we pasted some of those paper *ofuda* things around the house."

"You think that will keep them out?"

"See above re: no clue," she answered dryly. "Can't hurt though, can it?"

"Where do we get them?"

"The wonderful world of the internet?" she suggested. "Print them off and stick them on doors and windows?"

"Sounds like a plan," I agreed. "And we need to talk to the *tengu*. Things seem to be escalating."

"Agreed. I need to talk to him about . . . my thing. If I can't get a handle on this shape-shifting, I'm a liability. You get going with the *ofuda* while I talk to the nose."

"I won't be able to read them," I replied. "Aren't they specific to what you want? I'd hate you to come home and find I'd protected the house from runny noses and diarrhoea."

"Look for stuff connected to evil spirits or *yōkai*. Text me what you find and I'll run them by the *tengu*. Paste them in places that won't attract attention: on top of doors, under window ledges. That kind of thing."

"Deal."

But as it turned out, I didn't need to paste them anywhere. I did my online research, took a stab at the best results I could find, got the *tengu's* approval via Emily's phone and printed a few off. But when I got down on my back under the front window, glue stick in hand, I found that someone had beaten me to it. Somewhere on every door and window in the shop or the house, there was a slip of paper marked with carefully written kanji and marked with a red stamp.

What the hell?

Around the back door I found three different *ofuda* stuck to the jambs and lintel, each only visible when I got up on a step ladder. I called Emily and told her.

"How is that possible?" she said. "Can't be *Bāchan* because she hasn't been around the house in years."

"The *tengu?*" I suggested.

"Hold on."

There was an earnest muttering while she asked him, then she was back.

"Not him," she said. "Incidentally, he says the thing with the face that goes smooth like an egg is called a *noppera-bō* and it *doesn't* kill people. Just freaks them out."

"So we are dealing with multiple monsters whose brand of shape-changing is different."

"Exactly," she agreed, "and if our house is full of *ofuda*, someone knows about them."

I was still standing in the doorway considering the slips of printed paper pasted under the lintel, when I got the distinct feeling of being watched. I turned quickly.

"Hey, Emily," I said into the phone. "I'm gonna need you to come home, OK?"

I hung up without waiting to hear her response.

Standing there in the kitchen doorway, her eyes fixed on the *ofuda* but her face carefully expressionless, was my mother.

"Hey, Mom," I said. "You want to tell me what's going on?"

21

My father, Hirokuni Watanabe, had a difficult life. When he first moved to this country he set up a small farm in California, but that was in the 1930s."

I had heard this from *Bāchan*, but since Mom had never spoken to me about it before, I kept quiet for fear of derailing her, and gave Emily a significant look. My sister had raced over the moment I had told her who had been responsible for covering the house in *ofuda*, getting a ride with the *tengu* who was sitting in his truck out front.

"When the war came, my father was interred in a camp," she said, "and his property confiscated. He never got any kind of compensation. It's amazing to me that he stayed, but he believed in this country, despite what it had done to him. But there was nothing for him out west, so he moved here. He said the Great Smoky Mountains reminded him of Japan. By then he was married to my mother—your *obāchan*, though he was much older than her. He died when I was very young, and I remember little about him. He was often away, and when he was home he was quiet, spending most of his time walking in the mountains, like you, Caleb. He was kind to me and I loved him, but I did not know him. He died before you were born, before I met your father, which means that I had no allies to stand with me against my mother."

"Why would you need to fight against *Bāchan*?" I asked.

Mom smiled, a sad, knowing little smile.

"Your *Bachan* is . . . sure of her views, what she wants and how people close to her should behave. She did not like Stephen," she said, and there was a wistful look in her face, as if she was seeing Dad the way he had been when she first fell in love with him. "She wanted me to go back to Japan and meet a man there. It was . . ." but her face clouded and she couldn't find the words. "I married your dad anyway, and she never forgave me for it. And I never forgave her for that. For a while we did not speak, but then you two were born and she wormed her way back into my life. Wanted to bury old grudges, she said, be a family again, for the sake of the kids. But then one November, when Emily had just turned seven and you, Caleb, were about to turn six, a letter arrived from a lawyer calling me to a meeting in connection with my father's will. I was to go alone and not discuss the invitation on pain of forfeiting my inheritance."

"I was confused. My father had not been a rich man and, so far as I knew, anything he had owned, we already had. As for the secrecy . . . I did not know what to expect. I nearly didn't go. Sometimes I wish I hadn't."

"What happened?" I prompted. I could feel something coming. Something crucial.

"I received a box with a few bits and pieces which he wanted me to give you when you were old enough," she said with a dismissive gesture, as if none of it was worth mentioning, "and a letter."

"Saying?" Emily prompted.

"My father's English was . . . patchy. Some of it I didn't understand, and what I did understand I didn't believe. Some nonsense about ancient family history and old Japanese magic. He claimed that he was descended from some kind of warrior shaman or other."

"Raiko," I said.

She gave me a careful look, then nodded hastily, trying to reframe the dubious and slightly mocking expression.

"So the letter said," she agreed. "She said that my children—that is, you two—were the descendants of two powerful families, two magical lines."

"Wait," said Emily. "*Two* magical families? Meaning Raiko and Mayumi, the *Kitsune*?"

Mom frowned at that, and for a second I thought she was going to clam up, but then she shrugged and shook her head as if it was all crazy anyway. When she spoke, it was in a sing-song tone that suggested it was all fairy tale nonsense.

"He said he was descended from Raiko and Mayumi, a shape-shifting fox creature. Together those formed two strands of one powerful magical line. The other was from his wife's side of the family."

"*Bāchan?*" Emily exclaimed. She looked at me. "We thought she just married into the magic. She had some in her own right? Why didn't she say?"

"Because her side is evil," said Mom simply. "Or that's what my father said. I didn't tell you because it was all so ridiculous, but that's what he said."

"This is why you stopped *Bāchan* from hanging out with us?" I demanded. "Because you thought she was evil?"

"No, of course not!" Mom replied, her face reddening. "And in fact, your grandfather didn't say *she* was evil. He said she came from an ancient *yōkai* family, and though she was older than she seemed, she was not a monster herself."

"Older?" Emily echoed. "How old is she, like 75 or something right?"

Mom glanced away.

"How much older, Mom?" I pressed.

"A couple of hundred years or so," she said, with another dismissive wave. "I told you it was all crazy! He had obviously lost his mind. People didn't always identify dementia well back in those days, and he was gone so much of the time. I'm guessing it was some form of Alzheimer's."

I looked down, trying to process all this and the fact that it had been kept from us.

"Where is the letter?" Emily asked.

"I burned it," Mom replied.

"OK," said Emily, "but if you thought it was all the ramblings of a crazy old man, why did you banish *Bāchan?*"

"I didn't," said Mom, though she couldn't hold Emily's stare.

"Sure, you did," I said. "When Emily was seven, right? That totally tracks. She's barely been in the house since. Why did you push her out of our lives if you thought all this talk of magical ancestry was garbage?"

"Because she believed it!" Mom spat, her face full on fire-engine scarlet now. "She said it was all true and that we needed to plan for your future! Monsters and demons were coming, she said, and you would need to be ready."

We stared at her in a charged silence.

"You knew!" Emily exclaimed. "All this time, you knew and you said nothing?"

"Because it was madness!" Mom fired back, leaping to her feet, her voice rattling the windows. "There weren't demons and magic in our family history! How could there be? If I accepted that, then I also had to accept that my parents were monsters. But madness, disease and dementia? We had that in spades! I had to keep all that old country crap out of this house!"

"But it's here, Mom!" Emily yelled back, tears in her eyes now. "It's real and it's here and we aren't ready for it, because you never told us!"

"It's not!" Mom replied. "It can't be because none of it is real!"

"You pasted the *ofuda*!" I shouted. "You must have known it was true or you wouldn't have tried to protect the house!"

"Oh, big deal!" she replied. "I followed a few superstitious practices to be on the safe side! Doesn't mean any of it is real. I don't believe in any of it. I won't!"

"No?" Emily roared. "Then what do you make of this?"

And from behind her back the fox tail, long and full, its russet fur tipped with white, lashed back and forth in anger.

Mom stared, speechless. Emily glared back at her, eyes streaming now. She raised a hand to wipe the tears away, but it wasn't a hand any more. It was a paw, slim and studded with little black claws. I saw the horrified shock in Emily's eyes for a second or less, before they weren't her eyes anymore. Her nose and mouth pushed out, thinning and dappling with fur, tongue lengthening, teeth sharpening. And quite suddenly she was falling through her clothes, a complete and perfect fox, showing no sign of the girl she had been.

I got to my feet, craning my neck to see if I could spot the *tengu* still sitting in his pickup out front, so I didn't see right away what Mom had done. She had scooped up the animal into her arms, exactly as if it had been my sister, and buried her face in its neck, weeping, and hugging it to her as if her life depended on it.

"Oh hi," said a familiar face, peering round the door from the shop. It was dad, grinning wide and guileless. "Whose dog is that? Cute. Make sure you wash your hands afterwards. Where's Em?"

Mr. Saito brought Emily back. It took a good ten minutes and he was sweating like he was sawing wood, even though all he was actually doing was holding her face against his, his eyes shut, whispering the same unintelligible Japanese phrases over and over, but he brought her back. Mom had cleared Dad from the room, obviously, and the *tengu* had insisted upon a ring of candles and silence, though he said that was mostly for his benefit rather than Emily's. The transformation process itself was even more unnerving this way round, and I had to turn away long before the fox became anything resembling my embarrassed and frightened sister. Why she was frightened became clear as soon as she was dressed and coherent.

"I couldn't stop it," she said, her face still tear-streaked. "The angrier I got with Mom, the more I could feel it coming, but I couldn't stop it. I didn't want to. The passion of the thing, the sheer simplicity of its being. It felt stronger, more honest," she said. "I know that makes no sense, but suddenly everything we were doing seemed so ridiculously indirect, coded, polite. I can't explain it. But all the words and the clothes and the humanness of it all made me want to smash things. All the things. As a fox everything burns hotter, clearer . . . but then I couldn't get back. Wasn't even sure I wanted to."

"This will happen again," said the *tengu* gravely to me. "I will not always be there to help. If she does not learn to control her gift . . ."

"I know!" she said. "My *gift* will trap me and probably get me killed."

"Then we must work harder," said the *tengu*.

"And faster," I said. "I don't know what is happening, but things are coming to a head. I can feel it."

"Speed is irrelevant," said the *tengu* in full *sensei* mode. "Nothing is achieved by rushing. We will proceed with the scheduled training plan."

"No, Caleb's right," said Emily. "We can't wait on this."

"You acquire knowledge and skill at the rate you are fit for," the *tengu* replied, his huge nostrils flaring. "You people want everything now, but even you know you cannot run before you can walk. If you move too quickly, you will fall. You must learn each step or you will not understand. That is very dangerous."

"Maybe so, but there's no time," Emily said. "People have been killed on our doorstep. There will be more and we aren't ready to help fight for them or for ourselves. We need it now."

The *tengu* shook his head.

"Americans," he muttered.

"What do you make of what Mom's father told her in his letter?" I said, redirecting. "That *Bāchan* has some demon blood in her?"

"Any other day I'd make nothing of it," said Emily, picking up one of the *ofuda* slips Mom had papered all over the house. "But after seeing those CCTV pictures of her up at the cave . . ."

"Demon is a mistranslation of *yōkai*," said the *tengu*, still in school master mode.

"I don't think the finer points of language are really the issue right now, do you?" I said.

"The finer points of language are always essential," said the *tengu* with the kind of dignity which shouldn't have survived that colossal nose. "More so when the stakes are high."

"Ok, smart guy," I said. "Why does it matter? *Bāchan's* husband thought she was evil and descended from monsters and demons. Not sure a dictionary is going to give her the all-clear."

"*Yōkai* are not demons," said the *tengu*, irritatingly unflappable as ever. "I have told you this already. You should pay attention. *Yōkai* are supernatural beings, creatures, presences. Some have physical being and some do not. Some appear as distortions or hybrids of animals, people or objects."

"Like *Bāchan's* teapot," said Emily.

"Some are mischievous and playful," the *tengu* went on. "Like the *noppera-bō*."

"The what?"

"The thing which appeared to the high school boys," said the *tengu*. "The thing with no face. It can take different forms according to what you are thinking about."

"It sees into your head?" said Emily. "I knew it!"

"A little," said the *tengu*. "It creates its appearance, its behaviour, the things it says by accessing your short-term memory and the parts of your brain which control desire and expectation. That is all. It has no sense of who you are outside of those things. But this is my point. Usually such creatures are tricksters. They scare people and that is all, but the one here in Portersville is working with others toward a darker purpose. Some *yōkai* are terrible and bloodthirsty. But they are not demons in the sense you understand that term, because they do not have a single moral orientation. They are not creatures of absolute spiritual evil. *yōkai may* be evil, but they also may not, and a single *yōkai* may change its behaviour depending on how it is treated."

"You're saying they are like people," said Emily, "only with supernatural abilities."

"Perhaps," said the *tengu*. "And though it is clear that some types of *yōkai* are frequently dangerous, their goals focused on the destruction of the human world, its culture and its people, very few—such as *oni*—are consistently malevolent."

"What's an *oni*?" I asked.

"A little like what you might call an ogre," said Mr. Saito. "Very large, very powerful, very destructive. They hate humans and will kill and devour them when they can."

"Lovely," said Emily. "But none of the things we have encountered in Portersville sound like that."

Unexpectedly, the *tengu* laughed. It was such a surprise that we found ourselves wanting to join in with something like relief.

"No, no!" said the *tengu*, wiping his eyes. "In Portersville?! Ha! *Oni* are massive creatures. It could not stay hidden, and its trail of destruction would be very easy to see. No," he said, still laughing, "if an *oni* was involved, we would know and would have very good reason to be afraid. But only for a little while."

"Why only for a little while . . .?" I began.

"Because it would quickly kill us all!" roared the *tengu*, laughing so uproariously he almost fell off his chair. "Then it would tear us into small pieces and eat us. We would be very scared but only briefly because soon . . ."

He slapped his big hands together and made a squelching sound, then lifted his palm to his lips and pretended to chew.

"Right," I said. "Good one."

"OK," said Emily with a little shudder of distaste. "Then I guess it's a good thing there's no *oni* involved."

The *tengu* roared with laughter. "Yes, *very* good thing. Since we would be dead!"

"Yeah, thank you," I cut in. "I think we got it."

"Best thing about this country," sighed the *tengu*. "No *oni*."

Emily sat up.

"You encountered them in Japan?" she asked.

"Long ago," he said. "Mostly at a distance. Raiko fought one many times."

"I'm sorry?" I said, inching forward on my chair, suddenly anxious.

"There was a terrible *oni* in the Yamanashi mountains," said the *tengu*. "Very large. Very ferocious. Raiko fought it many times."

"This is the thing that killed his wife?" I said. Mr. Saito gave me a sideways look. "*Bāchan* told us. She said he defeated it but did not kill it."

Emily was picking up on my unease, I could tell.

"So that means what?" she said. "He imprisoned it?"

"He trapped it in a place of *yōkai* energy which was not in our world," said the *tengu*. "A mystical prison cell entombed in a far-off mountain."

"He bound the *oni* in a mystical dimension but located it in an actual place," said Emily, her eyes half-closed as she thought it through.

"Yes," said the *tengu* proudly. "For extra security. Many other *yōkai* were trapped in there with it. Not just the *oni*."

"And just how far off was this mountain?" I asked.

"Far from Yamanashi," said the *tengu* blithely. "Raiko passed through what you might call a 'dimensional gateway' to find a suitable location far from the villages which the *oni* threatened."

"Like, beyond Japan?" said Emily.

"Possibly," said the *tengu*. "It would need to have similar terrain to the place where they had fought for the magic to work."

"Mountains and forest," I said. "Warm, sub-tropical summers and cold winters."

"Probably," said the *tengu*, still confidently calm.

"Which is why you like it here, right?" said Emily. "Reminds you of Japan."

The *tengu* stared, his great eyes bulging.

"Here?" he said.

"Which is why Hirokuni brought his wife out here, right?" said Emily. "Keep an eye on things, just in case."

"And this dimensional gateway," I continued, reaching for a scrap of note paper and a red pen from the mug by the phone. "Might it have looked like this?"

I scribbled a pair of columns with a horned cross piece at the top.

"A *torii*," said the *tengu*. "Perhaps."

"Not just any *torii*. The *torii*," I said to Emily. "The one where all this started. The one outside the shrine where Raiko called us by our names up on Red Scar Mountain."

"Oh my God!" Emily exclaimed, glancing at one of the paper slips. "The *ofuda*!"

"What about them?" I asked

"Not these," she said. "The one in the cave! It wasn't there to keep evil forces *out*. It was there to keep them *in*! It was part of the mystical prison, buried deep in the mountain."

I suddenly saw it all so clearly I couldn't believe I hadn't seen it earlier.

"And the physical part of the prison was ruptured by the quake set off by the fracking!" I said. "The cave-in tore away some of the bonds keeping the *yōkai* confined!"

"They've been leaking out," said Emily. "Escaping. Which is bad, obviously, but if they can get out, then maybe at some point . . ."

"The *oni* will get free," said the *tengu*, getting hastily to his feet, his face pale. "It is very large, but if the breach in whatever is binding it in place can be expanded, eventually . . . you are right. We must work fast."

"What can we do?" I asked.

"Fight whatever is already out," he replied. "Confine those *yōkai* which have not yet escaped by restoring the *ofuda* and sealing off the physical prison."

"Can we do it in time?" asked Emily.

"I cannot say," said the *tengu*. "For all we know the *oni* is already freeing itself."

"And if it's already out?" I asked.

"Then we will die," he said, "and so will this town. Your world is not ready for an *oni*."

Emily looked stricken.

"Sounds kind of doomed," she said. "Pointless."

"Yet we will try anyway," said the *tengu*. "There is dignity and virtue in struggle even if it is in vain."

Not quite the uplifting speech I had been hoping for.

"*Ja*," said the *tengu* with clear resolve. "*Ganbarimasho*."

"Any chance that means that you sure we'll prevail no matter how bad things are?" I said.

"I'm not sure," said Emily, "But I think it's more along the lines of 'there's a shit ton of tough stuff to do, maybe more than we can handle, so let's get on with it.'"

"Ah," I said miserably. "Excellent."

"And *Bāchan*?" said Emily. "What do we do about her?"

"If she is working on behalf of the *yōkai* from this side of the dimensional barrier," said the *tengu*, "than she could be very dangerous."

"But she's in prison!" I said. "How much harm can she do in there?"

"If she is what we fear she is," the *tengu* replied, "she is only in prison because she feels no need not to be."

"And if she's on our side like she said?" I demanded. I wasn't ready to give up on her just yet.

"Then she could be a valuable asset," the *tengu* conceded.

"So we need to figure out her intentions," said Emily. "But how?"

"We could ask her," I suggested.

"Because if she's an evil monster trying to release a massive people-eating demon into the world, she'll be honest if we ask nicely?" my sister retorted.

I shrugged.

"There may be ways," said the *tengu*, "to ensure that she tells the truth."

I wasn't sure I liked the sound of that and gave Emily a quick look which the *tengu* read.

"It will not harm her," he said. "It requires only the eating of a certain bean prepared by special ritual and fed to her inside something else, an *onigiri*, perhaps."

"A rice ball," Emily translated.

I considered them.

"Let me get this straight," I said. "We are on the verge of some kind of mystical apocalypse, and our strategy is that you're going to make magic beans?"

"It will take several nights of good moonlight," said the *tengu*.

"We could just trade the family cow for some," I said.

"You do not have a cow," said the *tengu*. "Nor do you know anyone with whom you could trade."

"I was kidding," I said. "It was *A Jack and the Beanstalk* joke."

The *tengu* considered me seriously.

"Perhaps such jokes will stop the *oni* from pulling your legs off," he mused.

"Dude!" I exclaimed.

"I too am just kidding," he said. "But not really. I will begin preparation of the bean. You should train. And be on your guard. The *yōkai* are getting stronger and they are coming. I cannot say what their intentions are beyond escape, but I am sure you will be their primary target. They will want to deal with anyone who might be a threat, however weak and unprepared they may be."

"Thanks," I said.

"You forgot to say half or diluted," Emily added, but the *tengu* was unabashed.

"You are not strong enough to fight like Raiko," he said, "but you are close enough to him to be suitable targets. The *oni* and the other *yōkai* have been entombed for over a century, and they will want revenge on the man who put them there. He is gone, so they will come after his blood. They will come after you."

The *tengu* went home to start his magic bean ritual—and there's another sentence I never thought I'd say with a straight face—while Em and I ate in preparation for a mammoth training session back at the school. Mom was uncharacteristically subdued and Dad watched her throughout the meal, his eyes anxious, but I could think of nothing honest that would put his mind at ease, so I pretended everything was normal. Maybe when this was all over, we'd tell him everything, but even if we survived the danger pressing in on us daily, I wasn't sure how you segued into that particular chat: *Oh, here's a funny thing; we've been targeted by ancient Japanese shape shifting monsters . . .*

I left him to his chicken-fried steak. Half an hour later, my sister and I were sitting in the little clearing just west of the barn site, listening to the crickets and cicadas getting their early evening chorus on while the *tengu* opened a long pouch and drew out a couple of wooden swords. My heart sank.

"Can't we use the real ones?" I asked.

"The best swordsmen are the ones who still have most of their limbs," said the *tengu*, speaking in that booming voice of his that sounded like a temple bell. I guess he had a point.

"How goes the bean?" asked Emily.

"Marinating in herbs and *sake*," said the *tengu*. "I will boil it when I get home and then leave it in a special bowl overnight in the moonlight."

"And then anyone who eats it will tell the truth?"

"There are some words to be read over the final preparation," he said, "but yes, so long as the eater does not know, they cannot lie. There are countercharms which will take away its power. I say them every time I eat food I did not prepare myself."

"Paranoid, much?" said Emily.

"The mountain is full of enemies," he replied.

"Fair point," she conceded.

"We should begin before it gets too dark," he said, taking a battery powered lantern from his bag, switching it on and setting it in on the ground. It cast a flat, greenish radiance around the clearing, dying at the tree line. "I will train with Hideki . . ."

"Caleb," I corrected automatically.

"While you transform into your fox form and attempt to change back at will," he went on. "Write the characters of your name in the earth. You will focus on this in your fox shape and use it to bring you back to your human form."

"The characters?" said Emily. "What characters?"

"*Kazuko*," said the *tengu*. "Your name." He hesitated, considering her. "You do not know how to write your name?"

"Her name is Emily," I said.

He closed his eyes, head bowed, and breathed a little sigh. Then he looked up again.

"Look," he said. He took a stick and scratched a series of complex marks into the dusty earth.

嘉壽子

"I can't read that," said Emily. "I certainly can't write it."

The *tengu* blinked.

"In *hiragana* then," he said. He rubbed out the characters and wrote in the dirt afresh.

かずこ

Emily considered the symbols, sounding them out.

"Ka-zu-ko," she said. "OK."

She didn't look convinced.

"You can read that?" I said.

"Just about," she said. "My *katakana* is wobbly, but I know *hiragana*. Mostly."

"OK," I said, cautiously impressed. "Go for it."

She glanced at the *tengu*, who nodded fractionally, and closed her eyes.

147

Nothing happened.

"Are you going to . . .?" I began.

"I'm trying!" she snapped. "I can't seem to . . ."

"Find the *kitsune* within you," said the *tengu*. "You are a fox and a girl."

"Young woman," said Emily quickly.

The *tengu* pursed his lips and took another breath.

"You are a fox and a young woman," he said. "Both, at the same time. You merely have to choose the aspect in which you present yourself, the form in which you choose to reside for the moment."

"Right," said Emily. "Maybe you two should start your own thing. I can't do this with you looking at me."

The *tengu* looked ready to contradict her, but I jumped in.

"Good idea," I said. "Come on, Mr. Saito. You're due a spanking."

His face clouded with puzzlement.

"A what?" he said.

"Get your sword," I replied, walking over to the edge of the clearing to give Em some space.

He joined me. I turned my shoulder toward him, holding the wooden sword in my right hand.

"You are not a fencer with a foil," he said. "Open up your body and use both hands."

"That gives you more of a target," I said. "This way you have less to hit."

"That is not how we fight."

"Maybe it's not how *you* fight . . ." I began.

He whacked me hard across the thigh.

"Ow!" I exclaimed.

"If the sword was real, I would have cut your leg off," he remarked. "Do as you are told."

"I'm not sure I feel like an equal partner in learning," I said, falling back on a phrase one of my teachers used. "Not sure this is the most progressive of pedagogical practices . . . ow!"

This time he had thwacked me upside the head, his blow swinging in from my left.

"This is what happens when you face me side on," he said.

"It works in Olympic fencing," I replied, petulant.

"Because that is a sport with rules," said the *tengu*, "and no one is trying to kill you. We begin with *chudan no kamae*, a middle posture balanced between attack and defense."

I mimicked his stance, right foot slightly forward, left heel an inch or two off the ground, the sword held in front of me in both hands, angled up. He eyed me critically, then walked behind me, adjusting my elbow.

"Now *sudan no kamae*," he said, moving fluidly into a new pose.

"This feels weird," I said, as he corrected my posture. "I can't learn to fight by numbers. Not in a couple of days. Can't you teach me something more instinctive?"

"You need to learn the basics before you can develop your own style," he said, raising the sword over his head. "*Jodan no kamae.*"

"I won't live long enough to get that far!" I said, lowering my sword.

"You are too hasty," he replied, holding his position.

"And you admitted we didn't have time to waste. Can't we just . . . spar?"

"Studying the essentials is not a waste," he said, indignant. "But if you insist . . ."

And he came at me. His face did not change, but he became a whirlwind of energy, lunging and slashing with studied precision. I swung wildly but couldn't block a single stroke. After he had hit me half a dozen times, I threw my sword down.

"Woah! Woah! Dude!" I exclaimed. "OK, fine! You've made your point."

He nodded fractionally, his body now as completely still as it had just been a tempest.

"*Chudan no kamae*," he said.

And I did as I was told.

After an hour or so, we had moved—quickly, according to him—through eight stances and four basic movements. I couldn't remember their names because the words meant nothing to me, but I could feel my body learning, even if it wasn't anything like fighting. I felt like, with a lot of work over several weeks, I might become a kind of walking Wikipedia article. If anyone attacked me, they'd kill me in seconds, though with my dying breath I may be able to point out the shortcomings of their technique.

Emily wasn't doing much better. While I had been drilling with the *tengu*, she had managed to give herself a tail and a pointiness to her ears which made her look like an elf from a video game. When the *tengu* checked on her she managed to add a snouty sort of nose rivalling his, and a few whiskers, but she was still very much human, albeit now one with a promising career in traveling sideshows. I gave them some space and worked, somewhat half-heartedly, on my fighting stances. When I looked back, she had made the complete transformation into a fox which was now sitting in the middle of the clearing, staring bemusedly at the characters the *tengu* had scratched into the dirt, her head tipped on one side. It was pretty cute, to be honest, though I didn't think she'd thank me for pointing that out.

I was sliding between stances when, in the corner of my eye, I saw movement in the trees. It was quite dark now, the only light coming from the greenish lantern in the centre of the clearing. But I was sure I had seen something more than the shadow of a wind-stirred tree. I paused, senses heightened.

There it was again! A careful movement and—this time—two pin pricks of emerald light.

Eye shine!

"Sensei!" I said. "Emily! There's something out there . . ."

But it wasn't something. It was three somethings. Cats, tall as a man and reared up on their hind legs. They all took up the exact same stance, each balanced on one clawed foot, with one forepaw held out in front of them and one held over their heads like dancers.

Three of them! I had been sure that one of them could have beaten me if they had wanted to. We weren't ready for this.

And then the *tengu* transformed. He threw his arms wide and the action created a pulse of pale light, blinding in the dimness of the trees, and when that uncanny energy subsided he was different: wild and powerful looking, great feathered wings spreading from his shoulders and a hooked beak in place of the comic nose. His eyes flashed and he flew—literally, *flew*, a long, leaping swoop like a thrown spear—at the nearest of the cat monsters.

My instinct was to help him, but the other two were suddenly moving towards us, their feet not so much running as making patterns in the air which somehow moved them forward. Emily—who was still a fox—looked up from the characters on the ground and barked. She wasn't going to be able to turn back.

"Go!" I shouted to her. "Get out of here."

I leapt in front of her, my wooden sword scything through the air at the cat which hovered over her. It leaned back, out of my reach, hissing its fury. The Em-fox yipped at the air, snapping its jaws in alarm. The cat shrank back, but the remaining one was almost on me. I turned and cut at it, all my lessons forgotten in the fury and panic of the moment. A few yards away, one of the cats yowled as the *tengu*'s wooden sword caught it hard in the gut, but it came up with a deadly slash of its claws. The *tengu* leapt backwards, somersaulting in the air and settling back into its fighting stance.

I was yet to make contact with either of the remaining cats. I swung and lunged, but they dodged and feinted, always a little out of reach. I was fast and strong, but they evaded at the last second, so that in the low light, there were times when I thought my sword had gone right through them.

The Em-fox was frantic, hopping and biting, but she was having no more luck than me, and however close she got to the cat monster, her teeth always closed on nothing but air.

"Switch!" I shouted, hurling myself at the one she had been harassing in the hope that the surprise would give us an edge. I spun and whirled, slicing through the night with all the speed and force I could muster, sure I would hear the crack of wood on bone.

There was nothing but the wind of my stroke, my grunt of exertion and the satisfied snarl of the elusive cats. The effort of my assault had thrown me off balance, but I came up in one spring—*pretty deft, Smith*—swinging my foot around in a crunching kick into one of the cat's muzzles.

It passed right through.

It was impossible, but there was no denying it. And in that moment I realized.

"There's only one *bakeneko*!" I exclaimed. "The others are just *noppera-bō*!"

I turned in time to see the true cat monster barrel under the *tengu's* parry and bundle him to the ground in a flurry of teeth and claws.

"No!" I roared, as the two cats facing me and Em took on their true forms, humanoid and wearing kimonos, their fur vanishing, their faces becoming blank and egg-smooth. They didn't bother blocking me now, and when I moved to help the *tengu* I passed right through one of them.

The *bakeneko* was clinging to the *tengu's* body, digging its claws in, worrying at his throat with its bloody mouth. His wings flapped ineffectually and he tried to angle his beak into the cat, but it had him in a tight bear hug. Try as he might, he couldn't get any kind of purchase on the monster.

I hit it hard across the back—my first true strike—and it released him, rolling and and bounding clear. I went after it, but it side-stepped my clumsy swing, and was able to look back through narrowed eyes to where the *tengu* lay on the ground, assessing whether it had done enough. Satisfied, it seemed to smile, and then it was just a cat again, small and lithe and impossible to catch as it leapt off into the trees and away.

I turned to see the *noppera-bōs* gliding after it, their eyeless faces turned on me as they too melted into the night. Ignoring them, I stooped to the *tengu*, who was a mass of savage-looking wounds. Blood pooled on the dusty ground beneath him.

"Em!" I shouted at the fox. "Come back! I need your help!"

But the fox which had been my sister could only huddle up to his bleeding body, whimpering.

I clamped my hands over the worst of his cuts, holding them hard against the warm, slick wetness as I'd seen them do on the TV cop shows.

Direct pressure. Slow or stop the bleeding.

It wouldn't be enough, I thought, as his wings withered away and he became once more Mr. Saito, restauranter and part time carpenter. He was sprawled on his back, his eyes closed. He was going to die because I had been too slow to realize that two of the three cats had been mere distractions. I squeezed and adjusted and pressed but there were too many wounds. I just didn't have enough hands.

"What the hell just happened?" said a voice on the edge of the trees.

I looked up, twisting my head round to face the sound. Someone was there. Not Emily. A boy, tall, black, athletic . . .

DeMarcus.

"Caleb," he said in an awed, stricken voice. "What did I just see?"

I stared at him.

"Help," I said. "I think he's dying. Help and I'll tell you everything."

23

"How long had you been watching?" I asked absently, my eyes on the wounded *tengu* in the glow of the lantern. Not that it mattered. I was just talking to keep my mind off the horror of what was happening.

"Long enough," said DeMarcus, who had torn a sleeve off his sweatshirt and was tying it round the *tengu's* ravaged arm. He didn't look at me and his voice was low and unsteady with tension. I couldn't really blame him. When he spoke again it sounded like he was lining the words up in his head, holding onto something normal, something rational, as if by pursuing the sentence to the end he would find that everything made sense after all. "I went to the gym after football practice. The janitor lets me stay late. I came out again to run a bit and saw the light. And you. And . . . this. What were those things?"

The million-dollar question.

"Not absolutely sure," I said.

"You looked pretty sure," he said, staying focused on the wound he was clamping.

"I've seen them before," I said. "We should call my Mom. Get her to come pick us up. We need to get him into the light."

"We need to get him to a hospital," said DeMarcus. "He's lost a lot of blood and we have no idea how much internal damage there is."

There was no hospital in Portersville. The closest was a half hour away in Hendersonville, and I couldn't help wondering what kind of madness would result from running basic tests on someone who, despite Mr. Saito's current appearance, wasn't technically human.

"Not sure that's a good idea," I said.

"Better than watching him die," said DeMarcus.

"Keep the pressure on here," I said. "I'm reaching for my phone."

I moved my hand and felt a trickle of blood before DeMarcus slammed a wad of cloth onto it. I wrestled my phone from my pocket with one hand and dialled Mom. As soon as she answered, I said, "I need you to bring the car to school. Now. Mr. Saito is hurt. Badly. We are in the trees behind the gym."

There was a stunned silence on the other end, then she said,

"I'll be there in . . . seven minutes."

"If you could make it five," I said, "that would be good."

I hung up, and turned my attention back to the *tengu*, though I could feel DeMarcus watching me.

"What is he?" he said. "A couple of minutes ago he had wings and a beak."

"He's a *tengu*," I said. My heart sank, as if saying it showed how completely I had failed. The secrecy which had seemed so important didn't matter anymore.

"Ok," said DeMarcus. "That doesn't help as much as you might think."

"I don't really know," I admitted.

"But it's a Japanese thing?"

I bit my lip and blinked. The *tengu*'s breathing was ragged and shallow.

"Yes," I said.

"And you have a pet fox because . . ."

"It's not a pet," I said. I had put a finger on the *tengu*'s throat but I couldn't find a pulse. "It's my sister."

"Ah," said DeMarcus. "Right." He seemed to consider this for a moment. "I wrote a story like this when I was in elementary school. The last line was 'and then I woke up and it was all a dream.' Am I awake, Caleb?"

"'Fraid so," I said.

"And this is somehow connected to all the other weird stuff which has been going on?" he said. He was turning out to be annoyingly smart. "Those cat things, the missing fracking guys and all?"

"Yes," I said.

"Blake Wilde?"

"Afraid so."

"OK," he said again. "And it's a kind of good versus evil thing, right? Like in the comic books. Because those cat things felt . . . not good."

"I guess," I said. "It's complicated."

"So, you're some kind of superhero?"

"No," I said quickly. "I mean, he was trying to train me to help out, but . . ."

I didn't bother finishing the sentence. Another thoughtful hesitation and then he tipped his head to look at me.

"This is why you caught the tangerine," he said. "And my passes the other day."

"I guess," I replied, not wanting to talk about it. Those little triumphs seemed so stupid now. I was ashamed of myself for having revelled in them.

The Em-fox shifted, nuzzling deeper into the *tengu*'s neck like a cub trying to get warmth from its mother.

"That's Emily?" said DeMarcus.

"Yes."

"This isn't some kind of wind-up, right?" said DeMarcus. "Some kind of candid camera, America's Funniest Home Videos BS?"

"No."

"No," he echoed, almost disappointed. "I didn't think so. Shouldn't your mom be here by now?"

"It's only been a couple of minutes," I said, though I knew what he meant. It felt like hours. The *tengu* was slipping away. I could feel it. I don't know what I expected Mom's arrival to do that would change that, but the idea of him dying before she got here, before someone wiser or more skilled at first aid could try to help, was just too painful. If he died now, it really was on me.

"Why is the fox glowing?" said DeMarcus.

I was about to ask him what he was talking about, and then I saw it too, a soft, strange luminescence that pulsed through her from snout to tail. It faded away, and then came back, brighter this time, so that the fox seemed not red but golden, the light seeming to come from within, radiating out from her fur. Her eyes, which had been tightly closed, opened and they shone like white hot metal at the heart of a furnace. She opened her mouth and a frail whimper escaped her.

"What's happening?" I gasped. "Em? Em, come back!"

As the light faded away this time, the fox seemed to shrink, its muscle sagging as if its body had been hollowed out. It looked smaller, flatter, and the color had leeched out of its fur, so that it looked like one of those bad taxidermy examples of local wildlife that you saw collecting mould and cobwebs in state park ranger stations.

"Em!" I shouted.

"Oh my God," said DeMarcus. "Is she . . .?"

But in the next moment, several things happened at once. First, I saw headlights splashing across the sports field and over the bricks of the gym.

Mom! I thought, relief and anguish spiking. *She can't see Emily like this.*

Second, the *tengu's* eyes and mouth opened. He sucked in air, his great chest filling like a bellows, lifting him up off his back as if someone had just sent a thousand volts through his heart. His eyes seemed to rake the trees overhead, and his face rippled with uncertainty, as he tried to patch together memories of what happened. Then, as if sensing her presence beside him, he rolled onto his left shoulder and cradled the shrunken fox in his arms.

He spoke to her in rapid Japanese, calling her Kazuko, over and over. The fox didn't stir. She was grey, wilting before our eyes. There was neither life nor any trace of my sister in its half open eyes.

The *tengu* struggled up into a sitting position and started scraping symbols into the ground, the characters for her name which he had written before.

"Kazuko!" he called, strident at first, commanding, then softer, imploring.

But the fox's eyes were empty.

"Kazuko!"

But my sister's name was Emily.

"Em!" I shouted. "Em! Come back."

And then my mother was there, pushing her way through, demanding to know what had happened and then falling silent, staring at the fox, then dropping to her knees and snatching the frail creature to her breast.

"Emily!" she whispered. "My Emily. Come back my darling. Em. My baby. My sweet Em. Mommy's here. Mommy loves you. Please come back."

And then there was a softening of the darkness, and I realized that it emanated from a point a few inches above the fox's belly, like some tiny spark of light in her heart. Mom stooped to it, still whispering her love, and it was like she was blowing on embers, which flared. The light around us strengthened, touching our faces with gold, and then the fox was not a fox anymore.

"Turn away," said Mom, something of her old self returning in the instant.

DeMarcus and I, even the *tengu*, did as we were told, and Mom folded my naked sister in her arms.

"Hi Mom," murmured Emily.

"I know it's hard to get your head around," I said.

"Understatement of the decade," DeMarcus replied.

We had helped the *tengu* to the car while Emily dressed. They were both very weak, barely able to stand by themselves, but they seemed to be strengthening by the minute. In the car headlights it seemed that, though streaked with blood which was turning thick and brown as it dried, the *tengu*'s wounds were mostly closed. Emily had done that somehow. It had cost her, almost more than she had to spend, but she had saved his life. I had no doubt on that score. But it was hard not to dwell on how close we had coming to losing them both, and the *tengu* wasn't going to be in any shape to train with me anytime soon.

Things were well out of hand and, since we were in cliché land, I was utterly out of my depth: like in the middle of the Pacific with bowling balls shackled to my ankles. And sharks gathering.

"Now what?" asked DeMarcus, as they all got carefully into the car.

"I don't know," I said honestly. I looked up at the sky but I couldn't see any stars. There were storms coming through the mountains and the cloud was already thick. I wondered vaguely whether the lack of moonlight would affect the *tengu*'s bean ritual. "Go home. And thanks. But I'd appreciate it if you didn't tell anyone about this."

"Man," said DeMarcus, taking my hand and shaking it, as if we had bonded somehow and were now friends. "I wouldn't know where to start."

In school, the next day, DeMarcus kept his distance except to stop by my desk as he was leaving English.

"How's Emily?" he asked with mock casualness. "I heard she called in sick."

"Better, thanks," I said. "Be her old self in no time. Physically, at least."

He hesitated, trying to decide whether to say more, but someone called his name and so he gave me an awkward, bobbing nod, and made his escape.

"Emily's sick?"

It was Madison, radiant in a navy-blue top that gave her hair this implausible Disney princess glow.

"Oh," I said, ever the smooth operator. "Hi. Yes. No. I mean, she's just a bit under the weather."

"Speaking of weather, did you see the rain last night?" she exclaimed, her mouth making a little cartoon 'O' of amazement. "More coming, according to Action News 12. They'll probably cancel cheerleading. I guess you won't be able to work on the barn either."

She sounded secretly delighted, though I wasn't sure why.

"Probably not," I agreed, heading out into the hallway.

"So . . . we're both free after school," she said.

"Oh," I said. I looked at her closely and felt something of her Disney glow blossoming in my chest. Could this be happening? "I guess so," I agreed, hardly daring to believe it. "I mean . . ." And then it all came back: Emily and the *tengu* and getting answers out of *Bāchan* and the possibility —no, the certainty—that the *bakeneko* would come back for me and I needed to be ready. "Actually, no," I said. "Sorry. I'd love to, but I have things to do."

"Oh," said Madison, as if I'd sneezed on her lunch. "What things?"

"Well, homework, and I'm grounded," I invented. "Because of the barn. And I have to take Emily to the doctor."

"You can drive?" she asked, baffled but hopeful.

"No," I said, feeling stupider than usual, which is going some. "Just have to, you know, escort her. My parents are busy."

"Oh," said Madison again. "Well, maybe later in the week."

"Yeah," I said. "Maybe."

She left, a little less bounce in her step than usual, and I stared after her.

"She's not in your league, weirdo."

I turned to find two people watching me from a little ways down the hall. One was a girl I didn't know. The other was Tyler.

I blushed, but I wasn't in the mood to be cowed by him. I had caught footballs and fought monsters.

"It's none of your business, Tyler," I said.

"In this school," he said, "everything is my business."

He stared at me, waiting for me to wilt and scurry away, but I held his eyes.

"What is it with you?" I said. "What is it that makes you think you're so special? Is it the football thing, or your dad being the mayor? What?"

He smirked.

"Guess I'm just the complete package," he remarked. The girl next to him, a hard-faced brunette who hadn't stopped sneering since I'd seen her, grinned in smug agreement.

"But a package of what?" I asked, genuinely baffled. "I mean, I get that you're big and sporty, but you're kind of dim and no one really likes you. Not really. They want to like you because you're sort of a bigshot in this crummy little school and this still crummier town, but they don't. Your family is rich and powerful by Portersville standards, but it's not exactly New York or LA rich and powerful, is it? Even if it was, it wouldn't take away from the fact that you are so personally unimpressive. So's your dad, for that matter. I mean, he wears the suits and smiles the smile, but every time I see him on TV I think that wardrobe people will show up as soon as he finishes talking, and they'll take the suit away, maybe the smile too, and there'll be nothing there. No mind, no skills, no real personality at all. It's like, they could wipe away his make-up and his whole face would go with it."

"You want to watch your mouth," said Tyler, taking a step toward me, his face darkening with real anger. "My father's a great man, and one day I'll be just like him."

"Well," I said, smiling, "half of that statement is true."

Tyler's face flickered with doubt and then he decided that nothing the school could do to him was enough to stop him doing what he wanted.

"My dad is the mayor," he said, his anger boiling over. "One day, I will be too. You will always be nothing: a weird little half-breed freak whose parents run a crappy little store."

And he came for me, one fist raised.

He probably wouldn't have actually thrown the punch, but I stepped up and caught it anyway, grasping it firmly in one hand and holding it. His eyes flashed first with pleasure at the prospect of me giving him the excuse he needed to pummel me, then confusion, and finally pain.

Because I held his hand exactly where it was and squeezed. It was easy. And the mixture of rage and agony which chased each other across his high cheek bones felt like the reward I had earned from days of misery.

Years...

"Though somewhat inconveniently located . . ." I said, inches from his face. "It. Is. A. Good. Store."

He gaped at me, his eyes watering.

"Going from deft to mean, huh, Smith?"

It was Joey. I wasn't sure how long they had been there, but they were eyeing me critically from over by the lockers.

"He had it coming," I said, releasing him.

Tyler fell back, his face dark with fury. He glared at me, wanting to attack again, but just unnerved enough to think better of it. The sneering expression on the girl at his elbow hadn't changed, and when he decided to turn and walk away, she went with him, though she gave me a long, baleful glance before doing so.

"'Treat every man after his desert,'" Joey said, "'and who shall 'scape whipping?'"

"What?" I said, still watching Tyler in case he changed his mind.

"*Hamlet*," said Joey. "If we only treat people according to what they deserve, we're all screwed."

"You didn't hear what he said," I replied, surprised at how annoyed their remark made me.

"I can guess," Joey replied. "I've heard all Tyler's witty little put downs. Including a few he hasn't tried out on you. But you can't let people like him define you."

"What's that supposed to mean?" I shot back, amazed that my moment of victory—a victory I had earned over a long period of mistreatment— was not getting the applause it merited.

"That guy there," Joey said, "the one who grabbed Tyler's hand and crushed it? I've never seen him before. It sure wasn't the Caleb Smith I thought I knew."

"People change," I replied quickly.

"Yeah," they replied. "They do. You might wanna watch that."

And they walked away.

24

Elsewhere

Madison Haynes rolled her eyes at the tall girl next to her.

"Yes, Mom," she said into her phone. "Of course, I'll be careful. It's not even dark out! Won't be for hours."

"When will you be home?"

Madison made another face. She didn't really mind her mother being a little over protective, but it was important that she looked outraged in front of her friends, especially new friends who she didn't really know.

They were walking into town from school at the height of what passed for rush hour in Portersville. A pair of pickups rolled by, one of them tricked out with oversized exhaust pipes, roll bars and stylized flames stencilled onto the side.

"Couple of hours, ok?" she said, sounding more indignant than she felt. "Jeez, mom. I'm just going to Tony's. They close at eight!"

Tony's pizza was one of the few non-chain restaurants in town and it was Madison's favourite.

"You won't be eating dinner with us?"

"I'll probably just have a milk shake and a snack," said Madison. "I'll have something with you when I get home, but don't wait."

"Well, OK. And who are you with?"

"No one you know," said Madison. No one *she* knew either really, but she wasn't about to tell her mom that.

"Oh Maddie, you know I hate you keeping secrets from us," said her mother in that slightly hurt tone she employed in situations like this.

Madison's annoyance was real this time.

"I'm not ten, Mom," she snapped, lowering her voice.

"I just want to know who you are with. It will put my mind at ease."

"And I said it's no one you know."

"Just one person?" her mother, ace detective, asked. "Boy or girl? You know I don't want you seeing that Caleb boy."

Madison permitted herself a private smile. She rather liked the fact that her mother disapproved of Caleb who, she suspected, was nice as well as unexpectedly cool. Cute too, in a way which was also unexpected.

Yeah, she thought, momentarily forgetting her new friend. She had high hopes for Caleb, and if Tyler and his pals didn't like it, that was their problem. The idea gave her a rosy glow inside, like she'd made a back flip and stuck the landing.

Her mother was still talking.

"Did you know his grandmother has been arrested?"

Madison didn't know that. It was weird, but not in the way her mother obviously thought, given her scandalized tone. Why on earth would they have arrested Caleb's grandmother?

"It's a girl," Madison conceded. "She's new in school. I'm just looking after her."

She mouthed a *sorry* at the girl, but still blushed a little. Anyone could tell the girl did not need looking after. It was a good part of what Madison liked about her.

She could have heard her mother's sigh of relief without the phone.

"Oh, I am glad," she said. "What's her name?"

Madison didn't know, which was probably weird, though for some reason it didn't feel it. They had just got chatting and the tall, confident girl, the girl who oozed cosmopolitan sophistication and a whiff of adventure, had suggested they go for coffee or something and Madison had said yes without hesitation. What did names matter?

"Sacha," said Madison, pulling the name out of the air and considering the girl next to her. She looked like a Sacha. It was an interesting and slightly haughty name, Madison decided, hoping that the girl's name really was along those lines. She'd be disappointed if it was Jane or something.

"OK, Mom," she said, "I have to go. See you later."

And she hung up, turning to her new friend in the same moment.

"Oh my God!" she exclaimed with extravagant disbelief. "What is the deal with parents? I'm like, hello? Sixteen! I swear she'd keep me on a leash if she could get away with it. I mean, what do they think is going to happen? It's pizza. Are they going to force-feed me anchovies?" She paused, conscious that her friend had been quiet for a long time. "I expect your parents are way cooler. Right?"

"About the same," said the girl.

Madison was delighted, and a little relieved.

"So how long have you known Tyler?" she said. "Are you and he . . . you know?"

To Madison's further relief, the girl shook her head.

"I don't really know him, or anyone really," said the girl. "I'm new."

"Yes," said Madison. "You said."

"It's good to meet someone so friendly," the girl replied, smiling so genuinely that she looked quite different from the girl who had been slouching around with Tyler looking cool and ironic. Madison was pretty, she had known that since she was small, but she wasn't cool or ironic.

"What did you say your name was again?" she asked.

"I don't think I told you," said the girl.

"Oh," Madison replied, slightly wrong-footed.

"Just kidding," said the girl. "It's Sacha."

Madison laughed, but the girl said nothing else, and she found herself staring.

"Seriously, though," she said. "What is it really?"

"It's Sacha," said the girl giving her a sincere look. "Why, don't you think I look like a Sacha?"

"No, I do!" said Madison, a little defensive and flustered now. "It was just . . . I said that to my mom to get her off my back but I didn't know . . ."

"Maybe you heard Tyler say it," said the girl called Sacha.

Madison opened her mouth to say that she didn't think so, then shrugged and dredged up a smile.

"I guess so," she said.

"So, you like this Caleb kid, huh?" said Sacha, grinning.

"I guess," said Madison, cagey now, afraid of blowing what little cool she had. "He's . . . nice."

"Nice?" said the girl, head tipped forward and eyes wide.

"I mean, he seems cool," said Madison, backpedalling and adopting her new friend's casual swagger. "We'll see. But for now, yeah."

"But he likes you," said Sacha, eyes narrowed with unexpected serious-
ness. "I mean, *really* likes you?"

Madison blushed and looked away from all that curiously intense
focus, but the temptation was too great.

"Oh yeah," she said. "He's totally into me."

"Good," said the girl.

"Why?" Madison asked, feeling a little guilty for being so casual about
Caleb's interest.

The girl shrugged, her laconic self again.

"No reason," she said. "Let's skip the pizza. I want to show you something cool."

"Oh," said Madison, caught between wanting to seem interested in
what this girl thought was cool and what she had promised her mother.
"Yeah? What's that?"

"It's this way," said the girl, nodding towards Bevington Street.

There was nothing along Bevington but a few houses and a pawnshop,
and not much between them. Eventually it looped round to the ravine
road and the bridge where Blake Wilde had been killed. Madison swallowed. She looked up at the sky but the swirling cloud had not delivered
its promised storms. She found herself wishing for a ripple of lightning
that would give her the excuse to go home.

"Come on," said Sacha. "It will be fun. Promise."

"Ok," said Madison. The girl had a big city aura about her, but her
accent was softly southern like Madison's own. Charlotte, maybe. Or
Atlanta. "Where did you move from?"

"Atlanta," said the girl.

"Oh," said Madison. "Another good guess."

Why, she wondered, did that ring the thinnest and most distant of
alarm bells? It was, as she had said, just a good guess. It's not like the girl
could look into her head and say what she thought Madison wanted to
hear.

Madison felt the pricking of the skin at the base of her neck, as if her
body knew something that her mind did not. She looked at the girl, main-
taining her jaunty smile, and hoping it didn't look as strained as it felt.
Sacha smiled back, and it was strange the way the shifting light seemed to
change her face, so that she looked quite different now from when they
had first got chatting in school. She barely looked like a Sacha at all now,
more like the Jane Madison had dismissed so scornfully earlier. She had
lost that big city swagger and didn't even seem as tall as she had before.

And hadn't Sacha's eyes been green and sharp? Now they were an ordinary muddy brown.

Madison looked around distractedly. Maybe she was coming down with something. She put the back of her hand to her forehead, half expecting it to be hot with fever, but it was quite cool.

"You know," she said, "I really think I should head home. I have some homework I had forgotten about and . . ."

"Just a little further," said . . . *Jane?* "Just round the next corner. I'll show you and then you can go home."

"Can't you show me now?" asked Madison, a tremor of desperation running through her. "I really should be . . ."

"There!" said *Jane.* "See?"

"What?" said Madison gazing into the gathering twilight between two abandoned buildings. "I don't see anything."

"There!" said *Jane*, smiling and pointing.

There was a movement in the tangle of weeds and a grey cat emerged. It sat on the far side of the road, sphinx-like, and considered them as if waiting.

"This is what we came to see?" asked Madison hesitantly. "It's cute, I guess. You knew it would be here?"

"Oh yes."

"Is it yours?" asked Madison, sure she was being lied to but with no idea why.

"Not exactly," said *Jane.* "We just . . . work together."

Madison gave her a blank look. The alarm bells which had been distant were clanging now in her head. She wished they hadn't left the main road.

"How do you mean?" she managed. "Work together?"

"For someone else," said *Jane.* "It's important work. It will change the world. This part of it at least."

"Well," said Madison, wholly at a loss as to what to say, "I guess change is good."

"You know," said *Jane*, raising a hand to her face, "it really is."

The fingers moved, a stroking, teasing gesture, and when she took the hand away it wasn't *Jane* anymore. But then it wasn't Sacha either.

Madison stared at the space where the girl's face had been and then she started to scream. She turned to run, but her path was blocked by something large behind her, something yellow eyed and malevolent, something covered in grey fur.

25

Emily had spent half her sick day tending the *tengu*'s magic bean under his grumpy direction. Neither were close to being a hundred percent and they both tired very quickly, but while Emily wasn't dealing with the *tengu*'s pain, she was clearly sick of dealing with him.

"He corrects everything I do," she muttered, "even when no one could tell the difference between the right way and the wrong way. *Turn the bowl three times to the right! No, move your hand like this! You've got the sutra upside down!* I'm beginning to wish I had let him die."

"Yeah, about that . . ." I began.

"I don't know how I did it," she said, anticipating my question. "It just became clear in my head. I could see what I needed to do and I did it."

"Without being shown," I mused, impressed.

"Yeah, but it was like the transformation thing," she replied. "Once I started, I don't think I could have stopped if you and Mom hadn't brought me back. It was like I'd opened a vein or something. All my life energy was flowing into him. Eventually I wouldn't have had enough left to stay alive."

"You think he forced . . .?"

She shook her head vehemently.

"No," she said. "It was all me. I felt like I'd pushed a heavy door open, but as I gave him my strength, I no longer had the energy to close it. I saved him. You saved me."

She gave me a frank look. Em and I had always been close, though we didn't always see eye to eye, and I wasn't used to this kind of honesty. Usually we relied on an eye roll or a knowing smirk because most of what bound us together was our shared dealings with our parents, that sense of being lost behind enemy lines. She was the master spy with the disguise, the maps and the foreign language phrase book, while I was the clown with the airhorn and a backpack full of fireworks: occasionally helpful, always annoying. I was used to relying on her to get me through the tricky stuff. I wasn't used to her gratitude. Or her hugs, which is what happened next.

"Is the bean ready?" I asked, keen to change the subject.

"He keeps checking it like it's the Hope Diamond," said Emily, back to eye-roll mode. "But I'm gonna get it from him now the rice is ready."

"What are you making?"

"*Onigiri*," she said. "A rice ball wrapped in dried seaweed. The bean will be in the centre."

Something occurred to me.

"What did Mom tell Dad about why there's an injured Japanese man on our kitchen floor?" I asked.

"She said he's working on the barn with you but got hurt by a power tool."

"Huh," I said. "That's pretty good, so long as you don't look too closely at his wounds."

"Good enough for Dad," she said. "He asked if there was anything he could do to help, then went to work on his model train."

"And *Bāchan* is still in Halpern's cells?"

"She refused a lawyer," said Emily, "so no one is pressing them to charge or release her. Apparently she's just sitting there, saying nothing."

"Time we took her home, then," I observed.

"I don't know," said Emily. "Tensions in town are running high. We don't want to force the issue. Halpern may not have the evidence he needs to make anything stick, but he can feel the mayor breathing down his neck. I don't want him scape-goating *Bāchan*."

"You're still not sure of her, are you?" I said.

"It's why we're doing this bean thing," she said.

I nodded grudgingly.

"OK," I said. "But we should swing by her place on the way to the sheriff's office. Make sure the locals haven't set it on fire in retribution. And we should feed her cat. Assuming it's not a homicidal shape-shifting monster which is waiting to kill us."

"Because if it is," she dead-panned, "it can probably find its own food."

"There's something else I want to get while we're over there," I said.

"What?" she asked.

"The only thing to yet strike terror into the aforesaid homicidal shape-shifting monster."

"You want her teapot," said Emily, grinning.

"I really do."

Bāchan's shotgun shack had not been torched by the neighbors, but it did look like it had been the subject of a rough search. Drawers and cupboards were open, but the place was relatively tidy. If the cops had been looking for missing bodies, they had abandoned the hunt as a nonstarter.

It was also hot and stuffy. There was no sign of Snowball, so I left a saucer of cat food on the stoop and dug out the little box with the cast iron teapot. I peeked inside, expecting it to buzz with excitement at seeing me, but it just sat there, black and old and lifeless. As in . . . a teapot.

"It was this one, right?" I said.

"I don't see any others," said Emily. "Maybe it's asleep."

"Hey! Teapot!" I yelled into the box. "Wake up!"

"Good grief, Caleb," said Emily, snatching it from me and putting the lid back on. "Can you try not to make this even weirder than it already is?"

"That's setting the bar pretty high," I said.

"And yet you manage to clear it."

"It's my new-found athleticism," I remarked.

She managed a bleak smile, but when she responded all the playfulness had drained out of her voice.

"They're coming for us, aren't they?" she said. "The attack on the *tengu* was planned, targeted. They wanted him out of the way and they succeeded. He's not dead, but he can't fight."

The same thing had occurred to me, but I hadn't wanted to say it. Words had a way of making things feel true.

"*Bāchan* too," I agreed. "Assuming she's not bad, I mean. She's locked up out of the way. She couldn't have fought alongside us, but at least she knows things, things which might have helped if . . ."

"When," Emily corrected.

"When they attack," I said.

"I hate waiting," she said. "I wish we could take the fight to them. But we're not ready."

"Not even close," I agreed. "You think we ever will be?"

"Based on what happened to the *tengu* . . .?" Emily began, but she couldn't finish the sentence and hung her head.

"No," I said. "Me neither."

"And the worst of them hasn't shown itself yet," she said. "If the *oni* is anything like as dangerous as the *tengu* thinks . . ."

"When it gets out, that's it," I said. "Game over, and not just for us."

"So we *do* have to take the fight to them," said Emily, "stop them before they can finish opening the breach in whatever mystical bond is holding the *oni* in place."

"The cave on Red Scar Mountain," I said. "That's where this all started. That's where they will be. But like you said, we're not ready."

Emily blew out a long sigh, her face scrunched up in the frustrated expression I knew so well. It was the face she made if she underperformed in the pool, or got a grade less than an A. It always led to renewed concentration, focused work, long hours at whatever she thought would get her up and over the hurdle which had been put in her way. It always worked out for her in the end. My sister could move mountains if she really wanted to.

Not this time.

The words materialized in my head unbidden. I felt the truth of them like stones settling in my belly.

She isn't strong enough, and the enemy are too many and too powerful.

We went back outside, and were locking the door behind us when there was a whoop of a siren, so loud that I jumped. Sitting by the road was one of the gold and tan sheriff's cars, its lights strobing. Williams, the young officer we had met before, opened the door and climbed out, beckoning us over.

"You're not supposed to be in there," he said.

"Why?" I asked. "It's not a crime scene. And it looks like you already went through it."

"You shouldn't interfere with a criminal investigation," he replied.

"Why?" I said again. Something about his casual air of authority was making me defiant.

"You want to dial it down a little, Robin Hood?" Emily muttered out of the corner of her mouth. "Look."

Williams had stepped round to the back and opened the rear door. Inside, huddled and frail looking, was *Bāchan*.

"She is being released on a temporary basis," said Williams, "but you should assume we will have more questions for her soon."

"So why let her out if you are planning to pull her back in?" I demanded.

"They can't hold her indefinitely without charge," said Emily. "Even without a lawyer."

"It's also that she has an alibi for the latest incident," said Williams. "On account of her being in custody, and all."

"There's been another attack?" I said, all my hostile indignation evaporating.

"I can't confirm or deny anything about that," said Williams, coloring as he tried to find suitable official words. "But your grandmother is not our primary focus at this time."

"What is this new incident?" I demanded.

"Another abduction," said the deputy.

"Who?" I pressed.

"I'm not at liberty to say."

I glanced at Emily. She breathed out, her eyes half closed, and I could feel the relief I felt coming off her like heat. She was satisfied that *Bāchan* was innocent. Whoever had been on that CCTV footage, it wasn't her.

"Come on, *Bāchan*," said Emily. "Let's get you inside."

The old woman beamed at my sister, taking her arm as she moved up the path from the car. She did not look back at the deputy who hovered for a moment, looking unsure of what he was supposed to do, before getting back into the driver's seat and pulling away, the lights off.

"Sit down," said Emily, once we were inside and the door closed. "Crank that AC unit, Caleb, will you? *Bāchan*, you look exhausted. What can we get you?"

"*Omizu*," said *Bāchan*. "*Onegaishimasu*."

"Water," Emily translated. "On it."

As we bustled about, *Bāchan* just sat there, still and quiet. She wasn't the type to pitch a fit about her treatment but I wondered what it had taken out of her, being suspected of something terrible, imprisoned, treated like a criminal. I remembered what she had said about her husband, Hirokuni, who had been interred during the war not because of anything he had done, but because his face worried people.

"You want something to eat?" called Emily from the kitchen, her head in the open fridge. "Not sure what's still good. Oh, I made *onigiri*! You want that?"

"You *made onigiri*?" said *Bāchan*, clearly delighted.

"Yeah," said Emily, picking up her bag and taking out a Tupperware box. "Probably not that great, but I did my best. I found a recipe online."

"Kazuko, these look excellent," said *Bāchan*, beaming.

It was a mark of how glad we were to see her free and apparently innocent that neither of us thought to correct her use of Emily's middle name.

"Caleb, you want one?"

Emily offered me the box. The rice balls were like rounded triangles with a layer of papery green stuff around the edge. They smelled of the ocean.

"Ok," I said, taking one cautiously and examining it. As I've said before, I had almost no experience with Japanese food.

"Just bite into it," said Emily. "Jeez."

I did, munching slowly, then nodded.

"That's actually not bad," I said.

"The Japanese people thank you for your endorsement," said Emily. "They will now be able to get on with their lives."

"What was this other incident that deputy was talking about?" I asked, ignoring her sarcasm. "*Bāchan*, how do I put your TV on?"

The TV was ancient, a grey cube big as a cupboard whose back stuck out at an odd angle.

"Just push the button," she said, between mouthfuls. "These are very good," she added to Emily. "I will give you my recipe."

I had the TV on but was struggling to figure out how to change the station.

"You have cable, satellite?" I asked.

"Just antenna," *Bāchan* replied.

I considered the metal rabbit ears sticking out of the back.

"Seriously?" I said. "How many channels do you get?"

"Three," said *Bāchan*, quite happy. "Four when the weather is good."

"Which is Action News twelve?" I asked, fiddling with the antennae. "Oh wait. I think this is it."

"My parents are always going on about how they grew up with only a few channels," said Emily brightly. "I expect you had no TV at all."

"When I was a girl?" said *Bāchan*. "No. No TV. No radio. We had to make our own games."

"I think there's a news bulletin coming after these commercials," I said, raising my voice slightly. I wanted to know what was going on. "Maybe keep the reminiscences down a bit," I shot at Emily.

"What kind of games?" Emily asked pointedly. "I want to learn more about where you came from."

"We used to play in the woods," said *Bāchan*, smiling faintly. "Long ago."

"What were your friends like?" Emily asked.

"Not many people lived nearby," said *Bāchan*. "So it was just us."

"Us?" asked Emily.

"Guys, do you mind?" I said. A BREAKING NEWS title had flashed up on the screen in ominous red letters.

"Just me and my sister," said *Bāchan*.

Emily cocked her head.

"Your sister?" she said. "I didn't know you had a sister."

There was a pause, filled by the dramatic musical sting of the TV as the lights came up on a reporter with a bright light on her face standing outside the Sheriff's office.

"What is in these *onigiri*?" asked *Bāchan*. Her voice was different now, low and careful, strange enough to tear my attention from the TV. I looked at her, and she was staring at the remains of the rice ball, her face ashen.

"You had a sister," said Emily, leaning in.

Bāchan looked stricken, her face tortured as if fighting some inner struggle, and when the words came out it seemed that she did not want to say them.

"Shio," she said.

Emily looked at the half eaten onigiri and her face registered shock and anxiety. Something was happening. My attention still half on the TV, I remembered what the *tengu* had said about the bean at the heart of the rice ball. Emily flashed me a look and I knew that she wasn't sure she wanted to hear what would be said next.

"That was her name?" she said. "What happened to her?"

"She changed," said *Bāchan*. "She went . . . bad. Became . . ."

"But she's dead, right?" said Emily, earnest. "I mean, that was a long time ago."

But *Bāchan* was shaking her head.

"Imprisoned, not dead," she said, her eyes full of tears as she fought the truth-spell.

"Like the *oni*?" Emily gasped, then leaned forward in horrified realization. "*With* the oni!?"

Bāchan nodded, as if some invisible hand was moving her head against her wishes.

"Her child," she said. "Shio had a son."

Emily's eyes went wide.

"The ogre which killed your mother was . . . your sister's son?" she said. "Your nephew?"

Tears ran down *Bāchan*'s cheeks and her eyes squeezed shut, but she nodded again, the same mechanical movement as before. I could do nothing but stare, and as they fell silent the voice of the TV reporter filled the room.

"Sources can confirm that the latest disappearance is East Portersville High School Junior, Madison Haynes . . ."

26

W here are you going?" Emily demanded.

"Home!" I shot over my shoulder. "Get my sword. Then . . ."

"Make a suicide attack on the cave? Should I order the funeral flowers now?"

"You said yourself: we should be taking the fight to the enemy," I returned.

"But I also said—and you agreed—that we weren't close to being ready!" she shouted.

We were standing on *Bāchan*'s porch, nose to nose. It was a good thing there were no neighbors to disturb or someone would have called the deputy back.

"We have no choice!" I yelled, matching her ferocity. "The longer we wait, the more likely it is that the *oni* will get free. We can't sit around waiting for the *tengu* to recover so we can go back to training like it's a class at school! Madison has been taken . . ."

"Yes," Emily cut in. "She has. And before you go playing knight in shining armour, charging to her rescue, ask yourself why?"

"You're saying she's involved?" I demanded, incredulous.

"I'm saying it's a trap!" she exclaimed. "You see that right? They probably tried to get into the store to get Mom or Dad but couldn't because of the *ofuda*, so they have taken someone they know you care about."

Even there, in my rage and desperate need to take action, the thought embarrassed me a little.

"They'll be ready for you, Caleb," said Emily. "Whatever they want from us, they figure this is how they get it."

For a moment I just stood there, knowing that what she was saying was true. Her words blew on my molten anger, cooled it some, but that just made it hard and cold, like a blade plucked from the forge and quenched in oil.

"You're right," I said. "But I have no choice. People are already dead, maybe more than we know, and it's my fault." She opened her mouth to protest but I kept talking. "Not because of burning the barn down or anything like that. It's not because of anything I've done. But it's still happening because of me. The *oni*, the *bakeneko*, the *noppera-bō*. They are here because of Raiko. We are his descendants. Not long ago I didn't even know that, but now I do and I feel it like a weight I have to carry. I thought I could walk away from it, but bad things have happened and will continue to happen. I don't know that I like this town all that much, and I'm pretty sure that lots of the people in it don't like me, but if I walk away now, if I sit on my hands because I'm not ready, then truly awful things will happen. Lots of people will die, and that will be my fault too, because no one else can stop it."

"And if you can't stop it either?" she said, her eyes full of tears.

I shrugged.

"Sometimes all you can do is try, right?" I said. "No one else can do it. I probably can't either, but so long as it's *probably* and not *definitely*, I have to try. What's that Japanese word you use when you are trying to do something hard, something you might not get through, but you're going to give it your best shot anyway?"

"*Ganbarimasu,*" said Emily. "Except that in this case it should be *Ganbarimasho.*"

"What's the difference? The second means the task is doomed to fail?"

"It's what you say to other people who are also involved in the task at hand."

"You mean . . . ?"

"I mean," said Emily, "that it's a terrible idea, but I'm coming with you."

I glanced away, ashamed of how pleased I was to hear that.

"You should stay with *Bāchan,*" I said, though my heart wasn't in it.

"She's not sick," said Emily, something of her hauteur flashing in her eyes, "and I'm not her nursemaid. You're not the only descendent of Raiko."

I considered her, then nodded quickly.

"Ok," I said. "Thanks, Em."

"Didn't think I'd let you get all the glory, did you?" she said. She grinned and winked, but when she turned back into *Bāchan*'s house to tell her what we were doing, I caught something stricken in her face, a drained stiffness I had never seen before, as if a part of her was dead already.

It didn't completely leave her as she told *Bāchan* what had happened and what we were going to do, though she tried to sound up-beat, sure of herself. My grandmother nodded solemnly, giving nothing away, then got to her feet.

"What are you doing?" I asked.

"I will come with you," she said.

"This is not your battle, *Bāchan*," said Emily, "and to be really honest . . ."

"I am old and will get in the way," said *Bāchan*. "I have none of my sister's magic and I cannot fight. If I come with you to the cave, you will have to protect me, and that will make you vulnerable."

"Well, yeah," said Emi, confused, "so where . . ."

"I am coming to your house, not to the cave," said *Bāchan*. "Before you go to the cave, I must speak to the *tengu*." She took a steadying breath. "And to your mother. It is time."

Emily and I exchanged a sharp, anxious look, but *Bāchan* was already bustling about in her stiff, old lady way, turning off lights and getting her purse together like she was going shopping.

"Ok," said Em, giving me a hopeless shrug. "I guess."

We thought better of this the moment we reached the inconvenience store, though it was too late to do anything about it then. A crowd—or the closest thing to a crowd Portersville could manage—had gathered outside and there was an ugly feeling in the air. Some of them had beer like they were tail gating. As we arrived, someone shouted "Where's Madison, Caleb?"

Amongst them I saw several kids from school, with their parents, including Tyler J. Miller the third, though his dad was nowhere to be seen. I could guess why. If things kicked off, he wouldn't want to show up till it was time to call for calm. Before then, there would be drinking and shouting. Some of the noisier hot heads would find themselves being interviewed by drama-hungry local reporters. And then what? Broken windows? A Molotov cocktail tossed into the store? A few guys in masks marching in with baseball bats to 'get some answers' from my parents?

"We should call the sheriff's office," said Dad.

"Assuming they aren't already out there," said Em, darkly.

My family were gathered in the back of the store by the fridge cases, and away from the windows. Mom had nodded wordlessly at *Bāchan* who had bowed and then gone into the kitchen to check on the *tengu*.

"You knew this girl?" said Mom. "The one who is missing."

"Know her, yes," I said. "She's sort of my girlfriend."

I had never been in the circumstance where I might discuss who I was dating with my parents. I hadn't anticipated it going like this.

There was a pregnant silence.

"Ok," said Dad at last. "Right. Maybe we should organize a search party?"

"There's already one gathering downtown," said Mom.

"Ok," said Dad again. "Then we can go down and join whatever search is being organized . . ."

"Not sure we'd be welcome," I said.

"And these people outside," said Dad. "Are they another search party?"

"I think they are more the pitch forks and torches delegation," said Em.

She still had that grey caste to her skin and her mouth was thin.

"When the deputy dropped *Bāchan* off at her place," I mused, "he didn't seem to know there was a connection between us and Madison."

"He will now," said Emily, eyeing the swelling mob across the street.

"So they will be coming and soon," I concluded. "Which means . . ."

"We should go," said Emily.

I nodded and got to my feet.

"We'll slip out the back," I said. "I have to grab something from upstairs. You check on Bāchan and the . . . on Mr. Saito."

"You're leaving?!" exclaimed my mother.

"That makes you look guilty of something," said Dad, as Emily slipped out. "Wait till the police arrive. I'm sure you can explain everything to their satisfaction."

I had to laugh at that, though it was what you might call a knowing laugh, full of teeth and darkness. I couldn't explain, and even if I could, they might not listen.

I peered between the shelved packets of cookies and loaves of bread, through the window and out to the street. The crowd looked larger. I thought I could see the lights of news cameras.

"Keep the doors locked until the sheriff arrives," I said. "Then request a lawyer and say as little as possible."

"What about you . . .?" Mom began.

"We'll be ok," I said, picking up the box I brought from Bāchan's.

"What's that?" asked Dad.

"Teapot," I said, my mind producing absolutely nothing useful.

"You're taking off before the police come to ask you about your missing girlfriend," said Dad carefully, "but you are taking a teapot with you?"

"Well," I shrugged, "the English and the Japanese seem to agree that the solution to all stress, hardship and imminent disaster is tea."

Dad stared at me.

"Caleb," said Mom. "This missing girl . . .?"

"Madison," I said. "I don't know where she is," I added, realizing I hadn't actually said it. "I haven't and would never hurt her."

"I know," she said, though she seemed to relax a little. "You're a good boy."

"Ok," I said, making for the door. "We won't be gone long, unless . . ."

We get captured and, you know, <u>eaten</u> by creatures from ancient Japanese legend.

"Wait," she said.

"Can't, Mom. I have to go."

"You said you had to get something from upstairs," she replied. "Get it and come back."

I nodded, then went through the dividing door at the back and upstairs to my room. I snatched the sword in its featureless wooden scabbard from under the bed, stowed it in a case for fishing rods, grabbed a backpack for the teapot, and was downstairs again within the minute. I peered round the kitchen door where Emily was standing beside Bāchan who was inspecting the *tengu*'s wounds.

"Ready?" I said.

Emily came.

"We will do what we can from here," breathed the *tengu*. He sounded, weak, dreamy. "But if we can think of a way to help, we will come to the cave."

"No," I said. "Stay here. Look after my family."

The *tengu* considered me seriously, those massive eyebrows knotting, then he hitched himself up a little and gave me what was clearly a peremptory bow.

I returned it and went back to the store, Emily at my heels, and found that Mom had got a wooden crate out from under the counter. It was dusty and stained with age. From it she had removed an odd-looking, almost spherical object the size of a softball. It was plaster or paper mache, crudely moulded and painted red and gold with a face on one side. The eyes were large and white, and surrounded by swirls of black eyebrows and moustache. With a broom handle nose it would have looked like the *tengu*. Mom had found a black marker and was diligently filling in one of the eyes.

I gave her a blank look. Whatever this was, we didn't have time for it.

"I don't remember what it's called," she said, focused on her handiwork, "but it's for luck. Blessing. Something like that. You fill in one eye when you ask for help or protection, and the other when the wish is granted."

"It's a *daruma*," said Bāchan from the doorway. "I will help."

Her eyes met mom's and something complicated passed between them. Mom reached for another of the pens she used to change prices when things went on sale. She offered it to Bāchan, and then they were both sitting together, absorbed in their work.

There was a sudden rapping on the glass door of the store. I looked round and saw the strobing blue lights of a cop car out front. The sheriff had put two and two together.

I glanced at Dad and he gave me an unreadable nod.

I left.

Emily and I emerged from the back.

"You could transform," I suggested. "They won't spot a fox."

"That won't help you," she replied, "and if I can't change back, it won't help me either."

"Make for the trees, then," I said. "We can work our way up Red Scar through the woods."

"You sure you know your way?"

"If we can get there before dark, yes," I said.

The first part was the hardest because there was no trail and we had to pick our way through steep hillside littered with patches of poison oak, eyes down for young copperheads which are impossible to see in fallen leaves unless you spot the neon green tips to their tails. A few hundred yards directly behind the derelict Walmart, we found the ridge trail that climbed steeply up through wide swaths of native rhododendron, beech and yellow birch trees. I'd seen foxes up here, along with possum and skunk. A couple of times a mother black bear and her cubs. Once even a bobcat. I had no idea what I would see today.

My stomach did a sort of lurch and flop like it was trying to wriggle away.

Once up on the ridge, things got a little easier, though the path was more exposed, and we fell silent, constantly scanning for other people. Once I caught the whine of distant machinery—a dirt bike or ATV, perhaps—but it faded away before ever getting close enough to worry us. A pair of young white-tailed deer, startled by our approach, bolted into the undergrowth in long, uneven bounds, but apart from the distant hooting of a slightly premature barred owl, the woods were quiet.

"You sure you know where you're going?" asked Emily in a low voice.

"Yep," I said. "Not sure whether I actually want to get there, but yeah."

"Right there with you, little brother. Right there with you."

The sun was low now and where the forest was thickest the shadows were long and deep. The temperature was dropping too. Down in the valley, sundown didn't make much difference to the heat, but up here where the hardwoods gave place to fir trees, you could feel it, a welcome coolness, just enough to remind you how hot you had been before. I breathed it in, catching the scent of resin, over the slightly fetid dampness of the woods. As the first bat flitted overhead, I figured we had less than half a mile to go. Over to our right somewhere was the site where Em and I had followed the *torii* path up to the Raiko shrine . . .

Feels like years ago.

I looked that way, hoping there would be some mystical presence, some light or statue which had not been there before, something that would give us skill, wisdom or hope.

Because that last thing was in short supply. It had felt right to say we would tackle the *bakeneko* without the *tengu*. It had seemed clear, as if there was no real choice to be made. People were in danger and only my sister and I could stop it. It would be hard, but it was also . . . necessary. But now that we were up here, in the still and darkening mountains, with visibility failing and no real sense of what we would encounter if we got where we were heading, it suddenly felt stupid and futile. The goblin cat had made short work of the *tengu*, a supernatural creature from whom I had hoped to learn enough to stay alive. I had a sword which had felt cool when I had been swinging it around in the safety of the school grounds, but now it just felt like a strip of metal, something with which I was as likely to cut off something crucial of my own as I was to do real damage to the enemy. My sister could turn into a fox, but since that was pretty much a one-way trip before she forgot who she was and took to chasing rabbits, I was far from clear how she was going to help.

"You ok?" asked Emily.

"Sure," I said. "Mostly. Ish."

"So, no, then."

"Not really," I admitted. "You?"

"Kind of hoping this all turns out to be some kind of shared hallucination," she said. "The whole of this month a fever dream."

"Spores," I said, grinning at the memory from the night this had all begun.

"Spores," she agreed. "Bring on the questionable fungi."

I looked up, and my smile wavered.

"Hold on," I said, and found we were standing under a tall stone crag, like a pile of books at one end, but rising into a fist at the other. "I think we're close."

The fracking site headquarters was on the other side of the crag, right by the well head. It was mostly static caravans, trucks, storage tanks and a whole lot of pipe and cable, all enclosed by chain link fence, but there might still be people, even though the site wasn't active, and I didn't want to stumble into them now. I paused to get my bearings. If I remembered right, we should reach the cave before we reached the fracking site, and if we were careful we could do it without hitting the access road.

"Caleb!" Emily whispered. I felt her stillness, her unease, caught it off her even more as I realized she was sniffing the air, like a dog. Or a fox.

Up ahead, also quite still, was a shadowy figure. It was standing beside a boulder which was a little taller than he was. I wasn't sure why I thought *he*, but I did. He was so close to invisible in the low light that even as I stared, I couldn't be sure he was there. It could have been the stump of a vine-hung tree, a curious stone formation, or an animal—the mother of the two fawns we had spotted earlier, perhaps.

But it was none of those things. I ducked my head slowly, like an owl bobbing as it gathers the data it needs to calculate its attack trajectory, then shifted from foot to foot, and inched forward, ignoring Emily's warning gasp. The fractional shift in angle revealed an elderly man—Bāchan's age or more—gaunt, bald and bony, wearing a belted robe, his eyes were squeezed tightly shut. He stood there, sightless and statue-like, but turned towards us like some strange sentry. Very slowly he raised one gnarled hand, fist clenched, high over his head.

noppera-bō? It seemed unlikely they would take a form so unexpected. Nothing that could dip into our thoughts, however shallowly, would choose a shape so guaranteed to put us on our guard.

Emily glanced at me, then made a kind of shrug with her face and took a cautious step forward. Then another. The old man didn't move, except to tilt his face down a little as if concentrating, though the eyelids stayed closed and, as we got closer to him, I became sure that they could not open at all. Though his face was heavily lined with age, there was no seam between his eyelids. It was as if the skin had grown over the sockets. Beside me I heard a low, wary growl.

It was Emily! Her head was lowered, her teeth clamped together, and her eyes were fixed on the strange man. The guttural snarl was coming from deep in her throat, though I wasn't sure she was conscious of it. The hairs on the back of my neck stood on end at the sound. She sniffed the air, a long, probing inhalation which was less about smell than it was data collection. I had no idea what the man's scent was telling her, but she didn't like it.

Some kind of *yōkai*? But what kind. He was just an old blind man.

And then he opened his clenched fist and I nearly leapt out of my skin. In the centre of his palm was an eyeball, round, bright and staring at us. As I stood rooted to the spot, he raised the other hand to chest height and snapped his fingers open.

Two eyes, yellowish in the gloom, stared at us from inside the skin of his hands. His mouth spread in a leering grin and the tip of his tongue flashed wetly along his lips. My guts shrunk in on themselves and I took a revolted step back.

But Emily did the opposite, she stooped, edging toward him, nose first, eyes rivetted to him, unblinking, her growl rising in pitch and volume. And in an instant I realized what was happening.

She was changing.

Whatever the awful little man was, he had tripped some switch in her and she was turning into a fox whether she wanted to or not.

"Em!" I shouted, forcing myself to go back to her and grabbing her hand. "Stay with me, Em."

But even as I took her hand in mine, I could feel it changing, shrinking, getting soft, then hard again, but different now, smaller and covered with stiff fur. I had a momentary sensation of the pads on the underside, the tough, sharp claws, and then the paw was snatched away and a fox was freeing itself from Emily's clothes and rushing at the *yōkai* with the eyes in its hands.

Those eyes widened for a moment, the fingers splayed, and then the old man was scurrying backwards, hauling himself over rocks and fallen branches in his hurry to get away. The fox zipped through the underbrush, yipping and snapping at his ankles, and I ran after, running hard, but struggling to keep up. The weird little man was supernaturally spry and agile, and the fox shot through the spaces between rubble and tree trunks which I had to climb over or go round. I was faster than I had ever been and I could jump and land and redirect with the best athletes in the world, but I couldn't stay with them. The sheathed sword I had slung across my back snagged on a vine and as I turned to free it, I put my foot in a divot between roots, and went sprawling. I managed to roll as I fell, but still clattered to an ungainly halt at the foot of an ancient cedar.

Getting cautiously to my feet I took a second to make sure I hadn't broken or sprained anything—including my sword—concluding that the only serious injury I had taken was to my pride. Then I processed the real disaster. My sprint had brought me round a massive granite outcrop and now I could see, yawning like a great mouth in the mountain side, the cave.

But there was no sign of the creepy old man with eyes in his hands and, worse—much, much worse—no sign of Emily.

I was alone.

27

There was yellow crime scene tape across the mouth of the cave. It seemed to glow unnaturally in the darkness, shimmering ominously as the wind touched it. I had half expected bright, portable lights, even special forensic exam tents like you saw on *CSI*, but apart from the tape, there was no sign anyone had been there recently. Apparently the police and rescuers had decided the cave had already yielded all its secrets.

I knew better. I just didn't want to find out for sure.

For a long moment I just stood there, listening to the rustle of leaves in the forest around me, telling myself I was trying to hear signs of the Em-fox or the thing she was chasing, but really I was stalling, waiting to see if I got brave or certain.

I didn't. There was only the wind and the dark and the mocking, gaping hole in the mountain, waiting to swallow me up. I unslung the sword from my back and drew it, the blade ringing very slightly as it slid out of the scabbard. I took up one of the stances the *tengu* had taught me, bowed my head and closed my eyes, focusing on my breathing. I wasn't sure what I thought was going to happen—a sudden rush of power, an uncanny wind touching my hair and clothes, and the voice of Raiko in my head telling me I was his heir, a warrior of righteousness and justice against the forces of darkness in the world . . .

Nothing happened. I waited and, when nothing continued to

happen, I opened my eyes, feeling small and stupid and, well, me. Not some samurai priest, part mystic, part fighter. Just the same kid I had always been, but now waggling a sword like an idiot, like it made him cool.

Caleb Smith, ladies and gentlemen. A loser's loser.

Emily was gone. And Madison. Blake Wilde was dead. Other people too, probably, and there would be more. Lots more, if the *tengu* was right. The *oni* would escape, and he would lead his *yōkai* through Portersville and beyond. People literally wouldn't know what hit them.

What could the likes of me do to stop that?

"Caleb!"

I looked up. Someone was calling me from inside the cave.

A girl.

"Emily!" I exclaimed.

"Shhh!" she hissed. "Come on, but be quiet! I can see where they are, and I found Madison. She's alive! I know what we have to do!"

I took a couple of quick steps inside.

"What happened with that guy with the eyes?" I asked.

"I caught him," she replied grimly, "and before he could raise the alarm. The rest are asleep. Now is our chance! Quickly. Round here."

She was moving into the depth of the cave. I followed, though that was less about courage than not wanting to be alone in the dark.

"How can you see where you are going?" I asked, as I stumbled into a solid granite outcrop.

"I still have some of my fox vision," she said. "Stay close. It's through here."

We wended our way round fallen rubble to where the cave constricted like the neck of a bottle. Pasted to the rock wall I could just make out the shreds of old *ofuda*, torn where the rock had been split by the quake.

"Through here," Emily whispered.

"Where?" I said. "It's a solid wall of rock."

"It's not," she answered. "There's some sort of illusion that screens it, but there's a way through. Follow my voice."

I took a couple of halting steps toward her.

"I still can't see it!" I said, feeling the dragging roar of panic in my ears.

And then, without warning, I could. It was as if the light had shifted. There was a sprinkling of glittery blue particles around me and there it was. A narrow vertical crevice had shivered the wall of the cave as if cut by a giant's axe. It was so tight I would have to turn sideways to enter it,

185

and inside was absolute darkness. I hesitated, but my sister stepped close to me, and I could see her again. Just.

"Come on!" Emily mouthed at me. "Before they wake up!"

"I can't see."

"You will when we get through," she replied, leaning in close, her voice quiet as the footfall of a spider. "There are lanterns."

And then she was pressing through the crack in the stone wall and I had no choice but to go in after her. I went in shoulder first, my face twisted to the side so I could see only the gloom of the cavern behind me, knees and elbows tight against the rock. I held the sword in my right hand behind me, as if covering our backs, though there was no room to wield it. The crevice turned, shutting out even the low light of the cave I had left, and the stony tightness pressing on my body felt like the jaws of some great vice. If there was another quake, I thought wildly, the crack might close up again, crushing me under the weight of the mountain. I reached one arm out in front of me, testing the surface of the stone with my fingers, pulling myself along in anxious, shuffling steps that set my heart racing.

I am going to get stuck, I thought. *I won't be able to go forward or back . . .*

I shifted suddenly, banging my head, and for a moment light seemed to flash through my head, and I had to stop moving. My chest was thumping, my breathing was quick and shallow. I couldn't seem to fill my lungs, so that it felt like the crevice was tightening on my chest. I shut my eyes and thought of what the *tengu* would say.

Stop, I told myself. *Breathe.*

I became still. I could not rush. I had to go at my own pace. I had to slow down, regardless of what Emily said . . .

And then a new thought came to me. I opened my eyes, and though that made no real difference, I felt a measure of composure, of certainty. I began to move again, inching forward until the darkness was flecked by a greenish light coming from somewhere up ahead. Another two steps, then four, and I could feel the pressure all around me lessen. The air, which had been hot and stuffy, cooled, and I sensed a new cave opening up around me.

As I extracted myself from the passage, I turned to take in the space, and gasped.

It was like being in a theatre hollowed out of the rock by an eternity of running water and other forces, not all of them strictly natural. Something of the glittering blue radiance which had screened the entrance was

186

present throughout the rock structure and that, with a scattering of flickering greenish lanterns gave the whole thing a pulsing phosphorescence which rolled in waves over the stone. It felt like being under the ocean, looking up through rippling shafts of moonlit water. By the unearthly glow I could see that part of the structure had collapsed and lay in great mounded heaps around me. If the cavern felt like a theatre, what would have been the stage area was the strangest and most fascinating part of the space. It was framed by broken stone, beyond which was an uneven pattern of coursing energy whose color shifted like the iridescence of a butterfly wing. At its heart, however, was a hard, irregular blackness like a bullet hole in a television screen. Beyond it was . . . nothing. And as I stared at it I was sure that the fractured rupture in the centre was getting bigger. Black stress lines spider-webbed out from the hole. Tiny fragments streaked with the colored energy fell away and turned grey as if they had died.

This was the edge of the mystical prison in which Raiko had entombed his enemies. But it was broken, and the breach was expanding. Even as I looked, something with a human face on a long, glistening body which might have been snake or centipede, peered out, considered the outside world, and slithered out.

The *yōkai* were coming.

As my eyes grew accustomed to the unnatural gloom I made out a series of large, lumpy bundles suspended from the ceiling like chrysalises. They looked like they had been lashed together with kudzu vine. For a moment I couldn't make out what I was seeing, but as I tilted my head and stared at them, features came horribly into view: a work boot, a blue tie and a few inches of suit jacket, a face so desiccated it was little more than yellowing skin over bone.

I had found Southern Shale's missing workers.

The sight should have sent me running, but somehow it did the opposite. I felt a strange calm descending on me, a certainty which brought strength, as if my veins had filled with molten steel which now congealed and set. Only, you know, in a good way, rather than something that would kill me painfully.

I brought my sword up in both hands and took up a balanced stance.

"Hey Em," I said, not bothering to keep my voice low. "How come you are dressed?"

There was a momentary hesitation before she said, without turning to look at me,

"I went back for my clothes. What does it matter? Quickly, come over here!"

"I don't think so," I said. "You were able to return to your human form —something you've never been able to do before without help—got past me, and got dressed all in a few seconds?"

"What do you mean?" said Emily, changing tack. "I'm not dressed."

And now she wasn't. She had her back to me, and even though I knew it wasn't her, I looked away.

"You don't know the real Emily at all, do you?" I remarked, remembering what the *tengu* had said about the *noppera-bō's* ability to reach only into the shallowest parts of your mind to determine its shape. "And you sure as hell don't know me!"

"Of course I know you," said what was now Madison. She was dressed —just—in a light *yukata*, belted very loosely in the front. Her hair spilled down her shoulders like the sun in winter. "You came for me. I knew you would."

I hesitated, but only for a moment. Expectation and desire. That's what fed the *noppera-bō*. You had to want something enough for the *yōkai* to side step the little flags your brain threw up, the things that said *no, this isn't right, it can't be real*.

"Enough of this," I said, stepping forward and swinging the blade of my sword in a long, lethal slash.

The *noppera-bō* reacted too late, and my blade caught it in a rough arc from left shoulder to right hip, but instead of blood, the edge caused a flickering line of black lightning to open across its skin. The creature's face opened in a wail of pain and rage, then went smooth as an egg, then —in a silent flash of pure white brilliance—it vaporized.

I turned my eyes from the glare and, in the stillness which followed, realized that I was hearing the soft, dry patter of slow and mocking applause. I turned in the direction of the sound and found an old woman in a cowled robe, clapping formally. For a split second I thought it was *Bāchan*, but then she raised her hands to the hood which shaded her face and pushed it back.

I took a horrified step back. The woman's face was not just old. It was ancient and creased with malice. Her black eyes bulged, and a pair of sharp horns protruded from her temples. But the worst part was her mouth. It was wide, and too full of long, pointed teeth. She reached a hand into her robes and drew out a long cleaver, which she regarded wolfishly. From behind her back, a cat threaded itself between her feet and padded out into the cave, its familiar yellow eyes fixed balefully on me.

"You can put the sword down," said the horned woman.

In fact the words came out in low guttural Japanese, or what I took to be Japanese, and I could just about make them out, but what I heard was the echo of her voice resounding through the strange cavern. Somehow the echo came back to me in English.

"But I'm just starting to get good with it," I quipped. I didn't feel jokey, but I had to take a tone that would distract me from those black hard-candy eyes and the impossible fanged grin.

"As you wish," said the horned woman, as the cat sat at her feet and purred like a high-performance car. "We only need one of you."

She glanced past me and flicked her long-nailed thumb across her throat. The casualness of the gesture, its dispassionate ruthlessness, spun me round.

Sitting on a cage made of lashed bamboo canes was the creepy old man with the eyes in his hands. One hand was held up, palm open and unblinking. The other held a curved knife. Inside the cage I caught the flash of russet fur and a pair of scared eyes.

Emily.

"No!" I shouted, turning back on the horned woman. "Wait."

And very carefully, I laid down the sword.

The moment my fingers came off it I felt weak and stupid, but what choice did I have?

"Better," said the horned woman. "Now come with me and you will see your purpose."

"My purpose?" I said, trying to sound flip and defiant. "I think my purpose is to kill demons."

"No," said the woman. She said it as if I had confused the dates of Declaration of Independence with the Emancipation Proclamation, a casual dismissal of something stupid but to be expected in so poor a student. She didn't even look at me, but shuffled toward the hole in the mystical prison wall, moving almost exactly like *Bāchan*. "That is what the *tengu* wants you to be, but his kind have always been deceivers."

"While you are just out for my best interest?" I said. "That totally tracks."

"Our interests overlap," she said, still not looking at me. The knife in her hand was at her side now, seemingly forgotten. Even the cat walking with her had its gaze on her rather than me. "There is something I want which you can give me," she said.

"And if I refuse?"

She stopped, shrugged very slowly, as if nothing could be less important, then turned to face me.

"You will help me, whether you want to or not," she said, the cavern continuing to give its strange translation echo. "That is not a question. The question is whether you choose to help—to give—or if I have to take."

"Oh," I said, recognizing the trope. "This is one of those *we can do this the easy way or the hard way* things. I know you've been sealed up in here for like a thousand years or something, but you really need to brush up on your pop culture. Your dramatic interrogation technique needs work."

She ignored that, so I regrouped.

"Doesn't sound like I have much of a choice," I said, stalling while I thought what to do. "The end result sounds the same."

"Not exactly," she said, beginning her little mouse-footed pacing again. I followed cautiously. "Not for you, at least."

There was a heavy silence.

"I'm listening," I said.

"I am the *onibaba*," she said, her voice deep and churning with hatred. "Your great grandfather bound my child into this prison. My child, myself, and many other *yōkai*. The space inside it is vast and terrible, an entire dimension of hell in which we have been captive for centuries, and through that time the one thought which sustained us was what we would do on our escape, the revenge we would take on Raiko and his heirs."

"You're not out yet," I said. "Raiko's power lives on in us."

She laughed then, a wide, toothy smile which tipped her head back and turned into a wet and satisfied chuckle.

"You, Raiko's heirs?" she scoffed. "A pet fox and a defenseless school boy ignored even by his own classmates?"

I blinked as if she had slapped me but found something of my old defiance.

"If we matter so little," I demanded, "why have you gone to such pains to bring us here? Why didn't your cat monster kill us when it had the chance?"

Her smile softened then, became thoughtful.

"So," she said. "The American is not completely stupid, even if he knows nothing of the old world, the world which matters. You are right.

We do need you. These others," she said indicating the mass of desiccated bodies, "were just food. But you are special, in one way at least."

"Madison too?" I asked. "You ate her?"

She beamed at that.

"Oh, you do like that little blond creature, don't you?" she said, pleased. "Very well. Since you are going to do something for me, I will do something for you."

She snapped her fingers and the webbed corpses in the ceiling crashed down with a thump. She raised one long nailed finger and slashed the air with it. Along one of the corpse-shaped chrysalises, a long gash appeared. Pale yellow hair spilled out. And then a hand, its fingers waking slowly, then an arm, and Madison emerged.

She was dressed as she had been for school the day she went missing, but her face looked more than blank. She looked hollowed out, her mind scared away.

"She will be fine," grinned the *onibaba*. "For a little while."

Madison got awkwardly to her feet and turned to take in the various horrors around her.

"That way, idiot child," said the *onibaba*, pointing in delight to the crevice.

Madison stared, then ran, a stumbling, sprawling, staggering run accompanied by a protracted sob which rose in pitch as she went.

"Sweet girl," said the *onibaba*. "I look forward to eating her at a later date."

"You let her go . . ." I said, baffled.

"For now. She has served her purpose."

"Which was?"

"She brought me you."

"So you can revenge yourself on Raiko," I said.

The *onibaba* grinned.

"In part," she said. "But there is a little more to it than that. You have a special, honorable, even poetic purpose."

"Yeah?" I said. "Like what?"

"The *yōkai* prison is partly open, but strength alone will not force the portal wider. There are charms, old magics which must be countered. Look."

She pointed a bony finger to a place in the cavern floor directly below the breach in the energy field. A hollow had been carved into the stone, round, like a basin, and from it a channel ran into the irregular black fissure. The channel was brown and stained. Some of the deeper cracks in the rock were clotted with something slick and sticky, something with the alarming, metallic tang of blood.

I swallowed and looked up at the carcasses suspended from the ceiling.

"Yes," said the *onibaba*, "we tried using them to open the portal, but they are merely human. What we need is the blood of our old enemy, mixed and diluted though it is."

"I'm still not seeing this choice you promised," I said, keeping my eyes off the stinking basin.

"It is simple," said the *onibaba*. "We can bind you and your mongrel sister, drain you into the portal, sacrificing your lives to the dawning of the age of *yōkai* in America. Or you share some of your blood willingly. We can keep you alive and you can join us in our conquest, give you full access to powers the *tengu* could never teach you. You have lived the mediocre lives of unwanted humans long enough: bullied, ridiculed, content to be ignored. Now you can celebrate the other half of your heritage. Be what you were meant to be! Throw off the petty limitations of human morality! Draw on your *yōkai* selves and be, for once in your lives, magnificent. An easy choice, I think. Perhaps you did not know it, but it is what you have always wanted."

Her voice had a curious, hypnotic quality to it, as if her words were being poured into my head like water, and I found myself just standing there, listening, my brain switched off. That last line stirred something within me, however. I felt my brow pucker with uncertainty as the words swirled through my mind, this time trailing a question mark. That I had been bullied and ridiculed was undeniable. But to be special, to use the gifts other people did not have in ways that made me, in her words, "magnificent" . . .

Was this what I had always wanted?

I thought of facing down Tyler J. Miller the third, not as Caleb Smith, the loser's loser, but as Hideki, Heir of Raiko, with a sword in my hand and a *yōkai* army at my back. No more slinking about hoping to be ignored. No more of the sick and defeated feeling inside when I went home to the inconvenience store which would become my adult life. No more dread and fear. I could be strong. I could be confident. I could do what I wanted, and people would love me for it. I saw it all in my head, and the horned woman's word shone like the afterglow of a firework.

Hideki the Magnificent.

Distantly I heard a dog barking, a high, shrill sound.

Not a dog, I thought vaguely. *A fox*.

I turned to the cage where the hand-eye man stood, palms turned towards us so he could watch. Emily was barking, but somehow I felt sure she was not barking at him but at me.

As a true *yōkai* she would also access whatever abilities her *kitsune* form would bring her. Was it not a kindness to make the decision for her? Give a little blood, and no more would my sister be trapped, caught between selves and unable to control her own shape?

"Yes," said the *onibaba*. "Open the portal and she will be a *yōkai* princess, a beautiful and powerful fox goddess, answering to no one."

I guess my glance to the cage had given me away, though even so the *onibaba's* insight was a little too on the money.

"It is not only your sister who is caged," whispered the *onibaba*. "You are both locked up in the petty forms of your humanity, your weak bodies made still weaker by the rules you follow. You do not need to. People can change."

The phrase caught me off guard, reminded me of something similar I had said to Joey after my encounter with Tyler. I couldn't quite remember what it was. I had said that people changed and Joey had said . . . something. I concentrated, reaching for it, and at last Joey's response came back to me:

"Yeah. They do. You might wanna watch that."

I frowned.

"You're in my head," I said. Even in my own ears it sounded vague, uncertain.

"What?" said the *onibaba*, momentarily off balance.

"You're doing what the *noppera-bō* does," I said. "Reading what I want. Or what you think I want."

"I know what you want," said the horned woman. "Don't bother to pretend otherwise. I have always known how to read people. When it comes to understanding the true desires of the hearts, I am never wrong."

"No," I agreed, my eyes straying back to the corpses of the dead workers. It occurred to me that I didn't know their names and that suddenly seemed profoundly wrong. I felt first shame, then fury, and then something harder and simpler, clear as the resounding of an old bell. It was . . .certainty. "You're not wrong," I said. "But wanting something isn't enough, is it? If we take everything we want because we can, we become monsters. You wouldn't understand that, because you are one already, though maybe you weren't always. You say you are *onibaba*. Once you were something else. Some*one* else. Once you were Shio."

The old woman reacted as if I had thrown boiling water in her face. She howled with anger and pain, shrinking away, her hands going to her ears. Then she was babbling in Japanese, and now there was no translation echoing back to me. Her hard little eyes fixed on me and there was none of the friendly persuasion in her face now. Just rage and a deep bitterness. The heavy cleaver which had hung loosely at her side was now up in a gnarled fist.

The cat at her feet reared up and swelled, growing to its full six-foot height. As before, it hovered an inch or two above the ground, and its loose-fitting kimono floated around it, as if stirred by a wind I could not feel. Its eyes fastened on mine and its claws slid out like knives.

My sword was all the way over near the mouth of the cave.

I was defenseless.

28

Death, the philosophers say, comes to us all. Which is fine, I guess. A bit defeatist, perhaps, but fine, and in so far as I had really thought about it before I imagined it would come many years from now, after a long illness or a car accident or something similarly rational. Slashed to death by the claws of a six-foot floaty cat thing had never been on the agenda.

So it was with something like outraged disbelief that I leapt backwards, flipping head over heels in mid-air and landing neatly on my feet, an action which bought me the second I needed to shrug out of my backpack and yank it open. I pulled out the wooden box which was vibrating like my PlayStation game controller and yanked the lid off. The cast iron teapot exploded out toward the *bakeneko* on its little legs, its lid chittering, like something between a toy steam train and a robot terrier with a spout where its nose should be.

The great robed cat hissed and shrunk back, but I knew this wouldn't be enough to cancel out those feline teeth and claws. I just wanted it to buy me a little time. I turned and dashed across the cave to where my sword lay. It was only yards from where the Em-fox was caged, and the creepy eye-hand guy saw me coming, flicking his hand around like he was shining a flashlight on me. The other hand pointed at the sword's long handle. With my new found speed, I was pretty sure I could beat him to it.

So I hesitated. Just for a heartbeat. Just long enough to ensure that he reached it a fraction before I did. He seized the katana and came up ready to swing it, but it was a long sword, especially for a small man: a two-handed sword. The moment he grasped the handle in both clenched hands, he was blind. I took a sideways step and brought the wooden teapot box down hard on the side of his head.

He hit the floor with a soft thud, and I snatched up the sword. In the same movement I took a step toward the cage but somehow, moving with uncanny speed, the *onibaba* had crossed the cavern in a pair of long, unnatural bounds on all fours, her long cleaver gripped between her teeth. She moved uncannily, like a crab scuttling sideways. My mind and body rebelled at the sight of her, wanted to turn and run, but I had to get Emily out, even if there was nothing else I could do. Back by the portal entrance the *bakeneko* sparred with the snipping teapot, the cat mincing on its hind legs, as if afraid of being touched. The *onibaba* roared something at it which I didn't understand, and the cat pounced. It caught the teapot, rolled, juggling it for a moment, and then swatted it with one giant paw.

The teapot slid hard into the rock wall of the cave, spun around, and died.

"Any more children's toys you expect to save you?" cooed the *onibaba*, scurrying cockroach-like towards me on hands and feet. "Such poor warriors! Raiko must be turning in his grave. A *kitsune* who can't control her shape and a swordsman who can't control his blade."

"You're welcome to put that to the test any time you . . ." I began, but she came at me, snatching her own blade from her mouth and hacking at me.

I parried wildly, but on the rare occasion I could get a cut back at her, she deflected it easily. And all the time she grinned that impossibly wide grin of hers, her hard little eyes twinkling. I fought back with increasing desperation, remembering the *tengu*'s assessment with a sense of impending failure: I had the speed, the strength and the agility. I just didn't have the skill.

"Poor Hideki," mused the *onibaba*. "Raiko's American shame. You'll be better off dead. At least your blood can be put to good use."

Lit by a sudden rage at the injustice of so much more than this fight alone, I bellowed, raising the katana high over my head and bringing it slashing down onto her.

Or trying to.

In fact what happened was that just I was about to begin the downstroke, I felt my arms snagged by powerful clawed paws. In my fury I had not noticed as the *bakeneko* had padded up behind me.

The *onibaba* grabbed my hands and with fingers hard and dry as sticks but immensely strong, she wrenched the sword from my grip.

"Let us waste no more time," she said, pausing to kick the creature with the eyes in its hands until it stirred, palms blinking.

The old man got to its feet and moved behind me, snatching my hands and binding them with the cord of its belt. I could feel the cool, wet smoothness of its eye balls pressed up against my wrists as it knotted the cord. The *bakeneko* lifted me by the scruff of my neck, like it was carrying a kitten and I felt the fabric of my sweatshirt tear. Meanwhile, the *onibaba* picked up the bamboo cage and led the way. The Em-fox, which had been yipping excitedly throughout the fight, was now subdued, shrunk in on itself and trembling with fear. I had no idea if my sister was still in there, or if the creature's mind was now blank as a real fox, knowing nothing but hunger and fear.

We were marched back across the cavern to the rift. The *onibaba* clambered in, again moving on all fours like an animal, and I was shoved through after her.

The inside of what had been the mystical prison was a seething mass of light and noise, its walls shifting and contracting in chaotic undulations, as if we were within the spasming heart of some massive dying creature. The phosphorescence I had seen outside was more intense here, more varied and shifting, so that it was hard to keep your eyes open without being nauseated.

This, I thought, squeezing my eyes shut and scrunching in on myself as if I was going to fall over, *is what seasickness must feel like. Or vertigo.*

But as we pushed further into the deep, the velvety darkness I had glimpsed through the shattered breach smothered us. I could still make out the pulsing energy of the prison walls, but it gave no light to the ground where I stood. Something slithered over my feet and I sensed what felt like the hard tips of oversized insect legs running up my legs.

The *onibaba* raised her greenish lantern, but the light barely penetrated the featureless gloom.

"A fitting place for you to meet your end," said the horned woman. "Once we have freed my son and the other *yōkai* trapped inside, we will leave you here in the dark where you will suffer the tender mercies of your demon enemies. Perhaps they will kill you quickly," she said. "Or perhaps," she added with a leer that showed all her terrible teeth, and the pink wetness of her tongue, "they will take some time to show you the kinds of torment to which your great grandfather subjected them. A moment in hell feels like an eternity. What do you think an eternity feels like?" She snickered to herself. I had no reply. I had no words, no energy, no hope. "Now, we can't complete the ritual with your second rate *kitsune* in this shape. I shall have to draw her out."

She set her lantern down, reached into the cage and closed her fingers around the fox's throat, pulling it from the cage. The animal fought and whimpered, vainly clawing at the bamboo, but the *onibaba's* grip was like steel. She slipped the knife into the pouch at her waist and used her free hand to grip the fox's muzzle closed. Then she raised the animal's face to her own, till they were nose to nose, and muttered words I did not understand.

I had seen the *tengu* bring Emily back, but it had not been like this. He had coaxed her, invited her, reminded her of who she was, till she returned of her own volition. This was rough and violent, the spiritual equivalent of dragging the beast out of the cage, its nails scrabbling against the bars till they tore. It was sickening to watch, and I twisted my head away, so I did not see the moment when my sister spilled onto the floor, naked and sobbing.

All around us, the prison resounded with the incomprehensible wails of whatever was trapped inside. The *bakeneko* dragged me and I felt smooth, cold stone against my cheek. I had been positioned over the carved trench in the rock, my face held tight in the basin.

Would it be the *onibaba's* cleaver or the cat's claws which would open my veins? I fought, but they would have been too much for me, even if I hadn't lost both my sword and my strength. I heard rather than saw Emily being forced into a similar position. How much blood would open the portal, I wondered vaguely: a pin prick? A cup? More?

Not that it mattered. If we were alive when the *oni* emerged, we wouldn't be for much longer.

"Ladies first," snarled the *onibaba*, pulling a metal pin as long as a chopstick from her hair and placing its tip on the underside of my sister's wrist.

"Sorry Em," I muttered. "I tried but . . ."

"Shh," she said, and I felt her hand fumbling for mine. She interlaced her fingers through my own weakly. "It's ok."

And suddenly, it wasn't. The injustice of it all, the idea that we were to be sacrificed because of some ancestor we had never met, had never even heard of until a couple of weeks ago, filled me with an incandescent rage. I thrashed in my captor's grip, roaring my anger, and the *bakeneko* struggled to hold me. I felt its claws bite deep into my arm and shoulder, but I had surprised it, and for a moment I had more room to move than they would like. I jabbed with my elbows and stamped with my feet. When I made contact and heard the grunt of pain, I snapped my head back and felt the crunch of bone behind me. There was a yowl of furious pain, but I was momentarily free, though my hands were still tied behind my back.

I kicked wildly, and the *bakeneko* skipped back, regrouping. The creepy man was waving his hands around, trying to get a better view as I channelled all my strength into my arms, trying to snap the ropes that bound me.

The sound behind me was the last thing I expected to hear. It was a low, chuckling laugh, not just amused but delighted.

I turned to find the bug-eyed stare of the *onibaba* fixed on me, her fanged jaw open, her tongue like a pink eel, lolling.

"Very brave," she scoffed. "Except that your courage is really just a fear of dying. And a futile one at that. See?'

She nodded at my left arm and, in spite of myself, I looked. Where the cat had gripped me, its claws had punctured my shoulder. Three thin rivulets of blood had run down my arms and spattered into the stone bowl.

"Too late," said the *onibaba*, stabbing Emily's wrist with her iron pin.

The cavern began to shake as soon as the blood hit the rock.

"And so my beautiful, terrible son is born again," she intoned, "and the world will quail at his approach! Bow before him, for he is rage, and destruction, and death!"

Rocks fell from the cave ceiling, and the luminescent energy of the prison's energy shell flared in a whirling maelstrom of color and then went out. The cave went utterly dark. Not the darkness of a bedroom with the light out, where the window is grey from distant street lights or stars. This was the blackness of the deep underground, the kind of dark without even the memory of light, a darkness thick and stiff as concrete, where there could be only touch and smell and hearing because sight had never been invented.

I stood in it, unmoving, and for a moment I thought I was already dead.

And then it spoke.

"*Okasan?*"

It was a nightmare voice, deep and low as the space below the mountain, a rumbling growl like boulders moved by a flood, and just as implacable. It was a voice to break armies.

And then the cave was light again. There was a flash of red, hard and bright as a flare, and the *onibaba* was revealed, her hands raised above her head as if supporting the fiery radiance she had conjured, holding it up like it had weight. I winced away, shielding my eyes but I could not look anywhere that did not contain the *oni*.

It filled the cave, a massive, crimson skinned brute, horned like his mother, but rippling with muscle. It turned its immense head down to look at us, and its mouth was the same horror-show of pointed yellow teeth, though these were as long as my arm. It drooled great ropes of spit and its tongue was thick, brown and coated with bristling hair. It had three bulbous eyes, one in the centre of its forehead, and it wore a filthy loin cloth of animal hide. A broad leather belt held an ordinary human knife, though its massive fists were better suited to the club it held, which looked to be a tree trunk, its heavy end showing the root ball, as if it had been torn out of the ground by the monster which now wielded it.

Around its bare feet, each the size of a tractor, other nameless creatures swarmed, hooting and gibbering with glee at their release.

The *yōkai* invasion had begun.

29

The *onibaba* danced. I guess that what you would call it, though there was no music beyond the cacophony of the joyful, victorious *yōkai*. She leaped and pranced, shrieked with delight and waved her arms in mad rapture while her colossal son flexed and stretched and prepared to greet the world with a tide of blood and carnage. From time to time they spoke to each other, but whatever had translated the horned woman's words before was no longer working, though I could tell that they were swapping ideas, occasionally laughing uproariously. The *oni*'s laugh made the ground tremble. I did not want to know what they were talking about.

Emily had managed to shrug into the cat monster's kimono, but she looked defeated, broken even, her eyes glazed, her mouth closed as if she might never speak again. Not that we were going to be around much longer, and I had a nagging anxiety, given their scornful glances toward us, that it was this that the *oni* and his demon mother were discussing. Not whether to kill us, you understand. How. Which way would be the most satisfying, the most *fun*.

The *oni* favoured his tree trunk club which, I suspected told you all you needed to know about him. He kept brandishing it, making little smashing gestures and grinning at what he imagined would be the result. He made slurping noises as he imagined shovelling our remains into his great maw.

The creepy eye-hand guy pointed at the seething mass of monsters and at the now shattered prison membrane.

Seal them in, he was obviously saying; let a thousand *yōkai* take their time with us.

But the *onibaba* had another idea, one which lit her face with fiendish jubilation, as if the rightness of it satisfied all manner of urges.

"What's happening?" I muttered to Emily. "Why don't they just finish us already? They got what they wanted. It's over."

"Shh," said Emily, who had closed her eyes. "I'm trying to listen."

"You can understand them?" I asked.

She shook her head.

"Just the odd word," she whispered. "Be quiet."

I did as I was told, as much through weariness as hope. Hope was gone.

"*Tanto*," Emily breathed, echoing something the *onibaba* said. "What does that mean?"

There was no point asking me and I said so.

"*Raiko no tanto*," she said. "She keeps saying it. Something belonging to Raiko."

"So, what?" I replied.

"The *oni* says that whatever it is, it's *abunai*, which I'm pretty sure means 'dangerous'."

I frowned.

Tanto.

I had heard that before. I risked a look up. Amidst the chaos of the *yōkai* celebration, the *oni* stood hunched over, too big for the cave, his huge, ugly face distorted with doubt. His three eyes blinked simultaneously, and he put one hand to the knife in his belt.

Tanto!

I remembered it now from the book the *tengu* had given me about the different kinds of sword, and now, just as his massive fist closed around it, I saw something on the glossy black scabbard: a diamond inside a circle, under which a Chinese character was expertly sketched in gold lacquer. I had seen that symbol before.

"The knife!" I whispered. "It's Raiko's knife. That marking is the same as the one at the shrine."

"She wants to kill us with our own ancestral weapon," Emily breathed. "So why is he resisting? Why is it dangerous?"

Before I could respond I felt a curious tingling through the rope which bound my hands as if something was plucking—or *gnawing*—on it. I twisted my head round and, to my astonishment, saw the little black teapot. It had the rope between the hole where you filled the pot and its lid and was 'chewing' furiously. I felt my eyes go wide.

"Em," I whispered.

She looked at me and I made the barest of nods toward the teapot. She went stiff, then looked quickly around.

The *oni*, its mother, the *bakeneko*, and the hand-eye man were all engaged in earnest conversation. My sword was on the ground no more than four or five yards away, discarded and forgotten.

I felt the ropes give, but kept still, hoping against hope that the *yōkai* wouldn't look at us until the teapot had finished its work on Emily's bonds.

And then what? We run? Where to?

There was nowhere the *oni* wouldn't find us. I was free, but only kind of. I didn't see how I could defeat the towering ogre, but I had to try.

The moment Emily's bonds snapped, she rolled to her feet and I leapt for my sword.

With a bellow of rage which seemed to bring the cave crashing down around us, the *oni* swung his club. I vaulted clear, but the rock where I had been standing shattered in an explosion of grit and chippings which stung my face. The *yōkai* shrieked and the *onibaba* screamed, whisking out her cleaver and turning on us. The *bakeneko* flew at Emily, who seemed to vanish, reappearing a moment later as a fox, bounding around the cave. The *oni* saw her and forgot me, swinging his club as high as he could get it and bringing it down with a rush of wind and a crash that filled the cave with dust and noise.

I held my breath, braced for the worst, but as the dust debris cloud cleared I saw no mangled fur among the wreckage. The *oni* roared its frustration and then the Em fox was there again, running and jumping and biting, too close for him to club her. Her bounds got her as high as his waist. Again and again the *oni* tried to crush her, but she dodged and weaved, cutting between his legs and nipping at his ankles.

As if inspired, the teapot followed suit, harassing the cat monster, while I chased away the hand-eye man. The *onibaba* came for me, cleaver raised, her former joy replaced by spitting fury, but I timed my run, careful as any wide receiver. I leapt clean over her, landing blade first on the *oni's* crimson chest.

The sword tip should have skewered the monster where it stood.

But it didn't. The blade shattered as if I'd slammed it into solid steel, its shards falling harmlessly to the cave floor.

I stared in horrified dismay. After everything I had gone through, the *oni* was invulnerable to my sword.

And then the *oni* was laughing again, head tipped back, its barrel chest full, its mother joining in, releasing a high cackle that, even with everything that was going on, made my hair stand on end. The other *yōkai* joined in as the *oni* howled with mirth, exposing its throat to me, sure of its invulnerability.

It seemed like everything else stopped to celebrate this joke for the ages, and in that moment of hesitation, that half second as they revelled in the hilarious certainty of their victory, Emily came to me, still a fox, with Raiko's knife in her mouth.

I hadn't seen her snatch it from his belt and he hadn't noticed. But I knew what she was thinking.

"Abunai," he had called it. *Dangerous.*

The blade of his enemy which he had kept close, the blade he would have used to kill what remained of Raiko's line.

The blade which could kill him.

I took three long, strides, building speed and power as I went, and I hurled myself at him, leaping as high as I could possibly go, using every last once of strength and whatever magical reserves I had inherited. This was my shot, my one last attempt at victory.

He was too slow to react, too big. He swung the club at me but I was already past it, already on him and slashing with the razor-sharp *tanto*.

I barely felt it bite, so keen was the edge, but I saw the wound open in his neck, saw the thick, black blood bubbling up from the gash. My feet hit the ground, and I dived aside as he crumpled, clutching his throat. His mouth opened wide gurgling and gasping as the *yōkai* screeched their dismay.

"Em!" I shouted, extending my hand to where the fox was leaping over his sprawling body. In seconds she was halfway to the cave entrance. I ran after her, my mind blank, not daring to believe that we might yet get out into the world.

Em shot through the tight passage and into the outer cave, the teapot at her heels, but I was slower.

A little further, I told myself. *Get out, regroup, prepare for what comes next.*

The prison seal was broken and the *yōkai* would follow the *onibaba* out into Portersville, into the world, but there would be no *oni* to lead them, and I called that a win. What came next was tomorrow's task. We had beaten them once. We could do it again. I just had to get out.

In the tightness of the passageway I could only move sideways, and only by inches. I had no sense of how far I still had to go and my head was twisted so that I could only see what was behind me, and that dimly. But I saw her face, the mad ferocity below her horned brows and I knew that her cleaver was coming before I felt its edge.

I just couldn't stop it.

Somehow, the pain was less than the grief.

30

Elsewhere

Emily shed her fox form as she emerged from the crevice into the outer cave. It had served her well, but she needed to be a person again now, and found that that need was all she required. For the first time, the choice was clear in her head, and her route to the change required only a little concentration. She emerged bare foot and human into the beam of a flashlight.

In front of her was her mother and her grandmother, their heads bowed and—for the first time she had ever seen—their hands held. They were muttering simple Japanese phrases over and over. Emily did not know what they meant, but she stood between them, their hands in hers, and repeated the sounds.

She knew what they were doing. She didn't know how she knew, or if it would work, but she felt it like she felt the water in the swimming pool at a race, like it was an element she understood, a place she felt at home.

They were sealing the prison. Behind her she heard the *tengu*'s low voice breathing prayers of his own, and when someone draped a coat around her, she turned long enough to see DeMarcus Murphy, withdrawing quickly, looking embarrassed and uncertain.

The stone wall in front of them, the illusion that covered the narrow passage into the main cavern shimmered with energy and her brother staggered out and fell hard. Behind him she saw the familiar face of the *onibaba*, a mask of vengeful rage.

"*Bāchan*," said Emily.

The old woman beside her looked up and saw.

"No, sister," she said, moving with resolve to meet her, though her face was stricken with pain and sorrow. "You cannot come out."

For a moment the two old women were nose to nose, their gazes locked in some fearsome struggle, and then the one with horns was knocked back and something closed over her.

The *onibaba* bared her terrible teeth and howled her fury, but the energy bond was complete, and though she tried to scratch her way through, the surface of the prison pulsed with color which hardened till it shut out even the sounds of the *onibaba*'s screams.

And then there was stillness, and relief, and realization.

"Caleb?" said Emily's mother, huddled on the floor over the body of her son. "Caleb!"

Emily dropped beside her, folding her arms around her brother, reaching into him as she had reached into the wounded *tengu*, but he was still and cooling fast. Her mind searched for the spark of life that she might blow into a flame, giving him what essence of her own he needed, but there was nothing.

She sat back, eyes wide, tears flowing down her cheeks.

Her sweet, goofy, brave, loser of a brother, Caleb Hideki Smith, was dead.

The *tengu*, still pale and exhausted, hung his head. *Bāchan* held her daughter's hand, patting it absently, while DeMarcus sat with a dazed, horror-struck Madison.

And Emily raged.

She lowered her head, summoned all her strength, human and *kitsune*, and breathed into his lungs. When that did not open his eyes or quicken his heart, she lifted her brother in her arms and stood up.

"What are you doing?" asked DeMarcus. "We need to call an ambulance."

"It is too late for medicine," said the *tengu*.

Still cradling Caleb, Emily walked to the cave mouth.

"Em?" her mother managed. "Where are you going?"

But Emily did not respond.

She walked out of the cave, striding through the caution tape on the edge of the forest path, then moving with determined swiftness, her mind full of the outrage which gave her strength. She followed the track, or rather the scent of the track (she could smell as much as she could see), round and down and then up again, and the confused woodland creatures gave her room, sensing her purpose.

At last she saw the greenish torches and the vermillion *torii* gates which led to the shrine, which was not really there, and only then did she allow herself to stop. She lay her brother between the glaring stone fox statues, walked up to the great bronze bell and rung it as her brother had once done. The bell made the night air throb, a deep, resonant sound you could feel in your gut.

She inhaled the fragrant incense and waited. Around her the green torches leapt and the bamboo which only grew in this place at this time stirred in an unearthly breeze. In the shrine itself a golden light streamed from the crack between the lacquered box and its lid, a box marked with a familiar emblem of a diamond inside a circle. Emily stood her ground as the box burst its ornate rope binding and opened. The light which emerged was suddenly tall and roughly man shaped, though it hovered in the air before her.

Words appeared in her mind, old Japanese words which she did not know, somehow reframed into English.

"You have done well," it said. A man's voice, slow and dour as the *tengu*. "The threat has passed. You may leave your brother to his rest."

Emily blinked. The wind lashed her face and her eyes stung, but she would not turn away.

"Bring him back," she said.

"Hideki has served his purpose," said the voice.

"He has served your purpose, you mean," she shouted back. "He had purposes of his own which did not involve you or monsters or Japan."

"He has honored his ancestors."

"Great," Emily shot back. "Now they can honor him. Bring him back!"

"That is not how things are done."

"Not for you, maybe," she countered, "but we aren't you and this isn't fair."

There was a momentary pause and then the word came back shrouded in puzzlement.

"*Fair?*"

"Yes, fair! He's not Hideki. Or he's not just Hideki, as I am not just Kazuko. We are Caleb and Emily, and we have our own lives, our own way of doing things. It is not fair to weigh us down with your past! We have enough to carry of our own."

"You are shaped by history."

"Yes, but we are not defined by it. We are more than what was. You have to let us have our *now*! He did his part, now do yours."

"I did my part before you were born . . ."

"I don't care about that!" Emily roared, tears rolling down her face. "I want my brother back. He's not gone. Not completely. Doctors can't bring him back. I can't. But you can. I know it."

"It is not our way."

"Then make a new way!" she cried. "You owe him that."

"Respect is given to the elderly, to the dead."

"Respect is earned!" she replied. "Tell me he has not earned your respect!"

There was another long silence, broken only by the wind in the bamboo.

"And we're not done," she added. "We closed the breach in your dimensional prison, but our power is not equal to yours."

The voice, when it came back was brooding.

"This is true," it said.

"So what if it happens again?" Emily pressed. "Who will protect our world against the *yōkai*? Who will be your agents on earth?"

The silence this time was longer, heavier. The torches flared once more and Emily was sure the entity she thought of as Raiko had reached a decision.

"I will not do this," it said. "But if you wish it, you may. Once and once only. But consider this deeply. It is a great thing to restore a life whose time has passed, a great responsibility . . ."

But Emily was no longer listening.

"Yeah," she muttered, as she dropped to her brother's body and held him to her heart till she felt her energy become his. "Whatever."

There was a final rush of wind, and then silence and only the darkness of the woods. The shrine was gone.

Come on, she thought. *Come on.*

And then he stirred.

"Hey Em," said Caleb. "What's up?"

31

It took my sister a week to recover. Stress and over-exertion the doctors said, which fooled no one. They didn't know what was wrong with her. So for a week she lay in her room as close to being in a coma as it was possible to be, and then she opened her eyes and asked for *Bāchan*'s homemade *onigiri*.

What had happened at the shrine, no one rightly knew. I remembered waking up there with her in time to see Raiko's presence fade and the torches go out, and I knew she had saved me, but I didn't know how far gone I had been until she told me, and even then I think she held some stuff back. She made it sound like she'd done again what she'd done to save the *tengu* when he was attacked by the *bakeneko* but that didn't explain why she had hauled my ass all the way to the shrine and called on the spirit of our great grandfather. I pressed for more, but she dodged and smirked and said that I had been a brat and a pain in the proverbial, and that I owed her.

We left it at that.

My mother and *Bāchan* were sort of circling each other in what you might call an uneasy peace. They were polite to each other, which made a change, but kind of creeped me out, and my grandmother had been over for dinner most nights, which was just plain weird. They had even taken a few minutes to color in the second eye of the *daruma*, something they did in a strange silence like they were completing a ritual.

Dad, who had stayed to protect the shop on the night everything had gone down, seemed cheerfully baffled by the whole thing. Apparently DeMarcus had come over when he saw the news coverage of the mob gathering outside the inconvenience store and Dad had welcomed him in as an ally without question. Now, he didn't push to know why Mr. Saito had asked DeMarcus to drive him with Mom and *Bāchan* up to the cave the moment the sheriff had released them from questioning. Once I caught him watching me in a cautious, thoughtful kind of way, but when I met his eyes he just gave me that usual Dad grin of his and said nothing.

There was a lot of that about. Madison told the Sheriff and the press a frankly bizarre tale of hiking through the mountains and falling down a shaft from which she had not been able to extricate herself, and how my family had managed to find her and get her out. It was preposterous, but the town seemed to chew on it a bit in silence, and then decided to roll with it, as if they weren't ready to face stranger explanations. Geological investigators had found evidence of "structural instability leading to rock falls, tremors and subsidence" on the night of Madison's reappearance, and these seemed to be the direct results of the previous fracking events. A new excavation had located the bodies of the missing workers, and their dried-out condition was being blamed on a combination of animal predation and the unseasonably warm weather, somehow magnified by the caves.

I wasn't sure why everyone believed this, or if they did deep down, but it was tidy and gave people closure, which is what Portersville needed. There was a day of mourning for the dead, which was clearly pained and heartfelt, but then everything went back to normal. One minute the missing workers, the abductions and the death of Blake Wilde had been the only thing anyone could talk about, and then—without warning—it was as if we made a mutual agreement never to discuss it again. The out-of-town journalists all left, and Portersville became just another sleepy mountain town in the less touristy part of the Smokies.

"People don't always need to understand everything," said Dad cryptically. "Better to move on."

Southern Shale shut up shop, at least temporarily, pending other investigations, some professional and some legal. My guess was that they would be back soon enough, and plenty of folk in town would be happy about that, so long as they got paid and the company didn't put a hole in the fabric of reality, flooding the world with beings from another dimension. People hate that.

Of course, there are other things they hate too. On the night we had battled *yōkai* for Portersville's future, a huddle of irate locals had gathered outside the inconvenience store, and things might have gone very badly. That they didn't was down to a young sheriff's deputy called Kevin Williams who issued a few stern warnings, to DeMarcus who had stood alongside him, and to my Dad, who came out front and talked about the Panthers' weakness in pass rushing and whether or not this fall was proving to be hotter than last. In other words, he did his everyman routine for the town's more volatile members, and somehow that led to them not burning our house down, which you had to think was a kind of magic of its own. When we got back with Madison in one piece, not heroes exactly, but no longer suspects, he just said, "Good job, all. Who's for tea?"

And so normality was restored.

That normality included me being back to being the clumsy doofus at school. It was Em's idea, and though I hated it with a deep and fiery passion, it was probably smart. There could be no football stardom for me, even when I was out of barn-building detention. Drawing attention to myself was just too risky. Ironically, it was Madison who drove the point home for me.

I wasn't sure what she remembered, but she knew her story of a hiking accident was as fake as Mr. Grealish with hair, but when I sidled up to her at school to ask how she was, she practically set the carpet tiles on fire in her rush to get away. I gave it another shot a couple of days later when she seemed less jumpy, but she was stiff and distant, and made her excuses the moment I suggested getting together outside school for coffee or a study session or . . . anything really.

"She's not ready," said Emily wisely.

"When will she be?" I asked.

She made an apologetic face.

"Maybe never," she said. "She liked you when she thought you were special, different, but these things are relative."

"I'm now *too* special?" I snored. "Great."

"She's a regular person, Caleb. You are part of a world she glimpsed for one day, and it was a very bad day, the worst in her life, and the strangest. She doesn't want that world to be real, but every time she sees you, there it is."

"DeMarcus is handling it," I said sulkily.

"DeMarcus wasn't suspended from the ceiling with a bunch of corpses."

"There is that . . ." I conceded.

"People like special," Emily said, "in the same way they like going on holiday. Myrtle Beach is great for a week . . ."

"But you wouldn't want to live there," I concluded for her. "I get it. I'm good to have around when you need saving from demons, but when it's time for coffee and study sessions . . ."

"People like normal," said Emily. "Try not to take it personally. There'll be other girls."

"Yeah?"

"Almost certainly. Well, probably. I mean, there are other girls in existence. Whether they'll be interested in you . . ."

"And how come no one is freaked out by you?" I said cutting through her rapier wit like a band saw.

"I think this is where we came in," said Emily. "Because I'm cool and you, little brother, are not."

"But didn't Madison see you doing your shape-shifting *kitsune* thing?"

"*Megitsune*," Emily corrected. "Female foxes are *megitsune*. I'm not sure she realized I was the fox," she said, shrugging. "And she wasn't looking to date me."

"Fair enough," I said, grudgingly. "*Megitsune*, huh? You have been studying way more Japanese than I thought."

"Nah," she said, grinning. "That's straight up BABYMETAL."

I gave her a blank look.

"A band," she replied, shaking her head in wonder at my ignorance. "Trust me, you'll love them."

"You're overseeing my cultural education now?"

"Someone has to," she replied. "Speaking of which, have you seen the *tengu?*"

"No, but I heard he had recovered and was back to working on the barn."

"Yeah," she said, musingly, "about that . . ."

"What?" I said, sensing something odd coming.

"You might want to go check it out," she replied.

"Meaning?"

"You'll see."

And I did.

I wandered over to the barn site at lunch time, except that it wasn't the barn site any more. It was the barn. The whole thing, up and—so far as I could tell—finished. It glowed, a monument in clean new pine which smelled like a forest. It looked, I had to say, superb: a masterpiece of intricate carpentry and bold design which was way better than the original. It managed to look brand new and very old at the same times and had an exotic something that I couldn't quite put my finger on. No one seemed to be objecting. Quite the opposite, in fact. Mr. Watkins, the wood shop teacher, and Daren, his star pupil, were gazing up at it as I arrived, speechless.

"That was fast," I said. "Sorry I haven't been around the last few days. Family emergency . . ."

"Fast?" said Daren as if he was addressing a halfwit. "It's extraordinary! Impossible. And most of it Mr. Saito did by himself over night."

"Oh," I said.

"*Oh* is right," said Daren, his eyes sliding back to the building as if drawn to it. Mr. Watkins hadn't looked away from it the whole time I'd been there.

"It's beautiful," he breathed. "Exquisite. That curvature in the roof lines! I mean, it's still a barn but it looks like . . . feels like . . ."

"A temple," said Daren reverently.

"A shrine," I corrected.

"That something to do with you?" said Tyler J. Miller the Third accusingly.

I hadn't seen him sidling up behind me with his cronies at his elbow. They weren't smirking this time, and looked both hostile and frustrated, as if a certain victory had been snatched from them through a Hail Mary as the clock expired.

"I worked on it a bit," I said.

"But the architect or whatever he is," said Tyler, "that big-nosed . . ."

"Careful," I said, raising a warning finger.

For an uncanny moment the three of them looked at it like it was a gun, then remembered who they were and continued.

"He's like your uncle or something right?" said Bobby Davenham.

"Nope," I said. "No relation."

Their eyes narrowed suspiciously as they sought for something to target, and it occurred to me that they didn't fully understand why I annoyed them so much.

"The old barn was better," said Bobby, a lie so spectacular in its outrageousness that even Tyler glanced away. "A proper American barn."

214

"If you ask nicely," I said, "maybe they'll let you paint this one red, white and blue."

Irritation and confusion chased each other through Bobby's face.

"Wouldn't work," he ventured, though I knew that if I waited for him to defend this statement we'd be standing in silence for hours. He didn't know.

"This one isn't American enough, you mean," I said. "Maybe we should call in some builders from down the road in Cherokee; have them redo it. Doesn't get more American than that."

Bobby's face clouded and he balled his fists. I smiled, unconcerned.

"Come on," said Tyler. He had begun to lead his buddies away when he turned back, his face flushed.

"You're not fooling anybody, you know, Smith," he spat. "You think everyone buys that stuff about Madison falling in a gulley and your idiot family rescuing her?"

"It's what she says," I said, shrugging.

"And the bodies in the cave that were all dry and weird?" sputtered Tyler. "My dad says . . ."

"What?" I said, taking a step toward him. "What does your dad say, Tyler? What is he whispering about to the sheriff and the suits at Southern Shale, because I think Action News would love to hear about it? My family and I are heroes right now. Half the people who considered burning down my parents' store are ready to throw them a parade. Which side do you and your dad want to be on?"

Tyler just stood there, the storm clouds swirling in his face.

"We'll be watching you, Smith," he concluded. "You and your whole freakshow family."

I smiled and shrugged again.

"Enjoy the show," I said.

In spite of everything, when school ended for the day, I wandered to the fields where the football teams were practicing. Tyler was there, of course, but we ignored each other, though I thought he looked over when DeMarcus, coming off the field for a water break, spotted me and tossed me a perfect pass. With considerable effort, and feeling various pairs of eyes in the bleachers watching, I managed not to catch it.

"So this is the new you," said DeMarcus, eyeing me warily.

"Officially, yes," I said. "Kind of like the old me, actually."

"Just not the improved you."

"Right."

"Because you're not that anymore or because you don't want people to know about it?" he asked.

I probably should have gone with the former, said that whatever strange abilities I had developed had evaporated as mysteriously as they had come, but he had earned the truth and then some.

"The second one," I said, "but I'd appreciate it if you kept that to yourself."

He inclined his head and then glanced into the bleachers.

"Even from Madison?" he said.

She was up there with DeMarcus' pretty sister, Ayisha, and, a couple of seats over, Emily.

"I think she's been through enough strangeness, don't you?" I said.

"I guess so," he said.

"I never said thanks," I added. "For protecting the store, getting my family to the caves, and for keeping my secret."

He gave a grunt of acknowledgement and looked away.

"And now?" he said. "Is it safe?"

I blew out a long sigh.

"Honestly," I said, "I don't know. For now."

"Guess we'll take that," said DeMarcus. His eyes flicked over my right shoulder and I turned. Someone who had not been in the bleachers was coming over. It was Joey.

"Not playing today, huh?" they said.

"Or any other day," I said.

"I thought you wanted to be, you know . . ." they nodded toward Tyler who was celebrating a touchdown pass to a smattering of applause from the bleachers. "All that."

"Changed my mind," I said, grinning.

"Change is good," said Joey, who I guessed knew better than most.

"Speaking of which," I said, acting on an impulse I hadn't fully clarified in my head. "From now on, I want to go by Hideki."

"Hideki?" said DeMarcus.

"My middle name," I said, suddenly self-conscious. "I'm just, you know, trying it out."

"OK," said Joey. "Hideki. Sure."

"Hideki," DeMarcus added with an approving nod. "Cool. I'll get the word out."

"I thought you wanted to keep a low profile," Emily remarked over dinner that night. "You think being called Hideki will do that?"

Bāchan and Mom both looked up and, not for the first time, seemed to exchange a glance which was at once cautious and knowing.

I colored.

"I'm going to attract attention no matter what I do," I said. "I may as well own it."

"So you want us to call you Hideki?" said Dad who had just come in from the inconvenience store. He looked perplexed but indulgent, willing to go with it if that was what I wanted.

"Not you," I said. "Not here. I'm still Caleb to you guys. But out in the world, yeah."

Emily gave me a long, considering look, then nodded with what I took to be understanding.

A thoughtful silence descended on the table. I gave up on my chopsticks and jabbed some scampi. Sorry, *shrimp tempura*. I was being educated again. It was actually pretty good.

"Where do you want to put those rice crackers?" asked Dad.

"In the corner by the window," Mom replied. "With the other stuff."

Something in her manner caught my attention. She was being as close to furtive as her careful restraint permitted.

"What stuff?" I asked. "What rice crackers?"

"*Osembe*," said *Bāchan*.

"Not helping," I said.

Emily rolled her eyes.

"*Rice crackers*," she said, as if she was dealing with an idiot. "From Japan. Mom ordered a bunch of Japanese snacks for the store. Seaweed and dried squid. Strawberry Pocky and Green tea Kit-Kats. All kinds of stuff."

"Just experimenting," Mom cut in, hurriedly getting to her feet and starting to collect the empty plates. "See if people will buy them."

I stared. Emily grinned.

"Looks fantastic," said Dad. "No idea what most of it is, but they make a great display."

"And if no one buys them, we can eat them," said *Bāchan*.

Mom flashed her a look as if she was going to argue, to protest that this was simply a business venture, but she changed her mind and shrugged.

"Most of that stuff I haven't had since..." she began, but the sentence tailed off and she smiled a little sadly.

"Well," said Dad, "we have them now." He took her hand and squeezed it. "Come on," he added. "Leave the dishes to the kids. Come show me where you want the display. I'll even let you sneak some of the stock."

"I will go home," said *Bāchan*. "Call me if you need anything."

That last was directed at Emily and me.

"Thanks, *Bāchan*," we chorused.

"For everything," I added.

She gave us a broad, genuine smile which creased her face, the first such smile I could remember from her since we were very small.

———

That evening, after the store was closed, Emily and I sat on the stoop gazing up at the wooded mountains. They had just started to show the beginnings of their autumn colors, but it was too dark to see them now and the woods looked blank and a little ominous.

"So you've pretty much mastered the human-fox change thing?" I said.

She shook her head.

"Not yet, but I'm working on it. In the moment when I really needed to change, I could, but I'm not really sure how."

"Does it matter?" I asked.

"Not being fully in control of what shape you are and whether or not you can smell in color?" she shot back. "Yeah, I'd say it matters. The *tengu* has given me exercises: meditation type things. I'll work on it but being able to shift from one form to the other and back whenever I like? That's going to take time."

"Well, you're further along than me," I said, admitting it aloud for the first time. "When it came down to it, my sword fighting was useless. I am quick and strong, but I don't know what I'm doing, so I can't really fight."

"You killed the *oni*."

"That was luck and observation. And you gave me the knife. If I'd been by myself..."

"You weren't," she inserted. "And you won't be. We're in this together."

I gave her a quick look.

"You don't think it's over, do you?" I said.

"The immediate threat is," she said. "But forever? We live on the edge of a mystical dimension, a prison in which thousands of *yokai* are bound for all eternity. But the physical and spiritual barriers which hold them in can be broken. We've seen that, and some of them may have slipped out before we re-sealed it. I don't want to believe it, but we'd be crazy not to assume that the *onibaba* will be trying to escape."

I nodded gravely.

"And when she does," I said, "we will be top of her list. This time we were just the way to release her son and get revenge on Raiko. She didn't really know us. She does now, and I'll bet she hates us more than she ever did our great grandfather."

"The news said that Southern Shake are setting up an exploratory committee to explore restarting work on Red Scar mountain," said Emily.

I gave a bark of derisive laughter.

"Exploratory committee!" I sneered. "What are the bets that they get another good sniff of the methane under the mountain and will magically discover safe and efficient ways to get to it?"

"Unless the mayor and the town council forbid it in order to protect the environment."

She gave me a look and we both burst into laughter.

"Good one," I said.

We listened to the settling night.

"Do you feel different?" I asked. "After all we've been through, I mean, all we've seen."

"Not sure," she said. "In some ways. I understand the fox part of me better now, which you'd think would be a huge change but in other ways, no. I feel the same."

"Still Emily," I said.

"Still Emily," she agreed.

I thought of the cicadas that began life in one shape and ended it as something so completely different they were barely recognizable, and of those Russian nesting dolls which contained different versions of themselves. Even without the supernatural turn our lives had taken, I thought I would have felt that way, like lots of people inside one body, each one thinking and feeling a little differently, each one shouting to be heard. That had used to bother me, but now it didn't seem so bad.

"OK, Hideki," said Emily, as if reading my thoughts. "I suspect that even super heroes have homework."

"If I meet any, I'll ask," I said. "And to you, I'm still Caleb."

"For now, right?"

"For now."

Something nibbled my hand in an affectionate sort of way and made little chirruping noises like an aggravated squirrel. I glanced down.

"Come on," I said to Emily. "I have to feed the teapot."

Across the street from the convenience store, a young white-tailed deer stirred in the trees, its head up and ears pricked. Its big, glossy eyes widened and it sniffed the air. Something was moving stealthily along the forest path.

That something was an old man in a stained and ragged robe. He moved slowly and creakily, his head bowed, but when he reached the edge of the tree line he paused. The deer which had been frozen for several seconds, flashed its tail and bounded off into the underbrush. The old man watched it go, then turned his attention to the store. The lights were out, but he could just make out muttered voices coming from the porch. He shifted to get a better look over a raft of kudzu, raising his hands high above his head. In the palms of each, a glossy eye winked open, focused and staring at the point where his mistress's enemies sat, talking and laughing as if they were safe.

As if it were over.

THE END

AFTERWORD

This book was long in the making. It began, I suppose, in the late nineteen eighties when I was living and working in Japan, and where I met my Japanese-American wife, Hisako. I had developed a fascination with Japanese folk culture—the myths, monsters, and legends which underpin this story—and for years I tried to find a way to incorporate them into my fiction and screenwriting. It didn't work, because so long as the stories were set in Japan (a culture I had grown to know pretty well but which did not truly belong to me, was not in my bones) I couldn't find a way to tell the story which felt authentic. It always felt like an outsider looking in, a common and troubling trait when it comes to representation of Japan (think of all those movies which—often bafflingly—are set in Japan but hinge on foreigners, the locals reduced to background color).

Fast forward thirty years or so. My wife and I were living in Charlotte, North Carolina, and had a teenaged son, Kuma. As a mixed race family we had had our share of awkward moments, like the (surely well-meaning) lady in the grocery store who asked what agency I had used to adopt my boy, the minor officials who always talked to me on the assumption that my (Harvard- and Yale-educated) wife might not speak English, the waiters in restaurants who assumed we were two groups rather than a single family and so on. Small stuff, mostly. But as my son grew up I started to see the world a little differently, and found myself more alert to what have come to be called "micro-aggressions": those—often unintentional—sleights that come from unacknowledged prejudice and ignorance. And let's be honest, some of them aren't unintentional. Some of them are flat out racist. I heard the things my son reported from school, the jokes at his expense, the assumptions about who and what he was which came from the classmates of a large high school in which he was one of the only Asian students. Again, little stuff, but irritating nonetheless. And I remember the first time we took him to Japan. He loved it, but struggled to articulate what exactly he had liked so much. At last he said, "It's nice to be a in a place where everybody looks like me."

Heart-breaking, right?

Except, that he mostly didn't feel sad or tortured. He was and is a resilient and centered kid who doesn't much care what people think of him, particularly if their opinions come from ignorance. But what, I wondered, if he wasn't quite so self-sufficient? And what if we lived not in a comparatively cosmopolitan city like Charlotte, but in a smaller, more rural area? What would that be like? These impulses shaped the resultant story, a novel which felt more authentic because it was grounded less by Japan itself but by our own immediate surroundings and the experiences of our family. Most importantly, it became more expressly about people with feet in multiple cultures.

For decades my wife and I have discussed her experience growing up as a second generation immigrant and much of Caleb's fictional family history is derived directly from hers. Her grandfather was interred in one of the camps in Arizona during World War Two and her father, then a child, was sent back to Japan to spend the war years there. Her mother was born and raised in Tokyo. As adults they settled in the Chicago area and raised their children to be successful Americans, sometimes experiencing what today we would call racism, though they mostly accepted those conditions as the price of immigration. Different generations process such things differently, particularly as cultures evolve and become more conscious—and less accepting—of behaviors and institutional practices which work to suppress, marginalize or reinforce a sense of Otherness in minority populations. Our collective conversations about such issues shaped this book at its core, and we were particularly keen to write something which foregrounded the special sense of cultural displacement experienced by people who come from mixed race backgrounds, people whose identity emerges out of the both/neither binary, a third option which we often struggle to articulate.

In order to engage with these issues of course, particularly in fiction, you have to show some of the problems, some of the difficulties, which people actually face, rather than papering over them. I understand that some readers want simply to celebrate their heritage or sense of self without having to face the attendant trauma, and that's perfectly understandable. In this, however, we felt that we couldn't resolve the characters' identity issues without first wrestling with the issues, and that meant representing some of that trauma and the resulting sense of inner conflict. We tried to do this accurately but without dwelling on it longer than necessary, and without going so dark that (though all too real) the showing of it would feel exploitative.

The arc we were trying to trace here was about the mixed race immigrant's struggle to find themselves when they are always, in a sense, between worlds. We wanted to explore how they draw from the various aspects of their heritage while also claiming a sense of self which is not entirely defined by either. We hope the book provides an anchor for people in similar circumstances, and helps explain what they might be going through to those who aren't. It is both the task and the special gift of fiction to help us see the world through the eyes of others, to build that most fundamental of social building blocks, empathy. We hope our little story has achieved something of that, and that you have had fun along the way. Hopefully we'll share more of Hideki and Każuko's adventures in the future. Till then, be well, and look after each other.

- A.J., Hisako, and Kuma

GLOSSARY

Yōkai (**mystical creatures/beings**)

Bakeneko: cat monster: though it looks like an ordinary cat, it has the capacity to change into human form. Bakeneko are often thought to have been ordinary cats which have acquired magical powers, sometimes by licking human blood.

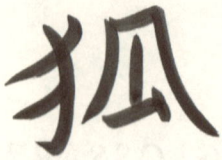

Kitsune: a mystical fox which has various powers including the ability to possess humans or to convincingly take human form, sometimes for many years at a time. Their power increases with age and is sometimes apparent in their having multiple tails. Some kitsune have the ability to control fire and some have healing powers. They can be benevolent or mischievous.

Tengu: an ancient and powerful creature, sometimes considered a god, the tengu have affinities to animals such as birds and dogs, but usually appear as humanoids with long, bulbous noses. They are particularly associated with wisdom and martial arts, with mountains and forest.

o *Noppera-bō:* a supernatural trickster whose natural form is human but without a face though it can simulate the appearance of ordinary people, at least for a short time. When it meets humans it uses this disguise, but then will startle and terrify its victims by revealing its true form. It is sometimes thought of merely as a form taken by animals which can shape-shift such as foxes and tanuki, but the true *Noppera-bō* is a separate entity.

o *Oni:* an ogre-like being, usually large and physically very strong. They generally have single or multiple horns, claws and a wild appearance, often including a tiger skin loin cloth, and sometimes have a third eye in their foreheads. They are extremely dangerous, especially to humans who they will catch and eat, despising their very existence.

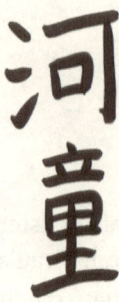

   ○ *Kappa:* an aquatic *yōkai* combining monkey and turtle forms, generally including a shell and a hooked beak. The tops of their heads feature a bowl-like depression which holds water and allows them to move around on land. They are surprisingly strong, are expert wrestlers, and are infamous for drowning humans and animals in order to extract mystical power from them. They are fond of cucumbers and fermented soy beans (*nattō*), and can—murderous tendencies notwithstanding—be very polite.

   ○ *Tanuki:* one of the most common Japanese *yōkai*, *tanuki* are raccoon-dogs which can shape-change into all manner of different people and things. They are usually mischievous and playful rather than dangerous and sometimes fall victim to their own trickery, particularly if they get carried away with drinking or other festive behavior. They often associated with shrines and temples and sometimes take the form of monks.

They are the stars of the Studio Ghibli film *Pom Poko,* and are an influence for the form of the title character in *My neighbor Totoro.*

○ *Megitsune*: the female form of the *kitsune*

Objects

○ *Torii*: the tall horned gateways symbolizing a portal into a mystical space used as entrances and the markers of pathways in and around Shinto shrines. They are usually brightly painted vermillion or russet.

○ *Tatami*: the mats of tightly woven straw which form the traditional floor covering of Japanese houses and temples. Never wear shoes on *tatami*!

○ *Yukata*: a light, cotton kimono belted at the waist with a sash, worn as casual dress, particularly indoors, and included for guests in tradition Japanese hotels and spas.

○ *Ofuda*: paper or wood amulets featuring powerful kanji or fragments of prayers. They are used to seal and protect from malevolent mystical forces, and are generally acquired from shrines and temples in return for an offering.

○ *Katana*: the most common form of Japanese sword. They are long, curved, with a point and a single cutting edge which is very sharp, and are generally wielded with both hands. Quality swords often have mystical associations acquired from years—or centuries—of use.

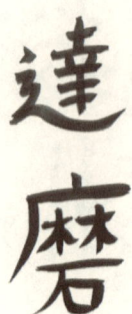

o *Daruma*: a stylized doll figure comprised almost entirely of a face. When purchased the eyes are blank. One eye is colored in when a wish is made. The other when the wish is granted.

Food

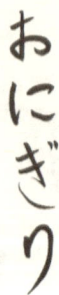

o *Onigiri*: rice balls (though they are usually triangular in shape) wrapped in *nori* (dried sheets of seaweed), usually with a savoury filling of something salty or pickled. Often served as fast food or taken in lunch boxes for a snack.

  ○ *Tonkatsu*: fried, breaded pork cutlet served as is or added to curry and other dishes.

  ○ *Tempura*: lightly battered and deep-fried items, usually vegetables (eggplant, sweet potato, okra, squash, onion etc.) and/or fish (shrimp, crab, squid etc.). When well prepared they are crisp and greaseless.

○ *Senbei*: salty rice crackers flavoured with soy sauce and sometimes partly wrapped in nori or spiced with hot pepper. They come in a variety of shapes and sizes.

ABOUT THE AUTHOR

A.J. Hartley (AKA Andrew Hart) is the award-winning and bestselling author of 25 novels in a variety of genres including mystery, fantasy, sci-fi, thriller, paranormal, children's and young adult. Recent work includes the comic time travel fantasy BURNING SHAKESPEARE, the ghost story COLD BATH STREET, the dark fantasy IMPERVIOUS, and the award winning STEEPLEJACK adventure trilogy.

He has written adaptations of *Hamlet* and *Macbeth* with David Hewson, and UFO thrillers with Tom DeLonge of Blink 182 (SEKRET MACHINES and CATHEDRALS OF GLASS). He is Professor Emeritus of Shakespeare at UNC Charlotte, and has a YouTube channel dedicated to Japanese rock music.

That interest, like HIDEKI SMITH, grew out of his time living and working in Japan, where he met his wife, Hisako, who is Nisei (2nd generation Japanese-American) from Chicago, and who is now a pediatrician. Their son, Kuma, grew up with them in North Carolina, and is now a university student in Washington DC. Find out more at www.ajhartley.net

OTHER FANTASY AND YOUNG ADULT BOOKS BY A.J. HARTLEY

Preston Oldcorn Series

Cold Bath Street

Written Stone Lane

Will Hawthorne Series

Act of Will

Will Power

Darwen Arkwright Series

Darwen Arkwright and the Peregrine Pact

Darwen Arkwright and the Insidious Bleck

Darwen Arkwright and the School of Shadows

Cathedrals of Glass

A Planet of Blood and Ice

Valkrys Wakes

SteepleJack

Steeplejack

Firebrand

Guardian

Impervious

Burning Shakespeare

FRIENDS OF FALSTAFF

Thank You to All our Falstaff Books Patrons, who get extra digital content each month! To be featured here and see what other great rewards we offer, go to www.patreon.com/falstaffbooks.

PATRONS

Dino Hicks
John Hooks
John Kilgallon
Larissa Lichty
Travis & Casey Schilling
Staci-Leigh Santore
Sheryl R. Hayes
Scott Norris
Samuel Montgomery-Blinn
Junkle